PLANET STORIES

T. T. SCOTT, Pres.   MALCOLM REISS, Gen. Mgr.   PAUL L. PAYNE, Ed.

A GRIPPING, FULL-LENGTH NOVEL OF A MAGIC OUTER WORLD

A SMASHING NOVELETTE OF THE FUTURE

SIX THRILLING PLANETTALES

AND PLANET'S REGULAR FEATURES

Winter Issue   Vol. III, No. 9
Sept.-Nov.   20c per copy
1947

PLANET STORIES: Published quarterly by Love Romances Pub. Co., Inc., 670 Fifth Ave., New York 19, N. Y. The entire contents of this magazine are copyrighted, 1947, by Love Romances Publishing Co., Inc. Entered as second-class matter, October 2, 1944, at the Post Office, at New York 1, N. Y., under the Act of March 3, 1879. All rights reserved. While due care is always exercised, the publishers will not be responsible for the return of unsolicited manuscripts. Yearly subscription rate 80¢ in advance. For advertising rates address: Advertising Director, Fiction House, Inc., 670 Fifth Ave., New York 19, N. Y. Printed in U. S. A.

2

WHAT MEN DON'T LIKE ABOUT WOMEN

WOMEN EXPOSED AS THEY REALLY ARE

NOTHING OMITTED . . . NO PUNCHES PULLED

Never before in the English language has the veil of secrecy been so thoroughly stripped from women. Never before has politeness, male deference, and smug courtesy been so completely disregarded . . . the truth so bluntly and unsparingly told. Thomas D. Horton figuratively takes the so-called "fair-sex" apart, reveals the callous and frank truth about the things that men think, yet rarely have the courage to say. In almost every sentence of this frank book you will find something to chuckle about, something that will bring to mind an experience of your own in your relationships with the opposite sex. Your wife or sweetheart may not enjoy watching you read this revealing book . . . but brother, YOU'LL LOVE IT!

THERE'S DYNAMITE ON EVERY PAGE

This amusing, often shocking book, does not talk in generalities. Based on the author's wide and frequently unusual experience, it discusses women, their thoughts, habits, speech and actions under almost every conceivable condition. You'll meet them in night clubs, in the office, in love, learn what they really say to and about each other, hear their candid opinions about men. Here, at last, is a man who is willing to stand up and fight for the superiority of his sex! You will gasp with amazement when you discover how thoroughly he covers the subject, how little he leaves to the imagination. Once you've read "What Men Don't Like About Women" you will regard them differently, understand them better . . . perhaps never again feel inferior or embarrassed.

DON'T READ IT TO A WOMAN!

"There is not the slightest likelihood of any male ever reviewing this book before a woman's club. The insurance premium would be prohibitive. Turn to any chapter, any paragraph and read it aloud in the presence of a female, and you'll have fury with its claws out"

COLUMBUS NEWS

**COMPLETELY
and HILARIOUSLY
ILLUSTRATED**

HERALD PUB. CO.
45 East 17th St., N. Y. 3, N. Y.

SEND NO MONEY

Learn the truth about women, at home, without risk. Send no money. Simply fill in and mail the coupon. On arrival pay the postman only $2.00 plus postage, or enclose $2.00 with the coupon and receive this book—delight postpaid. "What Men Don't Like About Women" must give you the most hilarious, rib-tickling nightsful of reading pleasure you have ever experienced, or return it within 5 days for full and prompt refund of your purchase price. Don't delay . . . send the coupon today.

Margaret leaped forward and slashed at Eldon's fingers.

BLACK PRIESTESS OF VARDA

By ERIK FENNEL

She was well-named—Sin, foul witch and raving beauty, Beloved of Sasso, the Dark Power striving to capture, with her help, a lovely little world. Their only fear was a whispered legend—Elvedon, the Savior ... But this crippled idiot blundering through a shower of sparks into their time and space—*he* could not be Elvedon!

THE PEN MOVED CLUMSILY in Eldon Carmichael's right hand. He had been left-handed, and the note itself was not easy to write.

Dear Margaret, he scratched. *I understand...*

When after a while the proper words still would not come he crossed the shadowed laboratory and took another long swig from the flat bottle in his topcoat pocket. He understood—he remembered his first one-eyed look in a mirror after the bandages were removed—but still he felt resentful and deeply sorry for himself.

He went back and tried to continue the letter but his thoughts veered erratically. The injury had been psychological as well as physical, involving loss of ability to face up to unpleasant facts, but still he could not force aside those memories.

There had been only a glimpse as the wrench slipped from Victor Schenley's hand and fell between the sprocket and drive chain of the big new compressor in the Institute's basement. He wondered. That look on Schenley's darkly saturnine face could have been merely imagination. Or horror. But there was something about the man... Still Eldon discounted his suspicions as the unworthy inventions of a disturbed mind.

Only the quick reflexes that had once made him a better than average halfback had saved him from instant death as the jagged end of the heavy sprocket chain lashed out with the speed of an enraged cobra. And often during the pain-wracked weeks that followed he had almost wished he had been a little slower.

The ring sparkled tauntingly under his desk lamp. Margaret had returned it by mail, and though the wording of her note had been restrained its tone had been final.

He picked up the pen again and moved the stub of his left arm, amputated just above the elbow, to hold the paper in place. But he had forgotten again how *light* and unmanageable the stump was. The paper skidded and the pen left a long black streak and a blot.

Eldon made a choked sound that was partly a shout of anger and partly a whimper of frustration. He crumpled the note, hurled the pen clumsily toward the far wall, and buried his disfigured face in the curve of his single arm. His body shook with sobs of self-pity.

There was only an inch or so left in the bottle. He finished it in a single gulp and for a moment stood hesitantly. Then he switched on the brilliant overhead lights. Liquor could not banish his tormenting thoughts, but perhaps work might. His letter to Margaret would have to wait.

His equipment was just as he had left it that night so many months ago when Victor Schenley had called him to see the new compressor. The setup was almost complete for another experiment with the resonance of bound charges. Bound charges were queer things, he reflected, a neglected field of investigation. They were classed as electrical phenomena more for convenience than accuracy. Eldon's completed experiments indicated they might be—something else. They disobeyed too many of the generally accepted electrical and physical laws. Occasionally individual charges behaved as though they were actually alive and responding to external stimuli, but the stimuli were nonexistent or at least undetectable. And two or more bound charges placed in even imperfect resonance produced strange and inexplicable effects.

Working clumsily, he made the few remaining connections and set the special charge concentrators whining. The vacuum pumps clucked. A *strain* developed in the space around which the triplet charges were forming, something he could sense without seeing or hearing it. Now if only he could match the three charges for perfect resonance...

THE lacquer on Margaret Mason's fingernails was finally dry. She slipped out of her robe and, without disturbing her carefully arranged pale gold hair, dropped the white evening gown over her shoulders and gently tugged it into place around slender hips. This should be the evening when Victor stopped his sly suggestions and made an outright proposal of marriage. Mrs. Victor Schenley. Margaret savored the name. She knew what she wanted.

Eldon had seemed a good idea at the time, the best she could do. Despite his youth he was already Associate Director of the Institute, seemed headed for bigger things, and a couple of patents brought him modest but steady royalties. And, best of all, his ridiculously straightforward mind made him easy to handle.

It had seemed a good idea until the afternoon Victor Schenley had sauntered into her office in the administrative wing of the Institute and she had seen that look come into his eyes. She had recognized him instantly from the pictures the newspapers had carried when he inherited the great Schenley fortune, and had handled that first meeting with subtle care.

After that he had begun to come around more and more frequently, sitting on her desk and talking, turning on his charm. She had soon seen where his questions about the Institute's affairs were leading. He was determined to recover several million dollars which the elder Schenley had intended for the research organization he had founded and endowed, the Institute of which Victor had inherited titular leadership. Victor did not need the money. He just could not bear to see it escape his direct control. He still did not suspect how much Margaret had guessed of his plans—she knew when to hide her financial acumen behind her beauty—and she was holding that information in reserve.

He had begun to take her out, at first only on the evenings Eldon was busy, but then growing steadily bolder and more insistent. She had been deliberately provocative and yet aloof, rejecting his repeated propositions. She was playing for bigger stakes, the Schenley fortune itself. But she had remained engaged to Eldon. She disliked burning bridges behind herself unless absolutely necessary and Eldon was still a sure thing.

Then one day had come Eldon's casual remark that as Associate Director he was considering calling in the auditors for a routine check of the books. That had started everything. Victor had appeared startled, just as she expected, when she repeated Eldon's statement, and the very next night Eldon had met with his disfiguring "accident."

VICTOR parked his sleekly expensive car in front of the Institute's main building. "You wait here, dearest," he said. "I'll only be a few minutes."

He kissed her, but seemed preoccupied. She watched him, slender and nattily dressed, as he crossed the empty lobby and pressed the button for the automatic elevator. The cage came down, he closed the door behind himself, and then Margaret was out of the car and hurrying up the walk. It was the intelligent thing to know as much as possible about Victor's movements.

The indicator stopped at three. Margaret lifted her evening gown above her knees and took the stairway at a run.

From Eldon's laboratory, the only room on the floor to show a light, she could hear voices.

"I don't like leaving loose ends, Carmichael. And it's your own gun."

"So it was deliberate. But why?" Eldon sounded incredulous.

Victor spoke again, his words indistinguishable but his tone assured and boastful.

There was a muffled splatting sound, a grunt of pain.

"Why, damn your soul!" Victor's voice again, raised in angry surprise. But no pistol shot.

Margaret peered around the door. Victor held the pistol, but Eldon had his wrist in a firm grasp and was twisting.

Victor's nose was bleeding copiously and, although his free hand clawed at Eldon's one good eye, the physicist was forcing him back. Margaret felt a stab of fear. If anything happened to Victor it would cost her—millions.

She paused only to snatch up a heavy, foot-long bar of copper alloy as she crossed the room. She raised it and crashed it against the side of Eldon's skull. Sheer tenacity of purpose maintained his hold on Victor's gun hand as he staggered back, dazed, and Margaret could not step aside in time. The edge of an equipment-laden table bit into her spine as Eldon's body collided with hers, and the bar was knocked from her hand.

Eldon got one sidelong glimpse of the girl and felt a sudden thrill that she had come to help him. He did not see what she had done.

And then hell broke loose. Leaping flames in his body. The unmistakable spitting crackle of bound charges breaking loose. The sensation of hurtling immeasurable distances through alternate layers of darkness and blinding light. Grey cotton wool filling his nose and mouth and ears. Blackness.

II

A SHRIVELED BLOOD-RED moon cast slanting beams through gigantic, weirdly distorted trees. The air was dead still where he lay, but overhead a howling wind tossed the top branches into eerie life. He was lying on moss. Moss that *writhed* resentfully under his weight. His stomach was heaving queasily and his head was one throbbing ache. His right leg refused to move. It seemed to be stuck in something.

He was not alone. Something was prowling nearby among the unbelievably tall trees. He sat up weakly, automatically, but somehow he did not care very deeply what happened to him. Not at first.

The prowling creature circled, trying to outline him against the slanting shafts of crimson moonlight. He heard it move, then saw its eyes blue-green and luminous in the shadows, only a foot or two from the ground.

Then his scalp gave a sudden tingle, for the eyes *rose upward*. Abruptly they were five feet above ground level. He held his breath, but still more wondering than afraid. A vagrant gust brought a spicy odor to his nostrils, something strongly reminiscent of sandalwood. Not an animal smell.

He moved slightly. The moss beneath him *squeaked* a protest and writhed unpleasantly.

The thing with the glowing eyes moved closer. *Squeak-squeak, squeak-squeak,* the strange moss complained. And then a human figure appeared momentarily in a slender shaft of red light.

Margaret! But even as it vanished again in the shadows he knew it wasn't. A woman, yes, but not Margaret. Too short. Too fully curved for Margaret's graceful slenderness. And the hair had glinted darkly under the crimson moon while Margaret's was pale and golden. He wanted to call out, but a sense of lurking danger restrained him.

Suddenly the stranger was at his side.

"*Lackt,*" she whispered.

The palms of her hands glowed suddenly with a cold white fire as she cupped them together to form a reflector. She bent over, leaving herself in darkness and directing the light upon Eldon as he sat in amazed disbelief.

Although the light from her hands dazzled his single eye he caught an impression of youth, of well-tanned skin glittering with an oily lotion that smelled of sandalwood, of scanty clothing—the night was stiflingly hot—and of hair the same color as the unnatural moonlight, clinging in ringlets around a piquant but troubled face.

"El-ve-don?" she asked softly. Her throaty voice betrayed passionate excitement.

He wet his dry lips.

"Eldon," he said hoarsely, wondering how she knew his name and why she had mispronounced it by inserting an extra syllable. "Eldon Carmichael."

His answer seemed to puzzle her. Her strange eyes gleamed more brightly.

"Who are you? And how in the name of sin do you do that trick with your hands?" It was the first question to enter his confused mind.

"Sin?" She repeated the one word and drew back with a suddenly hostile air.

For a moment she seemed about to turn and run. But then she looked once more at his mangled, disfigured face and gave a soft exclamation of disappointment and pity.

Eldon became irrationally furious and reached his single arm to grab her. She eluded him with a startled yet gracefully fluid motion and spat some unintelligible words that were obviously heartfelt curses. Her hand moved ominously to a pocket in her wide belt.

Then all at once she crouched again, moving her head from side to side. He opened his mouth, but she clamped one glowing hand over it while the other went up in a gesture commanding silence. Her hand was soft and cool despite its glow.

For a full minute she listened, hearing something Eldon could not. Then she placed her lips close to his ear and whispered. Her words were utterly unintelligible but her urgency communicated itself to him.

He tried to rise and discovered that his leg was deeply embedded in the dirt and moss. He wondered how it had gotten that way. The girl grasped his knee and pulled, and as soon as he saw what she wanted he put his muscles to work too. With an agonized shriek from the strange moss his leg came free and he tried to rise. The sudden movement made him dizzy.

Unhesitatingly the girl threw herself upon him, bearing him down while all the while she whispered admonitions he could not understand. She was strong in a lithe, whipcord way, and neither mentally nor physically was he in condition to resist. He allowed himself to be pushed to a reclining position.

The light from her hands went out abruptly, leaving the forest floor darker than ever. She reached into her belt, extracted a small object he could not see, touched it to his head. Eldon went rigid.

ONE of her hands grasped his belt. She gave a slight tug. His body rose easily into the air as though completely weightless, and when she released him he *floated.* ..

Her fingers found a firm hold on his collar. She moved, broke into a steady run, and his body, floating effortlessly at the height of her waist, followed. She ran quietly, sure-footed in the darkness, with only the sound of her breathing and the thin protests of the moss under her feet. Sometimes his collar jerked as she changed course to avoid some obstacle.

"I have no weight, but I still have mass and therefore inertia," he found himself thinking, and knew he should be afraid instead of indulging in such random observations.

He discovered he could turn his head, although the rest of his body remained locked in weightless rigidity, and gradually he became aware of something following them. From the glimpses he caught in the slanting red moonbeams it resembled a lemur. He watched it glide from tree to tree like a flying squirrel, catch the rough bark and scramble upward, glide again.

A whistle, overhead, a sound entirely distinct from that of the wind-whipped branches, brought the girl to a sudden stop. She jerked Eldon to a halt in mid-air beside her and pulled him into the deeper shadow beneath a gnarled tree just as a great torpedo-shaped thing passed above the treetops, glistening like freshly spilled blood in the moonglow. Some sort of wingless aircraft.

They waited, the girl fearful and alert. The red moon dropped below the horizon and a few stars—they were of a normal color—did little to relieve the blackness. The flying craft returned, invisible this time but still making a devilish whistle that grated on Eldon's nerves like fingernails scraped down a blackboard as it zigzagged slowly back and forth. Then gradually the noise died away in the distance.

The girl sighed with relief, made a chirruping sound, and the lemur-thing came skittering down the tree beneath which they were hiding. She spoke to it, and it gave a sailing leap that ended on Eldon's chest. Its handlike paws grasped the fabric of his shirt. He sank a few inches toward the ground, but immediately floated upward again with nightmarish buoyancy.

The girl reached to her belt again, and then she was floating in the air beside him. She grasped his collar and they were slanting upward among the branches. The lemur-thing rose confidently, perched on his chest. They moved slowly up to treetop level, where the girl paused for a searching look around. Then she rose above the trees, put on speed, and the hot wind whistled around Eldon's face as she towed him along.

It was a dream-scene where time had no meaning. It might have been minutes or hours. The throbbing of his headache diminished, leaving him drowsy.

The lemur-thing broke the spell by chattering excitedly. In the very dim starlight he could just discern that it was pointing upward with one paw, an uncannily human gesture.

The girl uttered a sharp word and dove toward the treetops, and Eldon looked up in time to see a huge leathery-winged shape swooping silently upon them. He felt the foetid breath and glimpsed hooked talons and a beak armed with incurving teeth as the thing swept by and flapped heavily upward again.

THE girl released him abruptly, leaving his heart pounding in sudden terrible awareness of his utter helplessness. He felt himself brush against a branch that stood out above the others and start to drift away. But the lemur hooked its hind claws into his shirt and grasped the branch with its forepaws, anchoring him against the wind.

A long knife flashed in the girl's hand and she was shooting upward to meet the monster. She had not deserted him after all. She closed in, tiny beside the huge shape, as the monster beat its batlike wings in a furious attempt to turn and rend her. There was a brief flurry, a high-pitched cry of agony, and the ungainly body crashed downward through a nearby treetop, threshing in its death agonies.

Eldon felt the trembling reaction of relief as the girl glided downward, still breathing hard from her exertion, and it left him feeling even more helpless and useless than ever. Once more she took him in tow and the nightmare flight continued.

Over one area a ring of faintly luminous fog was rolling, spreading among the trees, contracting like a gaseous noose. "*Kauva ne Sin,*" the girl spat, bitter anger in her voice, and fear and unhappiness too. She made a long high detour around the fog ring and looked back uneasily even after they were past.

ALL at once they were diving again, down below the treetops that to Eldon looked no different from any of the others. But to the girl it was journey's end. She twisted upright and her feet touched gently as she reached to her belt and regained normal weight. Eldon still floated.

The girl pushed him through the air and into a black hole between the spreading roots of a huge tree. The hole slanted downward, twisting and turning, and became a tunnel. The lemur-thing jumped down and scampered ahead.

It was utterly dark until she made her hands glow again, after they had passed a bend. Finally the tunnel widened into a room.

She left him floating, touched one wall, and it glowed with a soft, silvery light that showed him he was in living quarters of some kind. The walls were transparent plastic, and through their glow he could see the dirt and stones and tangled tree roots behind them. Water trickled in through a hole in one wall, passed through an oval pool of brightly colored tiles recessed into the floor, and vanished through a channel in the opposite wall. There were furnishings of strange design, simple yet adequate, and archways that seemed to lead to other rooms.

The girl returned to him, pushed him over to a broad, low couch, shoving him downward. She touched him with an egg-shaped object from her belt and he sank into the soft cushions as abruptly his body went limp and recovered its normal heaviness. He stared up at her.

She was beautiful in a vital, *different* way. Natural and healthily normal looking, but with an indescribable trace of the exotic. Her hair, he saw—now that the light was no longer morbidly ruddy—was a lovely dark red with glints of fire. She was young and self-assured, yet oddly thoughtful, and there was about her an aura of vibrant attraction that seemed to call to all his forgotten dreams of loveliness. But Eldon Carmichael was very sick and very tired.

She looked at him speculatively, a troubled frown narrowing her strangely luminous grey-green eyes, and asked a question. He shook his head to show lack of understanding, wondering who she was and where he was.

She turned away, her shoulders sagging with disappointment. Then she noticed that she was smeared with a gooey reddish-black substance, evidently from the huge bat-thing she had fought and killed. She gave a shiver of truly feminine repugnance.

Quickly she discarded her close fitting jacket, brief skirt and the wide belt from which her sheathed dagger hung, displaying no trace of embarrassment at Eldon's presence even when she stood completely nude.

Her body was fully curved but smoothly muscular, an active body. It was a symphony of perfection—except that across the curve of one high, firm breast ran a narrow crescent-shaped scar, red as though from a wound not completely healed. Once she glanced down at it and her face took on a hunted, fearful look.

She tested the temperature of the pool with one outstretched bare toe and then plunged in, and as she bathed herself she hummed a strangely haunting tune that was full of minor harmonies and unfamiliar melodic progressions. Yet it was not entirely a sad tune, and she seemed to be enjoying her bath. Occasionally she glanced over at him, questioning and thoughtful.

Eldon tried to stay awake, but before she left the pool his one eye had closed.

PAIN in the stump of his arm brought a vague remembrance of having used it to strike at someone or something. For a while he lay half awake, trying to recall that dream about a girl flying with him through a forest that certainly existed nowhere on Earth. But the sound of trickling water kept intruding.

He opened his eye and came face to face with the lemur-thing from his nightmare. Its big round eyes assumed an astounded, quizzical expression as he blinked, and then it was gone. He heard it scuttling across the floor.

He sat up and made a quick survey of his surroundings. Then the girl of the—no, it hadn't been a dream—emerged from an archway with the lemur on her shoulder. It made him think of stories he had read about witches of unearthly beauty and the uncannily intelligent animals, familiars, that served them.

"Hey, where am I?" he demanded.

She said something in her unfamiliar language.

"Who are you?" he asked, this time with gestures.

She pointed to herself. "Krasna," she said.

He pointed to himself. "Eldon. Eldon Carmichael."

"El-ve-don?" she asked just as eagerly as when she had found him, half as though correcting him.

He shook his head. "Just Eldon." Her eyes clouded and she frowned.

After a moment she spoke again, and again he shook his head. "Sorry, no savvy," he declared.

She snapped her fingers as though remembering something and hurried from the room, returning with a small globe of cloudy crystal. She motioned him to lie back, and for a minute or two rubbed the ball vigorously against the soft, smooth skin of her forearm. Then she held it a few inches above his eye and gestured that he was to look at it.

The crystal glowed, but not homogeneously. Some parts became brighter than others, and of different colors. Patterns formed and changed, and watching them made him feel drawn out of himself, into the crystal.

The strange girl started talking—talking—talking in an unhurried monotone. Gradually scattered words began to form images in his mind. Pictures, some of them crystal clear but with their significance still obscure, others foggy and amorphous. There were people and—things—and something so completely and utterly vile that even the thought made his brain cells cringe in fear of uncleansable defilement.

It must have been hours she talked to him, for when he came out of the globe and back into himself her voice was tired and there were wrinkles of strain across her forehead. She was watching him intently and he suspected he had been subjected to some form of hypnosis.

"Where am I? How did I get here?" he asked, and realized only when the words were out that he was speaking something other than English.

Krasna did not answer at once. Instead a look of unutterable sadness stole over her face. And then she was weeping bitterly and uncontrollably.

Eldon was startled and embarrassed, not understanding but wishing he could do something, anything, to help her. Crying females had always disturbed him, and she looked so completely sad and—and defeated. The lemur-thing glowered at him resentfully.

"What is it?" he asked.

"You are not El-ve-don," she sobbed.

With his new command of her language, perhaps aided by some measure of telepathy, he received an impression of El-vedon as a shining, unconquerable champion of unspecified powers, one who was fated to bring about the downfall of—of something obscenely evil and imminently threatening. He could not recall what it was, and Krasna's wracking sobs did not help him think clearly.

"Of course I'm not El-ve-don," he declared, and felt deeply sorry for himself that he was not. "I'm just plain Eldon Carmichael, and I am—or was—a biophysicist." Once, before Victor Schenley had tried to kill him, he *had* been a competent and reasonably happy biophysicist.

At last she wiped her eyes.

"Well, if you don't remember, you just don't, I guess," she sighed. "You are in the world of Varda. Somehow you must have formed a Gateway and *come through.* I found you just by chance and thought—hoped—that you were El-ve-don."

She went on with a long explanation, only parts of which Eldon understood.

HE WAS quite familiar with the theory of alternate worlds—his work with bound charges had given him an inkling of the actuality of other dimensions, and the fantastic idea that bound charges existed simultaneously in two or more "worlds" at once, carrying their characteristic reactions across a dimensional gap had occurred to him frequently as his experiments had progressed. He had even entertained the notion that bound charges were the basic secret of life itself—but the proof still seemed unbelievable. Varda was a world adjoining his own, separated from it by some vagary of space or time-spiral warping or some obscure phase of the Law of Alternate Probabilities. But here he was, in Varda.

He distinctly remembered hearing one of the resonant system components in his laboratory let go, not *flow* but *break*, and guessed that the sudden strain might have been sufficient to warp the very nature of matter in its vicinity.

"Your world is one of the Closed Worlds," Krasna explained. "Things from it do not *come through* easily. Unfortunately the one from which the Luvans came is open much of the time."

Eldon tried to think what a Luvan was, but recalled only a vaguely disquieting impression of something disgusting — and deadly.

"I hoped so much." Tears gathered in Krasna's strange eyes. "I thought perhaps when I found you that the old prophecy—the one to defeat Sasso—but perhaps I have been a fool to believe in the old prophecy at all. And Sasso—" Her expressive mouth contorted with loathing.

"How do I get back to my own world?" Eldon demanded.

Krasna stared at him until he began to fidget.

"There is but one Gateway in all Varda, the Gateway of Sasso," she declared in the tone of a person stating an obvious if unpleasant fact. "And only El-ve-don can defeat the Faith."

"Oh!" He laughed in mirthless near-hysteria at the thought of himself as the unconquerable El-ve-don. Her words left him bleakly despondent.

"What happened to the others who were near me when — this — happened?" he asked. "The man and the woman?"

Krasna straightened in surprise. "There were others? Oh! Perhaps one of them is El-ve-don!"

"I doubt it," Eldon said wryly.

BUT Krasna's excitement was not to be quelled. She spoke to the lemur-thing as if to another human, and the creature scuttled up the tunnel leading to the surface. Eldon thought once more of the witch-familiars of Earth legends. If he had *come through* to Varda, perhaps Vardans had visited Earth.

"We shall find out about them soon," she said.

"What happens to me?" Eldon wanted to know.

He had to repeat his question, for Krasna had suddenly become deeply pre-occupied. At last she looked at him. There was pity in her glance, not pity for his situation but pity for a disfigured, frightened and querulous cripple. She did not understand the overwhelming longing for Earth which was mounting within him every second. Her pity grated upon his nerves. He could pity himself all he chose —and he had reason enough—but he rejected the pity of others.

"Well?" he demanded.

"Oh, you can stay with me, I guess. That is, if you dare associate with me." There was bitterness in her voice.

None of it made sense. She had saved him from the forest, brought him to her home. Why should he be afraid to associate with her? But all he wanted was to find Margaret, if she were in this strange world, and escape back to Earth. There, though he was a cripple, he was not so abysmally ignorant. He knew he should feel grateful to this red-haired girl, but deep in his brain an irrational resentment gnawed. He tried to fight it down, knowing he had to learn much more about his new environment before he could survive alone. The last shreds of his crumbling self-confidence had been stripped away.

Suddenly he realized he was ravenously hungry.

"All right," the girl said. "We will eat now."

He stared at her in discomfiture. He had not mentioned food. She laughed.

"Really," she said, "you seem to know nothing about closing your mind."

Resentment flared higher. She was a telepath, and he was not proud of his thoughts.

The passageway into which he followed her was dark, but after a few steps her hands began to light the way as they had in the forest.

"How do you do it?" he asked. To him the production of cold light in living tissues was even more astounding than her control of gravity. That still seemed too much like a familiar dream he had had many times on Earth, and it probably had some mechanical basis.

She smiled at him as though at a curious child. "That is old knowledge in the Open Worlds. Your Closed Worlds must be very strange."

"But how do you control it?"

She shrugged her lovely shoulders. "You may be fit to learn—later." But she spoke doubtfully.

The food was unfamiliar but satisfying, warmed in a matter of seconds in an oven-like box to which he could see no power connections or controls. In reply to his questions she pointed to a hexagonal red crystal set in the back of the box and looked at him as though he should understand.

One of the foods was a sort of meat, and with only one arm Eldon found himself in difficulty. Krasna noticed, took his eating utensils and cut it into bite-sized bits. She said nothing, but he finished the meal in sullen silence, resentful that he needed a woman's help even to eat.

Afterwards Krasna buckled on her heavy belt with the dagger swinging at her hip.

"I must go out now," she said. "The not-quite-men of the Faith are prowling tonight, and Luvans are with them."

"But—?"

"You could not help."

The reminder of his uselessness rankled, but still he felt a pang at the thought of a girl like her going into danger.

"But you?" he asked.

"I can take care of myself. And if not, what matter? I am Krasna."

Once more she read his thoughts.

"No. Stay here." It was not a request but an order. "If you were to fall into the hands of—her—it would add to my troubles. And my own people would kill you on sight, because you have been with me."

III

AFTER SHE LEFT HE PROWLED restlessly around the underground rooms, looking, touching, exploring. He tried to find the controls for the illuminated walls, and there were none. Every square inch of the smooth plastic seemed exactly like every other. The other devices—even the uses of some he could not determine—were the same. There were no switches or other controls. It was all very puzzling.

He spent most of his time in the main room where Krasna had left the walls lighted, for the unfamiliar darkness of the others gave him the eerie feeling that something was watching him from behind. Some of the fittings seemed unaccountably familiar, although operating on principles he was unable to understand. The sense of familiarity amid strangeness gave him a schizophrenic sensation, as though two personalities struggled for control, two personalities with different life-patterns and experiences. A most unsettling feeling.

He thought of Margaret, longingly, and then of Victor. His fist clenched and his lips tightened. If Schenley were still alive, some day there would be a reckoning. Schenley had been sure of himself and had boasted. And now, he was sure, Margaret knew just what sort of rat Victor really was.

His thoughts turned to his anomalous position with the red-haired girl. Krasna had brought him out of the perilous forest purely because she thought he was this wonderful El-ve-don. And now he was living in her home, entirely dependent upon her sense of pity. It was galling.

He found a large rack containing scrolls mounted on cleverly designed double rollers, and after the first few minutes of puzzling out the writing letter by letter he found himself reading with growing fluency. Part of the same hypnotic and telepathic process, he reflected, through which Krasna had taught him her spoken language. At first he read mainly to escape his own unpleasant thoughts and keep occupied, but then he grew interested. Brief, undetailed references began to make pictures—the Gateway—the Fortress of Sin—the Forest People, evidently the clan to which Krasna belonged—the Luvans—Sasso. His mind squirmed away from that last impression. Gradually the disconnected pictures began to form a sequence.

He was still reading hours later when Krasna emerged from the tunnel. She gave a little sigh of fatigue, dropped her heavy weapon belt, and started to undress. But the lemur-thing interrupted. It raced down the tunnel, a furry streak that chattered for attention.

"Later, Tikta," Krasna told it, continuing to disrobe. "I'm too tired to understand."

The sight of her loveliness as she stepped into the warm pool gave Eldon no pleasure. If everything had been different . . . Instead it brought rankling resentment, of her, of his condition, of everything. She looked at him just as impersonally as she did at her lemur. It was evident she did not consider him a man, a person. He was just something she had picked up by mistake and was too kind-hearted to dispose of. Under the circumstances it would have been ridiculous for him to turn away.

"Now, Tikta," she said after her bath, sinking down on one of the couches.

The little creature ran to her, leaped to her shoulder and placed its tiny handlike front paws on opposite sides of her head. Krasna closed her eyes.

To Eldon, observing closely, it was like watching someone who was seeing an emotional movie. Hate, anger, hope, surprise, puzzlement, all followed each other across her mobile, expressive features, ending in disappointment and disgust. At last Tikta removed its paws and Krasna opened her eyes.

"Your—friends—" she hesitated over the word. "They are in Varda. Both."

"Is the girl all right? Where are they? How do you know? Did you see them?" The questions tumbled from Eldon's lips.

Krasna smiled faintly. "No, I have not seen them. But Tikta can catch the thoughts of all wild things that can not guard their minds, and tell me. The wild things saw your—friends." Again she hesitated, and this time made a grimace of angry distaste.

"Where is the girl? Can you take me to her?" he demanded excitedly.

"No. They are both beyond the Mountains that Move."

"So?"

"In the land of the Faith," she snapped.

"But couldn't you—?"

Pity was almost smothered in stern contempt as she looked at him. "We do not go among the Faith except for a purpose. And that purpose is not returning you to your—friends."

"But your people?"

"They would not help you if they could. For I am Krasna."

He did not grasp the significance of her words but the firmness of her tone indicated there was no use arguing with this self-willed, red-haired person. Nevertheless he resolved to try to find Margaret, and as soon as possible.

Krasna's eyes widened with apprehension at his thought.

"You are a fool. And if you must try you had better read all the scrolls first. Only El-ve-don could survive, and the death of the Faith is not easy."

Eldon cursed silently. This damnable girl, although beautiful in her own odd way, not only insulted him with her pity but invaded his mind.

"Well, shut your mind if you don't like it," she snapped angrily. "You're odd, too, and far from beautiful."

MARGARET MATSON opened her eyes. A strange man stood over her, and what a man! He was huge and hard looking, with dark, wind-toughened skin. He was dressed in some sort of barbaric military uniform, colorful and heavily decorated. And he was playing with a needle pointed dagger.

Her mouth opened. "Victor!" she screamed.

Her voice reverberated hollowly from the curved walls and roof of a small metal room. The big man screwed up his face at the shrill noise.

"Victor! Help me!" she shouted again.

Victor failed to answer.

"Eldon!" she yelled.

The big warrior spun his dagger casually, the way a boy would play with a stick. His lips curled back in a wolfish grin, emphasizing two of his strong white teeth that projected beyond the others like fangs. His whole appearance was brutal.

"Where am I? What do you want with me?" she gasped. Then her glance followed the man's eyes. Her form-fitting evening gown was torn and disarrayed. She snatched it down with a show of indignant modesty, and the man grinned widely. One corner of his mouth twitched.

Margaret would have been even more frightened except that the big soldier's reaction struck a familiar note that lent her confidence. He spoke, but his words were gibberish.

Then from a wall locker he produced two helmet-like devices, metal frames with pieces of some translucent material set to touch the wearer's temples.

She started to draw away as he stooped

to push one over her hair, but submitted when he frowned and fingered the point of his knife. He donned the other helmet.

"My name is Wor, *merta* of the Forces and *torna* to Great Sasso Himself." She understood him now.

"You and I might be good friends—if Sin allows," he continued. "You bear a great resemblance to Highness Sin, even though your color is faded."

Despite her position Margaret bridled angrily. Wor laughed uproariously. "Your temper is like Highness Sin's too," he declared appreciatively.

"Who—who is this Sin?"

"You will find out," Wor replied evenly. Then his face sobered and softened. "If you want a chance to be with me, take my advice and be careful what you say and even what you think. Sin is all-powerful—and jealous. She *knew* when you appeared in our world."

"Where is Victor?" Margaret asked. "Is he—?"

"The one-armed one, or the other?"

Margaret's face showed scorn. "Would I be interested in cripples?"

"Oh, the slender one. He too will be taken before Highness Sin."

"And Eldon?"

Wor looked annoyed. "Gone. *Came through* on the seaward side of the Mountains."

"But why didn't you get him, too?"

Wor was distinctly irked. "We looked. Either he *came through* below ground level, in which case he is dead, or the Rebels found him, in which case he is dead, too. Write him off."

Margaret let a couple of tears roll down her cheeks, but not from grief over Eldon. She knew that in this strange situation into which she had been flung she would need a friend and protector.

"What is going to happen to poor helpless me? Oh, won't you help me?" she asked plaintively. Her eyes expressed open admiration for the corded muscles rippling beneath Wor's military tunic.

It was an ancient appeal and Margaret realized it had been most obviously applied. But it worked. Men were so easily handled, even this Wor. Carefully she hid her satisfaction as he sat down beside her.

She moved a little closer to him as he talked, telling her about his land and what she could expect. After a while he sheathed his dagger.

Someone tapped on the bulkhead. Wor bellowed and the door opened. The man who entered raised his hand in a respectful salute, and Margaret would have given much to understand what he said. But Wor stretched out one enormous hand and snatched the helmet from her head. The words became meaningless but she could still see the deference with which Wor was treated.

After the man had gone and Wor had crammed the helmet back on her head she was careful by word and look to let him see she understood his importance. She could almost see his great chest swell. Men were so simple, when handled properly.

A whistle emitted a warning screech.

"We land in a few minutes," Wor told her. "Do nothing that might anger Highness Sin. Your life depends upon it."

He rose, snatched her to him in an embrace that was without tenderness and left her lips bruised. Before she could decide whether to resist or respond he was gone. A few minutes later the flying machine struck with a cushioned thump and the sibilant hiss of its engines died.

THE two soldiers who escorted her out looked suspiciously at the helmet Wor had allowed her to retain, but made no attempt to remove it. The ship had landed in the courtyard of a tremendous castle. Massive, weather-streaked grey walls soared upward to end high above in incongruously stream-lined turrets from which projected the ribbed and finned snouts of strange weapons. Windows were few and small, and the whole structure looked incredibly ancient.

The two guards hustled her through a circular doorway into a large hall that formed a startling contrast to the bleak exterior. It was richly appointed, and the walls were hung with heavy tapestries that glowed softly in patterns that changed and shifted even as she watched them.

There were many people in the room, soldiers and richly gowned women with olive skins and dark hair. But again there was contrast, for standing stiffly against one wall was a rank of perhaps thirty men and women, all stark naked and all staring straight ahead with blank unseeing eyes. They did not move a muscle as Margaret was led in, though other heads turned and the low hum of conversation ceased abruptly.

Margaret's attention centered almost instantly on the woman occupying a dais at the far end of the hall, and after that she could not tear her eyes away. This was Highness Sin, of whom even Wor stood in awe. Margaret stared and Sin stared back. Except for the difference in coloring this woman could have been Margaret's twin. She was beautiful, the white skin of her face and shoulders setting off her revealingly cut jet gown and ebony hair, and her haughty face wore an expression of ruthless power. Margaret knew that under similar circumstances she would have worn the same expression.

The woman raised one exquisitely groomed hand and the guards pushed Margaret forward, her feet sinking deep into springy carpeting at each step. Every eye except those of the stiff, unseeing people against the wall turned to follow her, and Margaret was uncomfortably aware of her torn and soiled gown and her tangled, uncombed hair.

She looked up at Sin and had an uncomfortable feeling the ruler was looking into her mind, *understanding* her.

"So you are the woman who *came through.*" Even her voice was remarkably like Margaret's.

Margaret said nothing.

"Why did you come to my world?" the ruler asked.

"It wasn't any of my doing," Margaret exploded petulantly. "I still don't know where I am, and I don't think I like it here, and I had nothing to do with coming. It was all on account of that Eldon's stupid experiments, and if he hadn't tried to kill Victor—"

"But you are here," Sin interrupted, tightening her sensuous full lips in a way Margaret recognized as one of her own mannerisms. "Perhaps I can find use for you."

"Can't you send me back—?"

"Why should I?"

There was no answer to that, and Margaret tried to hide her growing nervousness. Sin allowed herself a feline smile.

Wor came striding forward. "Highness Sin," he boomed. "I desire to claim my right to this captive."

Sin's eyes narrowed suspiciously, and Margaret's intuition told her the similarity between them had something to do with her hesitation.

"No. She is not of the Rebels, and therefore you have no captor's rights. You recognized her as an Outworldling yourself when you gave her a thought helmet. Thus by custom she is subject to a hearing —if I so choose."

"Then grant me, Oh Sin—"

"Go pick yourself another plaything. There are several in the slave pits who still have their minds. I must find out more about this one."

"But—"

"I have spoken."

Wor turned away, disgruntled but not daring to try the dark ruler's patience further. Sin returned her attention to Margaret.

"Follow me," she ordered. "We will talk in private."

THE ROOMS outdid any Hollywood production for sheer sybaritic elegance. Sin chose a couch and sank down with a languidness that did not fool Margaret in the least.

"Don't you want to thank me for saving you from becoming Wor's plaything?" she asked slyly.

Margaret decided on boldness. There was too much similarity between them for any successful deception as to character.

"Wor might have made an interesting plaything himself," she retorted. "But he is yours?"

Sin put her head back against the cushions. Her high, brittle laughter contained a trace of malice.

"Oh, I must read his thoughts when I tell him that," she said. "Earth Woman, Wor likes to consider himself rough and masterful. He's a mutant savage, you know, and if it were not for the Luvans of Great Sasso he would be only—"

"But he's yours?" Margaret broke in.

Without rising Sin assumed a regal posture. "All who serve Great Sasso are mine."

Margaret raised her eyebrows but said nothing.

Sin changed the subject abruptly. "There

were three of you who *came through*. One my Forces could not find."

"You mean Eldon?" Margaret asked.

Sin sat up, tensely alert. "Did you say El-ve-don?" she demanded harshly.

"No. Eldon."

Sin relaxed slightly. "What is he like?"

Margaret allowed herself a superior smile. "Why do you ask?"

"What is he like?" Sin's voice crackled.

Margaret held out the little finger of one hand and made winding motions around it. Evidently Sin understood the reference, for she smiled and leaned back.

"Why are you interested in him?" Margaret insisted. "He's crippled and disfigured, ugly, an honest fool. And Wor said he's probably dead."

Sin frowned. "We — myself serving Great Sasso — have almost won Varda. But the resistance of the Rebels provides an annoying delay. And there is a certain prophecy among the Rebels, a stupid story about a creature called El-ve-don, and the name was sufficiently similar . . . We understand each other, Earth Woman?"

Margaret nodded emphatically.

"Just what were your relations with this —this Eldon?"

Margaret explained.

"Oh, you have a monogamous society there," Sin commented.

"Theoretically, yes."

"We did here too, in the dark ages before the Faith. Stupid, isn't it? So restricting."

Sin had regained the poise Eldon's name had disturbed, and Margaret decided to press her advantage while she was in this friendly mood.

"I'd like to see Victor now, Highness. Wor said—"

Sin's eyes hardened instantly. "Sometimes Wor talks too much. No. I must see the Earthman first."

"But—"

"Remember, my dear, I am Sin."

IV

THE GUARDS WHO CAME FOR Margaret looked startled at their orders.

"Not the slave pens, Highness?" one of them asked.

"This woman will perhaps become Of the Faith," Sin snapped. "Treat her accordingly."

Margaret looked up, but Sin offered no explanation.

The suite of rooms to which she was taken were all she could have desired, but the windows looked out on a sheer drop and the guards bolted the door behind her. She had just time to glance around when the door opened again.

"Your first slave," a single guard announced. "A gift to you from Highness Sin."

The slave was a girl in her teens, scrawny and underfed and completely nude. Her face wore the same blank, uncomprehending look Margaret had noticed on the naked people in the audience chamber. Across her rigidly outstretched arms lay several rich dresses.

"One of the Rebels," the guard satisfied Margaret's curiosity. "They make good durable slaves when their brains have been treated and they have received the slave-mark of Sin, though of course you must think your orders in detail. Perhaps you had better speak your orders at first, until you grow used to giving thought-commands. In the Vat these Rebels are excellent. So vital.

"Highness Sin also sends you some of her own clothing." He withdrew, and this time did not lock the door.

"Put those dresses down," Margaret told her slave. The girl complied.

"Where is the bath?"

The slave girl pointed. She seemed to have no power of speech and her face was dull and emotionless.

"Get it ready for me."

At first Margaret felt faintly uncomfortable under the girl's mindless stare, but soon grew accustomed to it. The girl obeyed perfectly, like a machine. Sin's gowns clung as though made for Margaret alone, and there was a table loaded with cosmetics. When she was finished Margaret felt more herself. Fresh clothes did wonders for her morale.

Later the guard came again, bowed respectfully, and escorted her to the audience hall. He led her directly to Sin's throne.

"You will want a man, of course," Sin began abruptly. "Which shall it be, Wor or your victor from Earth? Or does some other catch your fancy?"

Margaret noticed for the first time that Victor was in the room, well back from Sin's dais. He looked worried and a soldier stood just behind him. Perhaps a guard. On Earth he had been an excellent catch, but here he had nothing except a certain sly venomousness to recommend him. And already she had sensed complex undercurrents of intrigue and hinted mysteries within the fortress. She must pick the one who could best help her, no longer by Earth standards but by those of Varda.

"I choose Wor," she announced.

Victor's head jerked in an angry gesture. A gleam of anticipation entered Wor's eyes as he stepped forward.

Sin's smile was definitely feline. "So be it. I believe you are a suitable candidate for the Faith, and tonight Wor will initiate you into the service of Great Sasso. Your Earth mind, my dear, has a certain potential value."

A BLOODY MOON leered through her windows. Wor came. There was a trace of diffidence in his manner that had been lacking earlier, and she wondered what payment Sin expected for this favorable treatment. For there was no doubt payment would be demanded. She must be sure it was not overpayment.

Wor guided her to an air car on the flat roof of the fortress. It was not the huge craft in which she had been brought in, but so small they lay side by side. The control buttons looked ridiculously small under Wor's huge hands.

With a hiss they were in the air. She was very conscious of Wor beside her, of his tremendous strength and blatant maleness, and she turned to watch him as he increased their speed. He had wanted her—other men had wanted her before and she knew the signs—but now he ignored her. He was excited, but about something other than herself. She wondered, deeply annoyed, what outlandish sort of religion this Sasso-worship could be to so captivate him. She asked him, but he only grinned.

"There! Over there!" He pointed suddenly in joyful excitement. A great dead-black globe loomed ahead. The stunted foliage of the flat, sandy plain ceased

abruptly in a circle around it, as though afraid to approach. *Something,* some intangible feeling that radiated from the huge ball, made Margaret shiver with a strangely apprehensive exhilaration.

Wor brought the ship down in a sickening vertical drop, and as it touched the sand he half dragged her from the cushions. She had to run to match his long-legged stride as he approached the base of the globe.

"Come on, woman. Great Sasso waits!" he barked, hustling her through a portal where the globe touched the footprint-tracked sand. His eyes were blazing with hungry madness.

The globe was hollow, and inside space itself was different and *alien.* The exhilaration was overpowering now, yet terrifying, with its undertones of ancient and unnamable evil.

"Great Sasso is near!" Wor spoke in a hoarse whisper.

He pointed upward. "The Gateway of Sasso!"

Hanging overhead in the center of the sphere, not suspended in any way she could see, was an area of glowing greenish-yellow luminescence that hurt her eyes. She lowered them to the shimmering, scarcely visible transparent platform beneath it. Sin stood there almost as though floating, enveloped in a voluminous black robe from neck to heels. Her lips, parted in an anticipatory smile, looked black in the greenish light.

Beside and just below the platform stood a huge cylindrical vat, also made of transparent material but plainly visible because it was filled to the brim with some pale lavender fluid. Beside the vat rose a long-boomed hoist, the hook on the end of its chain now hanging empty, and attached to the wall of the vat was a complex mechanism of distorted tubes, warped helical coils and irregularly shaped boxes studded with knobs and handles. An elevated chair was provided beside the controls.

A network of glittering woven cables, branching and rebranching, lying in loops, littered the bowl-shaped floor in seeming disorder. But all led to the machine on the Vat. One cable, as thick through as a large man's arm, curved upward unsupported and vanished into the glow of the Gateway.

Several hundred people turned in silent expectancy as Wor entered. The men almost without exception wore uniforms and the women were sleek and well dressed. A quick glance showed Margaret that the more glittering decorations were gathered toward the center, nearest the Vat and the platform upon which Sin waited.

Wor guided her to the front rank, shoving roughly aside those men and women who did not clear his path rapidly enough. Stooping, he found the end of a cable and buckled the metal strap in which it ended around Margaret's wrist.

"What do I do?" she wailed in uncertainty.

"You will know, and then I will know more about you. But so will Sin, so be careful."

He left her and turned to inspect the seven naked, mindless slaves who stood in empty-eyed imbecility beside the Vat. He exchanged a few words with two soldiers who stood near. They chose a girl slave first, and at their command she meekly extended her hands. With the quick skill of much practice they linked her wrists together and slipped a loop of the binding over the hook of the hoist chain. The eyes of the watchers turned appraisingly upon the girl's lash-scarred body, their faces twisted with expectancy and hunger, as one of the guards forced the girl's head back and popped a small pellet into her mouth. She gulped and swallowed obediently.

Wor climbed to the elevated chair and took his place at the controls of the machine on the Vat. Sin looked down, nodded to him, and made a beckoning gesture toward the doorway.

From the outside came a procession of —things. The Luvans. They looked like oversized, unfinished caricatures of men, but their faces were utterly inhuman. Except for beady black eyes they were a fuzzy, pasty grey all over. Repulsive wart-like lumps sprouted all over their bodies. Ominous looking creatures, as alien to Varda as they would have been on Earth.

The leading Luvan climbed stolidly to the platform. Sin turned, unfastening and tossing aside her cloak. Her bare skin gleamed yellow-green in the Gateway's glow. Then she and the Luvan met in the middle of the platform and *merged* in an indescribable way that stopped the breath in Margaret's throat, became one in a kinship of *alienness*. The faces of the watchers writhed in ugly loathing.

"Sasso comes! Great Sasso comes!" The words began as a mutter and swelled to a concerted roar that shook the sphere. It was a cry of exultation, but mingled with it was an unspoken, questioning longing strong enough to make itself felt.

"Tonight?"

THE GATEWAY was no longer formless light. *Something* was there. Margaret shuddered and had to lower her eyes.

The Sin-Luvan form on the platform leaped and *flowed* in wild contortions of a significance that made Margaret grow faint, yet held her enthralled. The thing in the Gateway became clearer in outline, larger, as though approaching from an immense distance. For an instant it seemed about to break the bonds of the Gateway, to enter into the world of Varda itself. An expectant, thrilled hum went up. Then the thing recoiled and the throng muttered in disappointment.

Sin spread her arms and arched her nude body backward, a living green-ivory statue as she gazed up into the Gateway. And the thing—Sasso—twisted as though communicating with her by its motions.

The priestess made a slight motion to Wor. Instantly his hands moved. Margaret had almost forgotten the cable attached to her wrist, but as Wor touched his levers force flooded her body. For a few seconds it was excruciatingly painful, as if it were liquid fire, but gradually through the pain she felt *alive*, fully and abnormally alive. She was acutely aware of every fiber of her body, of each separate hair, each pore of her skin, each muscle and tendon and bone.

That too changed, became an ecstasy of utterly alien vileness that overwhelmed and submerged her own consciousness. She was no longer herself alone. She was a part of Great Sasso and yet herself more than ever. She was powerful, and nothing was impossible or wrong. Only for an instant did she struggle, more startled than inherently repelled by the strange sensations. Then she surrendered herself completely and utterly—and gladly. She was floating in the exultation of an alien, unguessable obscenity. She had become Of the Faith.

And in that *oneness* many things became clear. She knew that Sasso the Conqueror, Sasso the Incomparable, came from afar to bring his boon to the Faith of Varda. And she knew that the machine and its cables were merely a temporary expedient, until Great Sasso should burst through the Gateway to his destined supremacy. Then They of the Faith, like Sin, the high priestess who was already old in the service of Sasso, could *merge* and become one more directly.

And she knew what bonds barred Great Sasso's way. The inimical thoughts of the Rebels, those ungrateful wretches who had not only rejected Sasso the Wonderful but through the concerted power of their thoughts managed to do *something* to prevent the passage of the Supreme One through the Gateway. The Rebels must be destroyed! They must! They must! Her only wish was that Sasso *come through*. She could sense the thoughts of Sasso's other worshipers, their intense desires so exactly like her own.

But *oneness* with Sasso was not without cost. She could feel herself weakening. Her knees sagged and her vision blurred.

Sin at last gave Wor a signal. The flooding force stopped abruptly and Margaret sank weakly to a sitting position. Around her many others did likewise.

The slave girl's thin scream of despair caught Margaret's attention as Wor touched the controls and the hoist raised her, swung her over the Vat. She was no longer a mindless automaton as she was lowered toward the seething lavender fluid, but a human fully aware of her impending doom. Margaret watched in horrified fascination.

The girl screamed again as her feet touched the surface, this time in agony, and drew her legs up in a convulsive spasm. Slowly, inexorably Wor kept lowering her. She screamed again and this time was unable to raise her legs clear.

Deeper and deeper she was plunged into the pale liquid. The slave girl seemed to dissolve as she touched, for although Margaret could see through the transparent Vat no part of her body was visible below the surface. Finally the screaming stopped.

The girl had vanished utterly. Wor raised the empty hook.

The cable and wristband led a new force into Margaret's body, a force that left her refreshed, replenished. The worshipers around her straightened and their dulled eyes grew brighter. Even the nebulous image of Sasso within the Gateway glowed with a more vivid fire, as though he too had *fed*.

Then once more the power of Sasso flowed, bringing dreams. Alien dreams—dreams of vileness so deep it became enthrallingly beautiful—dreams of conquest, world after world—dreams of great and very precious rewards for those who were Of the Faith.

Again the form of Sasso bulged at the Gateway, and once more drew back. Angry frustration entered the projected dreams—and yet the knowledge that an eternity of ageless tomorrows lay ahead.

Through her trance Margaret sensed the grey and boneless form of a Luvan beside her. It touched her tentatively, then withdrew, and she could feel its thought.

"Not yet—but soon for this one."

Seven times in all a slave was awakened from mindlessness by a pellet of restoring drug and lowered into the lavender fluid of the Vat to feed the Sasso-entity and revive its worshipers with the very essence of life. To Margaret the slaves were not human beings at all. She was now Of the Faith.

And then the last dream faded. The Gateway dimmed to a formless yellow-green glow as Sasso retreated. Sin wrapped the cloak around her white body. The Observance of Sasso had ended. All around her there was an awakening, a stirring.

Wor left his place and pushed his way toward her. He eyed her approvingly, for he had been watching and had found her suitable. She had not resisted Great Sasso. But his brows were creased in thought.

OUTSIDE the fresh night air brought her brain to full activity, thrusting forward half-memories of things she had not consciously noticed during the Observance.

At one time, cutting through the *oneness* of the group, had come a thought of different, more penetrating quality than the others. A thought not of the wondrousness of Sasso but of the beauty and desirability and irresistible attraction of Sasso's priestess. And she had seen Sin half turn, even in the very presence of that she worshiped, to locate its source. Oh, Victor was a sly one. Margaret frowned uneasily. His look when she chose Wor had been laden with malice, and he could become dangerous. Sin had been pleased by his thought.

Wor was silent until they were in the air.

"Soon—as soon as I am ready—the resistance of the Rebels will be crushed. Their forests can not protect them forever from the Forces that I, Wor, command." His eyes were alert for the effect of his words.

"Why don't you wipe them out immediately then?" Margaret asked, thinking of Sasso's *coming through.*

"For one thing, they are clever."

Something in his words made her realize he meant more than he had said, that his motives were not as simple as they appeared.

"You mean—?"

Wor looked at her searchingly. "One person, or two of opposite sexes, will acquire supreme power when Sasso *comes through.* Sin thinks because she is so old in the Faith that it will be she alone. But I have labored harder, devoted myself to the Faith even more wholeheartedly than she."

"But wouldn't that be treason against Great Sasso?" The thought left Margaret aghast.

Wor shook his head. "Sasso is far too great to care who receives the Power. With my knowledge of the Gateway and the Machine of Life, with your Earth brain that can project thoughts with such powerful intensity—"

"But—"

"Do you think you are safe?" Wor broke in angrily. "You are enough like Sin herself to know that she—" He did not need to complete his sentence. Margaret understood. She was well treated now—but Sin could change her mind.

"You and I — together," she agreed. Margaret was an ambitious woman.

With casual ease Wor landed on the fortress roof. Margaret started down the ramp toward her quarters but the big man seized her elbow.

"No," he corrected. "This way."

I N THE MORNING Sin sent a messenger to Wor's rooms. The priestess of Sasso had known exactly where Margaret had spent the night. But she did not know of the things she and Wor had discussed in quiet whispers.

"Did you find Wor a satisfactory companion?" Sin greeted her.

Margaret eyed her steadily. "He's scarcely a mental giant," she replied. "A bit uncouth, but otherwise adequate."

The answer seemed to amuse Sin. "And did you like the Obsevance of Sasso?"

"It's—it's—" Margaret was at a loss for words but her face betrayed the tremendous hunger to wallow once more in Sasso's alien vileness. "How soon again?"

Sin smiled at her enthusiasm.

"You are one of us now, and the inherent character of your Closed World brain will help overcome the Rebels all the sooner," she declared.

A nagging worry gnawed at Margaret's mind. "How about Victor?" she asked.

Sin's face became masklike and unreadable. "He has become Of the Faith too. He may amuse me—for a while. Something new, you know."

Margaret nodded. She dared not probe too deeply.

"Just remember that I am Sin, and that in Varda my word is law."

Margaret wondered whether the ruler was suspicious or had uttered the warning on general principles.

V

F OR SEVERAL DAYS KRASNA was out most of the time, and when home she was usually exhausted. Eldon was aware he was sharing her dwelling on sufferance only, because she pitied his maimed body and abysmal ignorance of this strange world, so in consideration he repressed most of the insistent questions pushing at his lips.

He spent many lonely, idle hours—when not indulging in orgies of self-pity—studying the scrolls he had found.

One dealt in scholarly fashion with the history of Varda, telling of a relatively small but highly civilized group, the Superiors, and a much larger number of uncivilized, barbarian Puvas. Most of the scroll dealt with the efforts of the Superiors to teach the Puvas the arts of civilization. It told of a populous, fairly happy world with a highly integrated culture of which Eldon had seen no trace, and it ended abruptly in the midst of a discussion of the economic system. The ending puzzled him. It was so—unfinished.

Whenever he tired of reading he investigated the marvelous mechanisms the girl used so casually. They left him perplexed, for they had no manual controls and he could not make them work at all. He dared not go out, for the girl had warned him that for her safety as well as his own he should remain underground. She had not explained.

The luminous walls bothered him particularly, and finally he asked her about them. She seemed surprised he did not understand.

"Just put your hand on a wall anywhere, so," she directed. "Now think of light. With your Closed World brain you should have no trouble."

Nothing happened.

"Think harder," she admonished. *"Believe* it will shine."

After a dozen attempts a wall suddenly flared into brilliance at his thought and touch. After that it became progressively easier.

"But why? How does it work?" he asked, still a scientist.

She frowned. "The detailed knowledge was lost many man-lives ago, when the Luvans *came through* and caused the Collapse." There was bitterness in her voice. "But of course it is by thought."

Eldon asked what she meant by the Collapse. She shook her head sadly and refused to discuss it, but before going out again she pointed out a small scroll he had overlooked. It was hastily written, an incomplete and fragmentary continuation of Varda's history.

The progressive civilization of the Superiors had been interrupted by alien creatures, Luvans, who had opened a Gateway from another world. They were few in number and the Superiors had not realized their danger until they had corrupted several individuals — the first of

whom was a woman called Sin—to the worship of their vile deity. Then a deadly, devastating conflict had ensued, with those who refused to embrace the Faith at a terrible disadvantage.

For something in the nature of the Luvans had caused the Superiors' radiation-type power weapons to backfire whenever used near them. And with horror the Superiors had discovered that no matter how cut or bullet-punctured, the gross grey bodies of the Luvans repaired themselves within hours. They utterly refused to remain dead.

Most of the Superiors had been destroyed during the first few months. The survivors had been forced to scatter, taking to the forests.

Then the Luvans, lacking sufficient converts to establish an effective cell of their Faith and unable to corrupt more of the Superiors, had deliberately caused mutations to take place among the savage Puvas, breeding individuals more suited to their plans. The mutants were intelligent, but they lacked some of the Superiors' telepathic ability.

Eldon added up what he had read. Krasna was obviously one of the surviving Superiors, the hunted folk whose coordinated thoughts and mental powers held Varda against the Faith of Sasso. He remembered the lighted walls and the other devices without manual controls. Evidently thought was a tangible force here in Varda. Anxiously he awaited Krasna's return, one question uppermost in his mind.

H E blurted it out as soon as he saw her. "Will you take me to your people? Perhaps they could return me to Earth."

Her body grew rigid and she stared at him in a silence suddenly grown hostile. Her hand hovered momentarily over the deadly radiant blast rod in her belt.

Then her eyes misted and her lips trembled. He knew he had unwittingly inflicted a deep hurt upon her, that somehow his words must have sounded like a taunt. He did not understand why, but he felt deeply apologetic and tried to tell her so. Finally the unfriendliness died from her eyes, but the hurt remained.

"My people?" she said in bitter unhappiness. "I have no people. I am an exile."

With an angry gesture she ripped her jacket aside, exposing the crescent-shaped red scar on her breast. "See this? It is the slave-mark of Sin."

Eldon stared blankly.

Jerkily, with words deliberately held to matter-of-factness, she told him. She had been captured by a raiding party of the Faith, gassed into unconsciousness, and had awakened in the slave pits beneath the Fortress of Sin. There she had been mistreated and tortured, dosed with a drug to reduce her to a mindless automaton, and in a bestial ceremony branded with the slave-mark. Her fate would have been eventual oblivion in the Vat.

But she had succeeded in poisoning herself before the drugs took full effect, and two mindless slaves under the direction of a mutant Puva guard had tossed her dying body on a rubbish heap outside the walls.

She had intended suicide, meaning to thwart the Faith, but a spying party of Rebels had found her barely breathing and rushed her to the Chamber, the only person ever to escape the clutches of the Faith.

"I went to the Thin World while the Chamber repaired the effects of the poison," she told him. "But even the Chamber could not remove *this*. Not so long as Sasso lurks at the Gateway."

Before Eldon could interrupt with questions she continued.

"They would have been kinder to let me die, even in the Vat."

The Forest People remembered the havoc traitorous adherents of the Faith had wrought among them, and would take no chances. Because she bore the slave-mark and was therefore suspect, Krasna had been sent into exile by the Council.

"The others can occasionally gather in small groups and fight their loneliness together," she sobbed. "But for two years they have even kept their minds closed against me. I'm completely alone, always."

Eldon felt a great longing to comfort the weeping girl. But even in her solitary exile she regarded him only as an object for pity, not as an equal and a friend. So there was nothing he could do but leave her alone with her grief. It made him feel more sorry for himself than ever.

NEXT DAY the alarm in the passageway hummed unexpectedly and Krasna leaped up as a man entered. His clothing was of the same blue-green material as hers, evidently intended to match the forest tints, and a bulging weapon belt encircled his waist. A long sword swung at his side, and he looked capable of using it well.

"Bolan!" Krasna greeted him with a happy cry and ran to his arms. He held her affectionately.

"How do you dare — ?" she asked through tears of joy.

The man made a disparaging remark about the Council. "After all, you are my sister."

Eldon felt a relaxation of the tension within himself. His hostility toward the man ebbed.

But Bolan glowered at the Earthman with black dislike.

"You certainly aren't helping yourself with the Council by keeping this Outworldling here," he told the girl. "You'd be well advised to send him into the forest."

"To die? But Bolan, he's harmless," the girl protested.

The man raised his eyebrows. "You think so? The other two *have not appeared in the slave pits*. You know what that means. And with their Closed World minds—"

Eldon interrupted in sudden anger. "Listen here. Margaret would never join that Faith. The man, perhaps, but not the girl. If she's there it is as a prisoner."

Bolan turned on him contemptuously. "Be quiet!"

Krasna intervened. "Your loyalty is touching—but I fear sadly misplaced," she said quietly.

Furious words surged to Eldon's lips, but Krasna refused to argue. She treated him like a sickly and petulant child. Enraged self-pity filled Eldon's mind. If he had both arms he'd show that big oaf a thing or two.

"Don't be a fool, sister, even if you have made a pet of this thing," Bolan said with brutal abruptness. "Get rid of him."

Krasna's mouth set in a stubborn line and her eyes flashed. Bolan shrugged, knowing the signs.

"There's a raiding party near," he

changed the subject. "I'm going to try an ambush."

At once the girl brightened. "I'm going too," she announced, gathering her weapons.

Bolan looked startled, then worried, and finally actually frightened.

"Don't worry," Krasna reassured him bitterly. "I'll go alone. I have no desire to be seen with you and make you an exile too."

"You know I don't believe—" her brother protested.

"Perhaps not. But the Council does."

Bolan went out first. Krasna followed a few minutes later with the lemur-creature riding upon her shoulder. Eldon was left alone with his own very unpleasant thoughts.

H E SLEPT, and was awakened by a skittering sound in the room. Silently he touched the nearest wall and *thought* light, and as the glow flashed he grabbed up the dagger he had placed near. His breath went out in a sigh of relief, for it was only Tikta, and then with a shock he knew something was wrong.

He tried to catch the agile little creature, but it eluded him easily. Then he remembered Krasna's lessons about the power of thought. He sat down again and concentrated on the idea that he meant it no harm.

At last, with desperation overcoming shyness, Tikta made a leap to his shoulder. It had never come near him before. He sat perfectly still as the handlike little paws moved to his head, remembering how he had seen it communicate with Krasna.

The room was gone. A forest glade blurred, cleared, blurred again, shifted from colors to colorblind tones of grey, widened, narrowed, as though seen through changing sets of eyes, finally settled.

Krasna was there, writhing in the grasp of a pair of lumpy grey creatures who towered above her. Luvans. One was using a device that Eldon guessed was calling an aircraft to pick up the prisoner.

He pulled Tikta's paws away and instantly was back in the underground room. Tikta glared at him reproachfully as he sat on the side of the couch. His heart was pounding and he was caught in the grip of uncertainty.

Finally he rose and fumbled in one of the wall cupboards for the extra blast rod Krasna had left behind. He knew he had to at least try, no matter what the odds, but he moved reluctantly.

Tikta pulled at his trouser leg to attract attention, and Eldon remembered with a gasp of dismay. Power weapons such as the blast rod were worse than useless against Luvans. They backfired. Slowly he picked up the heavy sword the lemur-creature had laboriously dragged to the middle of the floor.

Titka's chattering reached a frantic pitch. It leaped to Eldon's shoulder, clinging to his collar with one paw and pointing the way with the other in a manner almost human. The naked blade felt clumsy in his unpracticed right hand. All his life he had been left-handed, and he was no swordsman, and he was frankly frightened. But he had to at least try.

Huge butterflies flitted among the gigantic trees of the forest and rainbow-hued lizards raced over the rough bark, but Eldon hardly noticed. He was haunted by the vision of Krasna.

Tikta guided him straight to the clearing. It was not far. The two Luvans, indistinguishable duplicates of each other, still held the struggling Rebel girl between them.

Tikta leaped down in shrill, gibbering rage and raced ahead of Eldon to the defense of its mistress. One of the Luvans looked up unperturbed as Eldon tensed his muscles and forced himself to charge with sword swinging. One of them brought his knife hilt crashing down on Krasna's skull, and as she dropped unconscious both turned toward the Earthman.

Eldon staggered in mid-stride as his knees went rubbery with a chilling, unearthly fear surpassing his worst nightmares. His wrist drooped and his fingers were lax on the sword hilt. For an instant he came to a complete standstill, his body swinging involuntarily to run, and he knew himself as an arrant coward.

But, as he hesitated, through his terror seeped an impression of cynical *amusement*.

Then Eldon knew. Rage burned away panic. And with the rage came relief. He himself was not afraid—at least not that desperately afraid. The Luvans were

With a savage bellow Eldon leaped.

using a mental weapon against him, a lance of fear.

He took an unsteady step forward. Another. The third was easier, although his entire body still trembled. But now that he knew its cause the fear was less effective.

An expression that might have been amazement crossed the pasty grey features of the Luvans.

Eldon's sword slashed in a hissing arc, and as one Luvan moved sluggishly back it stumbled over Krasna's prostrate form. With a savage bellow Eldon leaped. His backswing bit deep. The Luvan's shapeless mouth opened soundlessly as blue-black fluid gushed from the wound.

Eldon's blade flashed bright in the sunlight as he brought it down again with all the strength of his arm. Then it was no longer bright and the ugly grey body collapsed slowly.

But the second Luvan had prepared. One splayed hand held a dagger while the other grasped an evil-looking whip tipped with a cluster of hooked blades.

The Earthman almost sprawled as projected fear gave way to a momentarily successful attempt to confuse the coordination of his leg muscles. Then he screamed aloud as his body burst into flames and he had the illusion that mile up mile of empty space lay between him and the Luvan. But with an effort of will he plunged ahead, heartened by the growing sense of consternation he could read in the monsters thoughts. Any creature of Varda would have shriveled and died under the

Luvan's psychic barrage. But not the cripple from the Closed World of Earth.

The metal whip licked out faster than eye could follow. The blades of its tip grated against the bone of Eldon's forehead and a gush of blood poured into his single eye. He lowered his sword momentarily to clear his vision with the back of his single hand, and in that defenseless instant the Luvan struck.

He felt the dagger snick against a rib and plunge deep into his chest. Automatically his foot came up in a tremondous kick that sent the Luvan reeling back, unhurt but thrown off balance.

Eldon knew he was bleeding internally but as yet his shocked nerves refused to transmit the full story of pain to his mind. Minutes to live. Something clogged his throat as he panted, and he spat a gobbet of red-tinged foam onto the moss underfood. Punctured lung.

He swung in a wide, clumsy lunge that missed by feet. And then he staggered, sagged, barely saved himself from falling. His sword point dropped weakly.

He felt the wave of triumphant, cruel gloating as the alien creature stepped in for the kill. And that had been the Earthman's last desperate hope, that the thing's inherent bestiality would not allow it to stand back and wait for him to fall. His time was short.

With a supreme, final effort he brought the sword up in a whistling uppercut. And struck. The point bit into the Luvan's chest. Into its throat. Snagged against the creature's jaw. Eldon stiffened his arm and let his body fall forward. The double-edged blade sliced through flesh and cartilage, then met with lessened resistance as the point emerged.

Eldon fell, blood from his wounds showering upon the obscene carcass, but he went down with the elation of the kill still in his mind.

KRASNA moaned and opened her eyes as three men in blue-green emerged from the trees. "Bolan!" she gasped.

Her brother took one shocked look at the carnage, misunderstood, raised his sword above Eldon's bloody head.

There was no time to argue or explain. The sword was descending even as she snatched out her blast rod and fired.

Orange fire blazed. The sword went spinning away, torn from Bolan's fingers. But power weapons used near Luvans—even hacked and bleeding Luvans—invariably backfired, and where Krasna's right hand had been there was only a shapeless mass of mangled, heat-seared flesh. For an eternity everyone remained frozen by the unexpectedness of the blast rod's discharge.

"The exile!" one of the men whispered fearfully. "She is truly a Sasso-creature! Kill her!"

"Wait!" Bolan spoke as though dazed. "Why did you—?"

Krasna did not answer. Instead she seized the Luvan's dagger in her uninjured hand and carved a gaping cross-shaped gash in the chest of the carcass beside her. Through glazing eyes Eldon watched as she plunged her hand into the slimy, quivering mess and felt disgusted at her exhibition of rank savagery.

She brought her arm out, fouled and defiled to the elbow with the Luvan's evil-smelling blood. In her hand was a tiny glittering capsule. She tossed it to the ground. "Smash it!" she said weakly.

Uncomprehendingly one of the men crushed it beneath his heel. Instantly the bloated, obscene, mangled carcass vanished as though it had never existed. Even its spilled blood was gone. The men drew unsteady breaths and a look of awed understanding appeared on their faces.

"The other one!" Krasna writhed as pain from her blasted hand penetrated her consciousness. "I—can't."

Eager swords hacked at the remaining monster and eager hands pawed among the filth of its body.

"We have killed a Luvan!" One of the men shouted exultantly as the second capsule shattered under his foot and the second carcass disappeared. "We know their secret now."

Bolan had recovered from his stupefaction. "The Chamber!" he ordered. "Be quick!"

"But it is forbidden," a man objected. "She is an exile. The Council—"

"Damn the Council!" Bolan picked up his sword and brandished it. "To the Chamber!" he repeated. The man looked to where the two Luvans had been and nodded.

"Take—him." Krasna spoke with great effort. "He—must—be—El-ve-don."

"Both!" Bolan decided instantly. He whistled and three more Forest People emerged from the trees. One was a tall, rawboned woman who took charge of administering first aid while the men prepared makeshift litters.

Eldon knew he was dying, but he tried to speak.

"Be still!" the woman ordered without rancor, continuing her ministrations.

One of the men picked up a small furry bundle and deposited it tenderly beside Krasna. The lemur-thing whined softly and snuggled against her.

Eldon felt no pain as he was rolled onto a stretcher. He was too far gone for that. As everything grew dark Krasna was looking at him, and now for the first time there was no pity in her glance. Instead there was dawning admiration. Her thought reached him, bypassing his ears and entering his brain as a telepathic whisper.

"Call me. I will be near."

VI

DEAD. DEAD. NO BODILY SENsations. No *being*. But still thought. The individuality of Eldon Carmichael looked without eyes, listened without ears. It was absolutely, utterly alone in *nothingness*. Nothing but terrible *aloneness*.

But something — someone — had said, "Call me." What? Whom? Shreds of memory began to coalesce.

"Krasna!" The individuality of Eldon Carmichael shouted without lungs or mouth. "Krasna!"

The nothingness was no longer quite so empty. A thought brushed his.

"Eldon? Where?"

"Here!"

"Think of your shape!" a thought commanded.

The individuality of Eldon Carmichael thought. Memory shreds were coagulating to remind him he had once had a body. This was not death. It was something else.

"Think of me—help me *form!*" The thought-appeal was urgent but unfrightened. "I can't alone."

"Krasna?" He sent out the wordless question.

"Yes!"

He remembered her as he had watched her bathing in the warm pool that flowed through her home. And then he could see her floating in nothingness beside him, tenuous at first, then solidifying. He saw her with a new three-dimensional clarity and depth, as though with two eyes. Instinctively he reached toward her—and his left hand clasped her right.

Krasna looked down at herself, at the crescent-shaped scar marring her loveliness, and winced.

"Even here I must bear that," her thought reached him. "Until Sasso is no more."

Confused memories were returning now, bringing horror of this unknown emptiness.

And then Krasna's thoughts were flowing around him protectively, soothingly—but not in pity. And her thoughts brought understanding.

They were in the Thin World, a—place —outside the more solid worlds. Here only thought had actuality. Their bodies here were nothing but thought-projections. And here they must remain until the Chamber had had its way with their torn, tortured *real* bodies, healing them. For such were the unique powers of the Chamber.

"But my arm? And my eye?" Eldon asked.

"You forgot you had lost them. Here you are as you think you are. And I—"

"Exactly! as I have dreamed." The thought left Eldon's mind before it could be altered by his loyalty to Margaret and his desire to return to Earth.

Krasna glanced at him sharply, but she seemed not displeased. And there was gratitude in her thoughts. Gratitude and surprised admiration for the way he had come to her rescue without thought of his own safety.

"We must stay away from our actual bodies long enough but not too long," she told him. "Otherwise we could not return at all."

She read his questioning thoughts. "No. A Vardan mind can not take knowledge of the Thin World back. I can rememebr almost nothing of the time I was here after escaping the Faith.

"But you, with your Closed World brain, can perhaps do what I can not."

With his new knowledge Eldon understood also that those crystalline capsules in the gross grey carcasses were the real essence of the Luvans. The bodies in which they had clothed themselves to live in Varda had been purely artificial.

"I learned the secret of the Luvans in the slave-pits of the Faith." Krasna's thoughts grew grim and bleak as she remembered the things to which she had been subjected there. Vardan memories could be carried into the Thin World, though not back again.

Eldon's thought-body drew hers close as they floated side by side in limbo, drew her to him comfortingly and protectively to thrust those memories aside. He thought she should be soft and warm to touch— and she was.

She pulled away—after a time that could have been either a moment or an age—with a tinkling laugh and a change of mood.

"Time here is *different* and it will seem long before we can return," her mind said. "Let us build a world to our own hearts' desires and live there until—until you can destroy Sasso and the Faith."

"But—"

She ignored his protest.

"I will go back to the Chamber occasionally—it will be necessary—but if you with your tenacious Earth mind went it would be disastrous."

"Understand this once and for all," he warned her. "If ever I can return to my own Earth I shall do so. I am not your marvelous El-ve-don, and I have no intention of fighting this thing you call Sasso. Those Luvans were bad enough."

Krasna frowned. Then her look of disappointment gave place to a knowing smile.

There was a hint of a surprising idea. Just the faintest sort of hint—and then she closed her mind, half laughingly and half in seriousness. But tightly.

"Let's build our world," she said.

IT WAS a Godlike sensation to *think* a world. It changed with their thoughts, part Earth, part Varda, and part the solidification of the non-existent lands of dreams. There were groves, streams, mountains, plains. There were towns too, but these could be seen only dimly, indistinct in the distance, the men and women in them tiny figures without individuality. Neither Krasna nor Eldon had formulated their ideas for an inhabited utopia concretely enough to fill in the details.

Krasna created for herself a wardrobe of wonderful gowns every fold of which draped in a perfection of beauty, and jewels of kaleidoscopic inner fires that shifted with her mood. After her hunted forest life in Varda she indulged her fancies to the fullest.

Eldon built a laboratory. He lavished concentrated attention upon it—and then it failed to give him the satisfaction he had expected. For he did not have to work to find solutions. He *knew*. Even the mysterious bound charges yielded up their secrets in minutest detail, and when he discovered his Earth theorizing about the close connection between interacting bound charges and life itself had been on the right track he felt no surprise. The experimental equipment he designed was worse than useless, answering so perfectly to his thoughts that he could make the needles of his meters swing by merely *willing* it. He gathered almost limitless knowledge.

Krasna asked about life on Earth, and occasionally Eldon created Earth scenes for her. Once he built a dream automobile, unhampered by the structural limitations of Earth materials, and any number of miles of broad highway. Everything but the traffic. Krasna was delighted at first, amused by the manually operated controls, but then she saddened as she remembered that once Varda had had its own system of roads. So Eldon erased the perfect automobile and perfect highway from existence.

Krasna looked at him peculiarly. She seemed almost afraid of him, so deep was her awe.

"You—you are most certainly El-ve-don!" she whispered. "Only El-ve-don could know how to do such a thing. My people will be grateful to you forever when you save us from Sasso."

Irrational anger stirred within him at her assumption. "No! I shall return to Earth as soon as I can—if I can. I am not El-ve-don."

Krasna was shocked. "Then some day Sasso will come to Earth."

Eldon shrugged, rejecting the thought, his mind still unwilling to believe in the very existence of Sasso.

Then it was time for her to visit the Chamber. Her thought-body *thinned out*, vanished.

Eldon found their private world dreary and dead without her. With the bright, vital waves of her personality missing there was no joy. He grew intolerably lonely, anxious for her return.

When she reappeared everything was right again in their self-created world. The news she brought was mixed. Their bodies were repairing satisfactorily, she reported, but outside the Chamber there was chaos and steadily deepening defeat for the Forest People. Many had been captured—she shuddered with horror—while others more fortunate had been killed.

Her eagerness to leave their dream world communicated itself to Eldon, but their reasoning was different. She was dedicated to the struggle against Sasso. He hoped with his newfound knowledge to escape the brutalities of Varda and return to old familiar Earth.

But the time was not yet.

Once more she went away and once more she returned, this time almost at once. "Eldon!" she wailed even as she materialized. "We must go back now!"

"Why?" he demanded.

"Because The Night approaches. Two Earth minds aiding the Faith have disturbed the balance. My people can not hold the Gateway much longer."

"But—?"

"If we don't we shall be lost here forever!"

Suddenly Eldon's homesick longing for Earth gave way to hesitation. Here he was whole, not a cripple. There—

But Krasna's absences had shown him that to be alone for all eternity on this self-created world would be unendurable. Even a disembodied brain could—would—go mad from loneliness. And there was Margaret, a prisoner of the Faith. He had no choice.

"All right," he agreed reluctantly.

"Now!"

Instinctively he knew the way.

"Eldon! El-ve-don! Stay near me!" He sensed Krasna's appeal even as their thought-world crumbled back into the featureless opacity of limbo, and he responded amid the *nothingness*.

VII

THE IRREGULAR WALLS, ROOF and floor were crystals of all shapes and colors. Some glowed, shedding polychromatic light. He rolled over—his body responded with a heavy stiffness— and beside him lay the red-haired girl. This was the Chamber, a natural formation possessing strange characteristics possible only in Varda. In the Chamber they had cheated death by giving their bodies complete rest.

He moved his left arm. It moved! His breath went out in a sigh of happiness as he looked at it, his two eyes' focusing with difficulty at first. It was less heavily muscled and the skin was white and tender. It looked *newer*. Here in the Chamber he had grown it like a—like a crawfish. And the mortal dagger wound had healed scarlessly.

Krasna opened her eyes and stretched. He looked over to see if she had fared as well.

She caught his look. Instantly her face flushed and she snatched up a cloak one of the rescue party had left beside her, wrapped it around herself. Eldon was surprised. The prudery of bodily modesty had seemed entirely lacking from her character. In her home she had always been charmingly natural and unembarrassed.

She saw he had discovered his new arm and eye.

"Pleased?" she asked.

He nodded vigorously, forgetting everything else.

He felt a pull, a tugging deep within himself. Krasna felt it too and jumped up.

"Come," she urged. "We must get out of the Chamber at once."

Together they climbed a crystal-lined passage so steep it was almost a shaft. His muscles felt stale, unused and stiff. They came out on the rugged slope of a mountain, high above the forest line, and the opening to the Chamber was a small black hole amid a cluster of boulders.

Eldon shivered in the chill wind after the tingling warmth of the Chamber, and Krasna drew her cloak more closely around the tattered remains of her clothing. There was a flash of movement among the rocks and Tikta came running, chattering happily. Krasna stroked its soft fur and the lemur-thing placed its paws on her head in the way Eldon had learned meant mental communication.

He watched her face become set and grim.

"Things are going—badly," she said.

She hurried him down the jagged slope, telling him as they went that the Forest People were gathering. It was risky, an unprecedented move of desperation, for if any large numbers were killed or captured Varda's entire defense against Sasso would collapse. The Gateway could be fully opened.

But Krasna was unable to maintain the pace at which she started. She tired rapidly, and often they rested at her suggestion. She seemed clumsy, unsure of her footing, and frequently he helped her over the rougher places.

"Do you remember the Thin World?" she asked during one pause.

"N—no," he admitted. He could remember Earth and Varda, remember his battle with the Luvans. But about the Thin World he could recall only that there was such a—was it a place?

"But you must!" she wailed. "You must!"

"I don't," he insisted.

She sighed. "Perhaps it will come back to you."

FINALLY they were out of the mountains, the blue forest moss squeaking beneath their feet as they walked. Once they stopped for a brief sleep, and although Eldon found it uncomfortably hot on the forest floor Krasna kept her long cloak wrapped closely.

"Where are we going?" he asked, very tired of this hiking and of the girl's reproachful glances. Even the little lemur-thing seemed to stare disapproval at his lack of memory.

"To my people, of course. Perhaps they will allow me to return now. Every one of us will be needed to counteract the two Earth minds working with the Faith.

"Ugh!" Eldon grunted, furious over her reiterated hints that Margaret—his Margaret, for she had come to him that last night on Earth—was Of the Faith.

They continued walking in strained silence.

"Can't you remember anything?" she asked again, her lips trembling. "About

the Thin World? That you are El-ve-don?"

"No."

His tone was unintentionally sharp, for he was irked by his inability to remember. There was something — something he couldn't quite grasp. She responded by bursting into a flood of tears and he stared at her, astonished. She had seemed such a well-balanced girl, one who did not cry easily. And so healthy and active too. But now—

She was still sobbing intermittently when three heavily armed men stepped from among the trees and approached with swords and blast rods drawn.

Eldon tensed instantly at their hostile attitude, and though he was unarmed he prepared to resist.

But Krasna grasped his arm. "No. They are my people. We must go with them quietly."

With a guard on either side and the third behind they were hustled through the forest. Krasna stumbled occasionally and Eldon took her arm. They were not allowed to speak to each other, and the guards were so watchful they seemed almost afraid of their unarmed prisoners.

Once three tubular silvery ships like the one which had hunted Eldon on his first night in Varda cruised overhead in echelon formation. Instantly their guards forced them into hiding.

"Kill both if they signal," the leading guard directed.

Neither Eldon nor Krasna had the slightest intention of signaling the aircraft of the Faith, and with their captors they breathed a sigh of relief when the ships vanished in the distance.

Their hurried progress continued, with Krasna panting and stumbling. Perspiration beaded her face, but still she kept the heavy cloak around herself.

Finally one of the guards whistled and almost at once they were surrounded by armed men who stared at them in hostile silence for a moment, then forced them into a black opening at the base of a tree.

The tunnel smelled musty and unused and the huge underground room smelled the same. But the room was in use now, packed from wall to wall with Forest People.

Sudden silence fell as the captives were led in, and hundreds of eyes turned toward them. Krasna gasped and her face grew pale.

"Oh, Eldon! They think we—"

"Be quiet!" one of the guards snapped, prodding her roughly in the back.

Eldon's fists clenched despite the swords ringing him in, but Krasna's look counselled to wait.

Something was very,very wrong with many of the Forest People. Their skins were red and raw and their bodies were swollen and bloated, as though they had been severely burned or were in the last stages of some dreadful disease.

A woman—she might have been good looking at one time—pushed toward them. Her feverish eyes were sunk deep in pockets of swollen flesh and her poor, distorted face twitched uncontrollably.

"You did this, red witch of Sasso—and you, Earthman!" Her voice was so cracked with hate that Krasna stepper back.

A middle-aged man put his arm gently around her, and she was sobbing and leaning heavily upon him as he led hear away.

"Sasso-creatures!" he growled, his eyes flashing venom.

All at once Eldon realized he could read thoughts, just as Krasna had read his. He knew what these Forest People were thinking and his face went tight as he felt their concentrated hate. For every one of them believed that Krasna had been deliberately allowed to escape from the Fortress as part of the Faith's dark plot. Didn't she carry the slave-mark? And they were sure that he, Eldon, was as much Of the Faith as his two fellow-worldlings.

The ancient, white-haired man in charge of the meeting pounded for attention. He peered at the prisoners with searing loathing and spoke to Krasna.

"The Council erred when it sentenced you to exile," he declared grimly. "It should have been death. But this mistake which has cost so many lives will be rectified."

There was a growl of approval.

"And this Earthman—"

Krasna straightened. "This Earthman is El-ve-don!" she shouted.

For a moment there was incredulous silence.

"You lie, Sasso-creature!" screamed one of the bloated, dying men.

"Kill them! Kill them! Kill them!" The chant roared deafeningly from the low ceiling and the old leader made no attempt to stop it.

Krasna raised her arms high in a plea for silence. She got silence, sudden and complete, but in an unexpected way. For as she raised her arms the cloak fell open and the tattered and bloodstained clothing beneath hid little. There was a startled gasp from the crowd, then a hum of shocked comment.

But it was not her semi-nudity that caused the sensation. Her condition, the heaviness of her body, were obvious.

She saw that her secret had been disclosed.

"This man is El-ve-don!" Her voice was firm and defiant now, pitched to cut through the noise. "Though he has refused to save our world, which only he can do, Varda must have another chance."

Eldon was held in outraged motionlessness as an angry mutter spread.

"Forest People!" Krasna lifted her voice. "The Earthman is the father of my child—although he himself did not know it until now!"

Eldon wanted to shout a denial. But he understood why she had been so unsure of her footing descending the mountains, why she had tired so easily.

"This Earthman *could be* El-ve-don of the prophecy if he would. He will not. But some day—if the Gateway can be held long enough—perhaps our child will accept the burden its father has shirked. The child will inherit characteristics of a Closed World mind. It was all I could do for Varda."

Her voice broke in a sob.

Eldon read a thought in her mind, a thought intended for him alone.

"And besides, I love him."

His brain was awhirl. It was all utterly impossible. But his confusion was interrupted by a stir in the back of the hall. Bolan entered, shoved his way to the dais. He spoke to the old leader and there were cries of angry protest from those near enough to hear.

"But—" the old man began.

"A trick to regain our confidence," someone broke in loudly. "Even Luvans would be sacrificed to defeat us."

The old man spoke to Bolan again, and

Bolan turned to stare at his sister with disbelief changing to undisguised loathing.

"But she is the only one who knows the arrangement of the Fortress," he said aloud. "Kill her and you doom our attack to failure."

There was a babble of disagreement.

"I say this not as her brother—if she has chosen a mate outside our own People I hereby declare her no longer my sister—but as chosen leader of our attack."

Amid the ensuing uproar the old man made a gesture to the guards, and with his newfound telepathic ability Eldon caught the thought-command.

"Take them to the side rooms, apart from each other. We must consider this."

A LONE in a tiny cell Eldon tried to bring his whirling thoughts to order. Krasna had lied. She must have lied. Why? But for a moment her mind had been so open to his telepathic sense that lying was improbable. And—

He felt a sudden mental wrench, a dislocation, a twisting— a million ideas spun through his brain—and he *remembered*. Memories of the Thin World—those very memories whose lack had made Krasna cry so bitterly—all at once. They had been there all the time, but buried, and the quick series of emotional shocks had brought them to the surface. Gone was the irksome, nagging feeling that had made him speak so harshly to the poor girl, replaced by a sense of surety and power.

Krasna had returned to the Chamber, to their real bodies, while he had remained in the Thin World. It could have—must have—happened that way. He remembered the secret, knowing smile she had worn, and the hints he had detected in her mind. And thought was a powerful force in Varda, controlling material objects. And time in the Thin World was different, variable.

It had been her patriotic urge to give Varda a chance at no matter what cost to herself. But he suspected there was also a shrewd feminine attempt to involve him emotionally in the fate of her world. It was most disconcerting.

Then that other thought—that most surprising thought of all. So she loved him. So what? He had not encouraged her. He tried to shrug it off, tried to tell

himself he had no responsibility whatsoever in the matter. But his heart spoke otherwise. He tried to grow angry at Krasna for the unfair advantage she had taken—and failed miserably.

H E MADE no resistance as he was led back into the hall. Memories of the Thin World, of the nature of interacting bound charges, were arranging themselves in his mind. And he understood how to use that knowledge. His was a triple mind with an understanding of Earth, of Varda, and of the Thin World. But somehow there was little satisfaction and no happiness in the belief that soon he could return to Earth.

The old man began, for the benefit of the crowd, with a lengthy explanation that there was still some doubt in Krasna's case. She had, after all, given them the Luvans' secret, and she was necessary to the plan to infiltrate the Fortress and assassinate the leaders of the Faith. But still she bore the slave-mark.

"She will be kept under guard and her mind will be intensively probed," the old man announced. "The child with the Earth taint will be destroyed at birth."

"No!" Krasna shrieked. "No!"

Eldon felt a twinge at her frantic, pitiful cry, but he hardened his heart and did not face her.

He did not wait for the inevitable death sentence to be pronounced upon him. He turned away, almost casually, and walked toward the passage. He must find Margaret, attend to the matter of Victor, and then return to Earth. And he must go first to the dread Fortress of Sin, for he would have need of the Gateway.

But he was filled with a deep sadness for Krasna and her—their—unborn child.

At first the Forest People did not guess his intention, for he screened his thoughts. Then two warriors leaped to block his path with upraised swords. Eldon *thought*, and for the fragment of time it took to pass them they remained immobile. A knife whistled toward his unprotected back. He *felt* it coming and with incredible swiftness whirled and caught it in midair.

"Up! Up! Higher!" Eldon concentrated as a blast rod was drawn somewhere behind him. The sizzling lethal charge passed over his head and tore a gaping scar in the plastic ceiling as the aim of the operator was disturbed by his penetrating thought.

He risked one look at Krasna. She was struggling to tear loose from her guards and follow.

"El-ve-don!" she called. In her voice was the anguish of one who has lost hope.

Then he ran, knowing that as soon as the Forest People recovered from their surprise he would be no match for their massed mental powers.

VIII

MOTTLED SPLOTCHES of tree-filtered sunlight flashed across his body. He ran, wishing he had not looked back at Krasna, guiding himself by the sun, and when he grew tired he used his new knowledge to postpone fatigue. His body would have to pay a price later, but for that he was prepared.

He knew now that he must inevitably come into conflict not only with the Faith, but with the Sasso-thing itself. For Sasso held the Gateway. He smiled wryly to himself as he considered fragmentary plans. Perhaps he was El-ve-don after all.

The forest thinned to allow glimpses of the Mountains that Move, and then he was clambering up the same barren, rock-strewn slopes he and Krasna had descended so slowly together.

He found the entrance to the Chamber without difficulty, for that black hole among the rocks was fixed indelibly in his memory. Then he had to drive himself, push himself step after lagging step down the steep tunnel until he stood amid the warmth and polychromatic glow of the crystal-lined grotto. He felt his spirit, his *self*, float free from his body. It was like swimming in a riptide, requiring a conscious and constant effort to hover near and not be swept out again into the Thin World.

And then, deliberately, Eldon's *self* did strange and terrible things to the body that lay crumpled on the rought floor. There was a psychic pain that ripped and tore at the *self*, more intense and poignant than any purely physical torment, and it continued for a timeless age.

When at long last a body staggered up

the tunnel its left arm was a stump and one eye blinked and squinted in a ruined, disfigured face. By his own choosing he was outwardly as he had been during those last unhappy months on Earth. The mental changes were invisible.

Above the Chamber the mountains grew steeper, rougher, and to an already exhausted cripple the difficulties were almost insuperable. Time after time he narrowly avoided rock slides loosened by the constant earthquakes, and there were ledges where the slightest misstep meant death, and crevices from which noxious, choking fumes puffed in irregular spurts. And always there was the howling, shrieking wind that strove to wreck his precarious balance and send him tumbling to destruction.

He wished he had an antigravity egg. With time and proper facilities he could have constructed one. He understood how. But he was not in the Thin World and could not produce one from nothing merely by thinking about it.

And he could not have used it anyhow. It was necessary that his maimed body be tortured almost to the point of collapse. The Gateway must be reached through Sasso, and Sasso could be reached only through the Faith. But one who was Of the Faith could not be false to Sasso.

Scratched and bleeding, half-frozen, his shoes worn through and the palm of his single hand shredded by jagged rocks, he crossed the summit and made the long descent to the semi-desert plateau on the other side. Near the bottom a small stream trickled across the rocks, and Eldon drank deeply although the water stank of chemicals leached from the volcanic core of the range.

The domain of the Faith was huge, and for three days he plodded across the drifting brownish sands. His breath whistled noisily in a throat parched with thirst and seared by alkali dust. Beneath the tattered remains of his shirt his ribs showed starkly through weather-scoured, sun-blistered skin, but he welcomed the emaciation and each scratch of the cactus-like plants. It was all necessary.

As the merciless sun rose for the fourth day he sighted a column of mist ahead. In the afternoon he topped a slight rise and looked down upon a small lake steaming in the brazen sunlight. On its shore two dozen mud and wattle huts huddled together for mutual protection. A settlement of the primitive Puva tribesmen, the original non-mutants. Eldon hid in the scanty shade of a boulder and slept a couple of hours.

Then he stood up, allowing the setting sun to outline him. It was only a minute before a savage saw him and gave a shout. Still Eldon stood in plain sight, and soon thirty Puvas armed with clubs and spears were racing toward the stranger who had dared invade their territory. To their primitive minds stranger and enemy were the same.

Eldon waited until they were near. Then he *thought,* and a moment later smiled to himself as he passed undetected within a few feet of the tribesmen seeking his blood. His peculiar Earth mentality, coupled with the control he had learned in the Thin World, made him completely invisible to the Puvas. But he knew well it was a trick which would never work against mentalities that were more nearly his equal.

Beside one of the huts he found a crudely made clay pot of water. He drank his fill and threw the remainder of the water over a Puva woman. She screamed. He shattered the pot at the feet of another woman who ran to investigate. Then he trotted away, leaving the village in turmoil behind him, trusting the wind-whipped sands to obliterate his footprints.

All night long he plodded steadily eastward toward the Fortress of Sin. Near morning he threw himself down on the sand, this time making not the slightest effort at concealment.

THE whistling ships appeared with the grey of dawn, heading for the Puva encampment. The first passed high and to the south, but as the second approached Eldon opened his eye, lurched to his feet, staggered a few steps. He did not look up as the sound of the ship changed. Then he let himself sink limply to the sand.

The ship skidded to a stop nearby and through a slitted eye Eldon watched two men emerge. Men—mutant Puvas of the Faith—and not Luvans. He allowed himself a sigh of relief before feigning unconsciousness.

One of them rolled him over with a booted toe.

"Hey, Thordan," he said to his companion. "It's the crippled Outworldling that Highness Sin ordered us to watch for."

"But how could this have—" Thordan began.

"Those Puvas!" The other mutant sounded disgusted. "They saw this thing; and when he hid from their clumsy searching they sent that false alarm that the Rebels had crossed the mountains. Superstitious fools!"

Thordan nodded and examined Eldon critically. "Bah! Who'd want such an atrocity as a slave? Not me! Let's blast it here and not dirty our ship."

"Blast it and you'll carry lash scars," the other warned. "That thing is—was—an Earthman."

"All right. Throw it in and let's get back," Thordan agreed sourly.

"And don't give it food or water either," the other reminded. "Highness Sin, or perhaps Lesser Highness Margaret may have other ideas."

Something inside Eldon died at the casual mention of Lesser Highness Margaret. The words did something Krasna's hints and the open accusations of the Forest People had failed to do. They convinced him, brought into sharp focus all the half-thoughts and doubts he had so resolutely pushed aside.

THE ship landed and Eldon was half-led, half-dragged across the courtyard of the Fortress and into Sin's audience hall. There he was given a final shove, tripped at the same instant, and made involuntary prone obeisance to the dark-haired woman on the throne. He had just time to notice with a start how closely she resembled Margaret.

Sin looked down in questioning contempt. Eldon could feel her mind probing tentatively at his and deliberately made incoherent thought-pictures of burning sands and torturing thirst, of howling savages with blood lust in their eyes, of the trembling hell of the Mountains that Move. He invented scenes of being hunted through an endless towering forest by murderous people. To set up a complete mind block would only have called attention to his ability.

Sin's mind displayed increasing interest at those pictures, so he took his thoughts back to Earth and reproduced the nightmarish, multiform and utterly horrible and meaningless images of morphine and delirium which had haunted him in the hospital. He had the satisfaction of feeling her mind withdraw in fastidious disgust.

"His mind is gone, Highness Sin?" a hulking, much-decorated warrior asked.

Sin nodded. "Curse those Rebels. He is of no value in this condition."

Wor nodded. "Could his mind be restored?"

"Not worth it," Sin decided. "It would be a tedious task, I fear. A third Closed World mind for the Faith would have made the victory simpler, but no matter." She shrugged.

"The Rebels still die under the new weapons?" she asked her military chief.

"Yes, Highness Sin," Wor responded. "It will end soon now. Shall I—?" He made a snapping motion with his hands.

Sin shook her head. "Not so quickly, Wor." She raised her voice slightly. "Margaret, do you want this thing?"

Eldon resisted the temptation to turn, for that would have betrayed that he understood every word.

Margaret's voice came clearly from behind him.

"No!" she declared, her tone indicating revulsion at the sight of his maimed ugliness and the grime that clung to his blood-flecked skin.

Then quickly she changed her mind.

"For the Faith, Highness Sin—yes. He was always a fool, but with proper care perhaps enough of his mind can be restored to hasten The Night."

"Granted." Sin sounded pleased at Margaret's devotion to the Faith. "This idiot creature could not possibly be El-ve-don. But have your slaves take it out of my sight. It sickens me."

Eldon heard the girl he had once loved give an order, felt himself lifted and carried. A few minutes later, still feigning semiconsciousness, he was deposited on a soft bed.

"What do you want with this thing?" It was the big man Sin had addressed as Wor, and he sounded suspicious.

Margaret answered calmly. "As an unexpected aid to our plans."

"How?"

"Victor hates me since I chose you. Now Sin has taken a fancy to him. She will use him against us—if she suspects. And we both know Sin is dangerously clever. But I hope we can use this one—against Sin through Victor."

"But can you be sure—?"

"This one will do whatever I say." Margaret laughed confidently. "But remember, Wor dearest, for a while Eldon must be my only love. Now leave me alone with him."

The big man muttered an oath.

"Jealous? Don't be stupid, Wor. This should be a real surprise for Sin."

ELDON lay motionless, the slow, unsteady rise and fall of his chest the only sign of life. But his brain was alert. He heard the tantalizing sound of water being poured. A vessel was held to his lips and water dribbled into his mouth. It took all his control to keep from gulping greedily, and he had not had nearly enough when Margaret took the glass away.

Once more there was water, this time mingled with perfumed soap on a soft cloth as she washed the dirt from his face. Once he had delighted to have this woman near him, but now it was all he could do to suppress a shudder. Whenever her hands touched his skin he could *feel* that she was Of the Faith in a manner possible only through her own free will.

She snipped the tattered remains of his clothing away and applied a soothing ointment to his cuts and scratches. He thought he understood why she did not leave such ministrations to her slaves. She wanted his first waking thoughts to be of her love and solicitude. His lips almost thinned angrily.

He waited until she was growing impatient before he opened his single bloodshot eye. And then he held his face blank and empty.

"Eldon," she whispered softly, in English. "Eldon, it's me, Margaret. The girl who loves you."

"Margaret?" His voice was thick and hoarse, and that was not acting. Thirst had left his throat cracked and dry.

"Poor Eldon!" Her tone was soothing, caressing. "What did those nasty Rebels do to you?"

Eldon twisted his face in an idiotic grin. He giggled insanely, and when she tried to touch him drew back like a frightened animal. He muttered vaguely of horrors.

"Poor Eldon," she said again, and kissed him. With his increased sensitivity it was all he could do to keep from retching as her lips touched his. But he clung to her with his one shaking arm as though begging her protection.

At last he lay back and gradually his trembling subsided.

Margaret bent over him. "Victor is here," she said slowly and distinctly. "You remember Victor. He tried to kill you. I tried to save you. Now you must get well and kill Victor. You hate Victor, just as you love me."

Eldon whispered obediently. "Yes, I must kill Victor!"

He found himself wondering why normal people so often speak to invalids and cripples as though they were feeble-minded. He knew full well that if his body had been whole and well Margaret would have been more careful and Sin would have been much more thorough in her examination. This tendency to discount the mentality of a cripple was particularly strong when the victim was full of irrational fears and whining self-pity. All Eldon's hopes rested upon this simple psychological fact.

"You must sleep now, lover," Margaret crooned. She gave him a pill and a swallow of water. "This will make you feel better."

He let his body relax as though drifting into slumber. He could not hear her footsteps on the deep, rich carpeting but the swish of her gown and the soft opening and closing of a door traced her movements. Quickly he removed the pill from his mouth and tossed it through the open window. Sleep he needed, but drugged sleep he could not afford.

A MURMUR of voices came from the next room. Silently Eldon rose and pressed one ear to the door.

Margaret was speaking. "Great Sasso! That thing clung to me like a slobbering baby. But he'll be easy enough to control, especially—"

"Careful! Want him to hear us?"

"It wouldn't matter. He couldn't understand a word. Besides I gave him a control pill."

"But we don't want to make a mindless slave of him," Wor remonstrated.

"Of course not," Margaret assured her alien lover. "He'd be useless that way. The drug will only paralyze his will so he will believe unquestioningly anything we tell him, and you can see that he does not receive the mark that would make him a complete slave of the Faith."

"Ssh!" Eldon heard the big warrior whisper. "I thought I heard—" A chair creaked and there were footsteps.

Silently but with utmost speed Eldon threw himself on the bed.

"You're nervous as an old woman," Margaret complained.

Wor's voice was deep in his throat. "One lives longer that way when plotting against Sin," he declared.

Eldon was lying on his back, breathing raspingly through his open mouth. Wor gave a satisfied grunt as he closed the door, and almost at once Eldon had his ear to the panel again.

"Ugh! What an ugly sight! How can you stand having that thing near you?"

"When the stakes are the control of a world one can endure much," the woman said evenly. "And it should not be for long."

Wor chuckled softly.

"There is one more problem," Margaret continued. "He *must* be present on The Night."

"An idiot Outworldling at an Observance! Impossible! Highness Sin would never permit it," Wor objected.

Margaret's tone sharpened. "Are you or are you not commander of the Forces? And aren't you clever enough to invent a story? Perhaps that a mild administration of life-essence from the Vat could restore enough of his mind to give you information on the Rebel defenses, and thus hasten The Night."

Wor gave a low whistle of appreciation. "It might be arranged."

Eldon had heard enough, but still he had no plan. He must improvise in accordance with developments.

About failure he did not dare to allow himself to speculate. Even El-ve-don could fail—if he were really El-ve-don. And the price of failure he must keep from his mind lest it confuse his thoughts at a moment when he would need all his powers.

But now the deliberate self-torment of his body had served its purpose, and well. To carry it further would be stupid. Carefully he closed his mind against telepathic probing and prepared for sleep.

But his last thoughts were not of his own safety, not of the disheartening shock of discovering that Margaret was not a prisoner but was Of the Faith, not of vengeance on Victor. He thought instead of poor Krasna as he had last seen her, and of their unborn child—the child she had hoped would one day save Varda—doomed to die at birth. He cursed himself for a fool while his mind groped in hopeless longing.

IX

GRADUALLY HIS BODY recovered. After the first day or two Margaret tired of the menial tasks of caring for his wants, as he had expected, and turned them over to her mindless slaves. But first she assured him carefully that it was all perfectly right and normal, and Eldon, supposedly under the hypnotic influence of the drug, nodded docile, unquestioning acceptance.

The slaves, two men and two girls, all carried crescent-shaped scars upon their chests, duplicates of the one marring Krasna's loveliness. One of the men had the racial characteristics of the Forest People. The other three were Puvas, evidently of the non-mutant group. Carefully Eldon suppressed the wave of indignant sympathy they aroused in him, and almost as though he too were mindless submitted as they rubbed his abraded skin with healing ointment, fed him, brought him clothes at Margaret's command, dressed him.

But Margaret did not abandon him. Each day she visited him and sat near him, often touching him. Her hypocritical, saccharine attentiveness was so revolting that at times it was all he could do to maintain his dazed, semi-idiotic pose. She spent the hours planting suggestions in his supposedly vacant mind—about trusting her implicitly, about obeying no one else, about preparing to exact a blood revenge from

Victor. Sasso and the Faith she did not mention.

At intervals she brought him more pills. After a terrifying experience in which she remained with him so long that a small portion of the drug dissolved in his mouth and left him unable to think for hours afterward he adopted the expedient of tucking a small strip of cloth beneath his tongue to absorb his saliva and keep the pills from melting before he could spit them out. Just one would seal his doom—and that of Varda.

He was glad now of the long hours he had spent reading Krasna's scrolls. One had been a medical treatise and the mental control he had acquired in the Thin World enabled him to dilate the pupil of his single eye, slow his pulse, and counterfeit the drug symptoms exactly.

On the sixth day Wor visited him, alone.

"Stand up!" he commanded. He spoke a queerly accented English, evidently learned from Margaret.

Eldon obeyed.

"Turn around...Bend over...Walk to the door...Now come back."

Eldon obeyed the warrior, although Margaret thought she had conditioned him to take orders from no one but herself. The time for a showdown was not yet ripe.

"Turn on the lights," Wor directed crisply.

Eldon hesitated.

"Turn them on!" Wor bellowed.

Eldon looked blank. It had been a trap, for the lights were mentally controlled. Wor tried another trick.

"Catch!" He pulled a blast rod from its holster and tossed it. Eldon caught it, but clumsily.

"Fire it out the window."

The weapon differed from the blast rods of the Forest People. This one had a button, evidently a trigger, while Krasna's had been entirely controlled by thought.

Eldon was sorely tempted. It would be so easy to whirl and burn Wor down. But he resisted the impulse, knowing he would have only one chance and must make it really count. And perhaps the weapon was not charged. Wor was not altogether a fool. He pretended stupid unfamiliarity with the device.

Wor appeared satisfied that Margaret had not been arranging some scheme of her own.

"We will teach you to use this weapon later," he said. "You will use it to kill Victor."

That gave Eldon his first ray of hope, a foundation upon which to build a plan.

Wor's eyes narrowed with jealousy as he spoke the Earthman's name, and Eldon had overheard enough to understand why. Since Victor Schenley's arrival the officer had found himself with a formidable rival for Sin's confidences and attentions. A smaller, physically weaker rival, but sly, and one who could not be removed by force without incurring Highness Sin's wrath.

IT WOULD have been pointless to hide the recovery of his body, but the concealment of his true mental condition— that the experiences he had undergone had not left him a mind-blasted dunce and that he was not even under the influence of Margaret's drugs—was of supreme importance. One incautious moment and he would die speedily, for the leaders of the Faith feared one thing only, Elve-don, and if they suspected—

By a stroke of good fortune the room in which he was kept in luxurious captivity adjoined the larger one in which Margaret and her companion held most of their conversations. Eldon overheard everything, from endless plotting to love-making.

Wor boasted endlessly, egged on by Margaret's open adulation and flattery, of the deepening plight of the Rebels. The slave pits below the Fortress were filling rapidly. In fact so many Rebels were being captured that no more Puva slaves were being processed. Eldon clenched his fist in helpless anger, and a nagging worry began to haunt him.

One thing puzzled Margaret. Several of the Luvans had dropped out of sight.

"But they are not really of this plane at all," Wor dismissed the matter. "They are a law unto themselves."

Eldon guessed what was happening. He had seen the first two Luvans sent into nothingness by a bleeding, dying girl who had paid a great price in discovering their secret.

Several score of Wor's mutant Puva soldiers had been killed in running battles with Rebel bands, but Wor was not disturbed. He had ample fighting men at his disposal and the troops had been indoctrinated to believe that if killed in battle they went straight to Sasso. Margaret patterned her attitude upon his.

Eldon felt a surge of admiration for the scattered remnants of the Forest People who still fought against such overwhelming odds, even though their sullenly suspicious minds had condemned Krasna's unborn child—her child and his—to death. He could not blame them too much for being overcautious.

One night he overheard the critical conversation which meant this forced inaction would soon end.

Wor was singing as he entered Margaret's rooms, and despite the mutation which had increased his intelligence his savage Puva ancestry betrayed itself in the roaring vocal antics he considered music.

Margaret asked a sharp question.

"The next Observance of Sasso," Wor announced ponderously, "will be The Night!"

Eldon heard Margaret gasp. "Are you sure?"

"As sure as anyone can be. Those Rebels had the effrontery to gather again, to actually plan an attack against our Fortress. But we found their meeting place. It was a most effective raid."

Eldon felt a stab of fear, not for himself but for Krasna. Killed? Captured? Escaped?

"The attack is broken up?" Margaret asked.

"Yes. And there will be little more mental resistance either."

"Why?" Margaret asked as she was expected to.

"Because one of the prisoners was an old man whom I am certain was acting as their thought-coordinator." Wor laughed. "I, personally, slit his scrawny throat from ear to ear. Without a thought-coordinator their barrier can not last."

"Does Sin know?" Margaret asked anxiously.

"She has no idea." Wor was very proud of himself. "The Night should catch her off guard, and when that precious creature of yours kills her Victor she will be un-receptive for the moment. Then I—we—shall receive the Power."

"What weapon?" Margaret inquired.

"A blast rod, of course. That way the backfire will take care of your creature too, automatically."

"You think of everything," Margaret said admiringly.

"Has Sin agreed that we bring him?"

"Not willingly," Wor admitted. "It was extremely difficult to persuade her."

"Why?"

"Because I couldn't let her guess how close The Night really is. I had to report failures and suppress news of victories. And after four man-lives of waiting Sin is impatient.

"Oh, the tongue-lashings she gave me. She called me stupid and incompetent and a strategic imbecile, and I believe if it weren't for memories of nights—memories of things that happened before she took that perverted fancy—I would have been relieved of command of the Forces."

"The ungrateful wretch, after all the victories you have won for her!"

"But she'll pay for those insults—soon. She finally gave her permission."

Margaret laughed, and then her voice became very prim and self-righteous. "It would serve her exactly right for treating you that way, Wor darling."

E LDON was never to know whether Highness Sin was suspicious or merely cautious. But while Margaret was away she came to see him. Victor accompanied her, dressed in a flashy uniform, an arrogant expression on his narrow face, very conscious of his position as chosen consort.

Eldon cowered, trembling and simulating fear and a total lack of recognition, keeping his real thoughts screened against Sin's mind and his disgust from finding physical expression. His heightened sensitivity made him acutely aware of what she was. At one time, before she had surrendered herself to an alien master, she had been just a woman. But not now. Her body was lovely enough, almost too lovely, but something *not human* had entered into it. And she was far older and more experienced in evil than any human had a right to be.

"Are you being treated well?" she asked in Vardan.

Eldon made a grunt of incomprehension.

Victor translated her question, but Eldon only stared. An expression of annoyance crossed Sin's haughty face.

She continued her questioning, with Victor translating, but received no intelligent response. Then she made a determined effort to read his mind, but he was on guard and screened his thoughts with the phantom images and chaotic emotions of mental disorder.

Then the high priestess of Sasso changed her tactics, spoke to him soothingly until he stopped trembling in fear. She put her arms around him, pressed her body close against his, and kissed him passionately full on the mouth while Victor glowered.

Eldon gave the she-devil her due. She was fiendishly desirable. There was something hypnotic about the insinuating motions of her body, the warmth of her skin, but Eldon's lips remained lax under hers and no light of desire kindled in his eye.

She shoved him brusquely away, convinced that he had lost not only his mind but his inborn, basic instincts.

"I doubt if we will gain any information from this thing," she said. "Come, Victor."

Without warning Victor struck at Eldon's unprotected face, a viciously unprovoked blow that sent him crashing to the floor. It took all his mental control to keep from leaping up and attacking the renegade, but he trembled and lay sobbing until they were gone.

The next day Wor and Margaret led him from the room for the first time, took him to an air car waiting on the roof, and flew him to a spot on the brownish desert away from all habitation.

The two instructors never dreamed their pupil was already familiar with the blast rod, as for a long while Eldon shivered at the spitting hiss of the discharge and consistently missed the desert shrubs they pointed out as targets.

"I'm afraid we'll have to use some other weapon," Margaret said at last.

"He'll learn, damn him," Wor growled. "We've been patient long enough."

Wor's educational methods consisted of brutal kicks and smashing punches in the ribs. Eldon's progress became almost dangerously phenomenal. He knew he had to improve rapidly, before the plotters changed their plans.

For the blast rod was a bound charge weapon, and he suspected that by mental concentration he could change the resonant frequency of the discharge, perhaps modulate it properly. He would need it, and badly.

"For a one-eyed cripple without the brains of a crawling *sbedico* he does well enough," Wor conceded at last. "All he needed was firmness."

THERE was more tiresome waiting, nerve-wracking tense days of it.

And then one evening as the sun was setting Margaret entered and he knew instantly by her avid, *hungry* look what was to happen. Conditions of shifting coincidence between Sasso and the world of Varda were now favorable and Sin had commanded an Observance. But Eldon shared a secret with Margaret and the scheming military commander. This was to be more than another Observance. This was to be The Night.

A thrill of mingled fear and expectancy ran through him. For an instant his body straightened, but Margaret was too deep in anticipation of unholy ecstasy to notice. "Come," she ordered.

A few minutes later he was in an air car screaming through the twilight at its utmost speed. They flew only a few minutes before Wor looked ahead, grunting a warning to his companion, and sent the machine plummeting downward. Eldon uttered a squeal of fear.

Margaret turned in her seat and spoke in the Vardan language he was not supposed to understand. She was smiling and her tone was gentle, but her words were, "Just you wait. This is nothing to what will happen to you later."

Wor laughed uproariously at her little joke.

The huge black globe of the temple of Sasso loomed ahead, and as the uncanny emanations of the alien structure struck his mind Eldon was seized with panic. He, Eldon Carmichael, putting his puny knowledge and even punier strength against— *that!* He was almost overpowered by an urge to fill his lungs and shriek a death-dirge for himself. But the effect on Wor and Margaret was entirely different. They were Of the Faith.

They landed among ranks of other parked air cars, in a space held open for Wor because of his rank. Eldon's arm was almost jerked from its socket in the eager haste with which Wor pulled him from the vehicle.

They entered the huge globular temple, and instantly Eldon felt the *strain* surrounding the formless hanging glow of the Gateway. It gave him a trace of reassurance, but he dared display no sign of understanding as he gazed at the tensely expectant people who were gathering.

"Margaret," he asked, his voice childishly high and naive. "What is this place? Why did you bring me here?"

Margaret leaned close. "To kill Victor!" she hissed in his ear. "See him over there?"

Victor stood at the base of the transparent, shimmering platform directly beneath the Gateway. For sheer magnificence of decoration his uniform surpassed even that of Wor. He outshone even Sin, who stood beside him, but there was about the priestess an aura of potent, evil power which the Earthman lacked.

Eldon allowed the scar tissue of his face to contort in a grimace of hate and took one long step forward. But Margaret's hand detained him and she smiled, well satisfied with her hate-conditioning.

"I will tell you when," she whispered. "You trust me completely."

The low-voiced hum of the Gathering of the Faith mounted to a new pitch and a cannibalistic leer spread over the faces of Sasso's devotees. The sacrifices were being brought in. A man in the throng bumped into Eldon. The Earthman allowed himself to be knocked off balance, and as he recovered he was facing the door. Without the bump he could not have turned, for that would have betrayed volition.

Only one guard accompanied the file of naked prisoners. One was enough, for the sacrifices were mindless ones, deadened to unquestioning obedience by drugs and the slave-mark of Sin. Two men, a woman, another man— and then Eldon's breath caught in his throat and the fingernails of his single hand cut into the flesh. For the fifth in line was a red-haired girl whose unclothed body was no longer as slender and lithe as it had once been. Krasna! Krasna and her unborn child—their child—destined victims of the obscene Faith!

There was cruel amusement in the hum of the gathering, amusement and anticipation.

"Two lives at once," Eldon heard a woman remark to her companion. "I wonder what the vitality of the unborn one will be like."

Sin's eyes settled on Krasna and her lips drew into a thin snarl of recognition. This slave would never escape a second time.

IN AN INTUITIVE FLASH ELDON knew why he had deliberately ruined his restored body, tortured himself, placed himself in a position of deepest humiliation and direct peril. And it was not for a chance to escape to Earth. He would try to save Krasna—and their child—even if he jeopardized all Varda in the attempt.

But for the moment he could do nothing. The girl who stood so abject and robotlike beside the Vat was not really Krasna, his Krasna. Only during the brief interval before her vital essence was to provide sustenance for Sasso and rejuvenation for the entity's vile followers, only when she had been given the pellet which would restore her numbed mind, only then would he dare strike. And if she were chosen to be lowered into the Vat before Sasso's one vulnerable moment arrived—

Margaret picked up one of the cables that snaked in seeming confusion across the concave floor and eagerly snapped the band around her wrist. Wor picked up another cable end. .

Eldon's heart sank. Even his Thin World was very inexplicit, but he feared that being coupled to Sasso through this mechanism would result in a transference that would transcend all mental blocks.

But Wor and Margaret had no desire that he be subjected to the full Sasso-force. That might destroy their carefully developed control over him. Margaret produced a square of flesh-colored fabric and wrapped it around his wrist before Wor

attached the cable. They had planned this all in advance.

"Give him the rod as soon as the Observance begins," Wor directed in a low voice. "But don't let him fire until the Gateway turns red. And hold enough of yourself aside so we won't miss our chance."

Margaret nodded understanding and Wor turned toward his place at the controls of the Vat, beside and below the platform which Sin was just mounting. The priestess looked down and the big man inclined his head to signify readiness.

A white hand emerged from Sin's enveloping black cloak, touched the fastening at her throat, and as the garment fell away she drew her slender white body erect and raised her arms in invocation to Great Sasso. The Observance had finally begun.

Eldon felt his scalp prickle as a huge grey shape appeared beside her on the platform. After a moment of symbolic gyrations the figures of the woman and the Luvan *merged*, seemed to interpenetrate each other and become something that still looked like Sin but was only partly human. He heard Margaret's indrawn breath, felt the psychic wave of her lustful, panting impatience, saw her face masked in unearthly expectancy as *something* took on nebulous outlines in the Gateway, throbbing evilly.

The guards bound the wrists of the first sacrificial victim, a girl, and at a touch of Wor's hands on the controls she was drawn up until her bare toes just touched the floor. There was a hush of tense expectancy as the restorative pill took effect, and then a satisfied whisper swept the gathering as she screamed and struggled in sudden horror. The glow of the Gateway brightened, shaded from green to yellow, and Sasso showed more clearly in all its alienness, glorying in the terror of the victim.

Wor's fingers flashed to the controls and a thrilled shudder shook the gathering as the Sasso-force flowed through the maze of woven cables. Eldon felt rather than saw Margaret's slender body, so exactly like that of the high priestess, shiver and go rigid beside him.

Then he was too occupied to notice. For the fabric around his wrist was not a perfect insulator. His entire body tingled. His heart was pounding and blood raced through his body and throbbed in his temples under the leaking influx of the Force of Sasso. It was a terrible sensation, evil and yet compelling. The eerie waves surging through his brain called upon him to surrender, to give himself now and utterly and forever to the service of Sasso—for Sasso was the All, the Everlasting.

Almost he succumbed. But then for an instant his sight cleared and he looked upon Sin's cruel face, on the screaming girl who hung above the Vat in readiness for sacrifice, upon Krasna, the piquantly smiling face he remembered so well now dull with idiot emptiness. Soon she too would be screaming above the Vat.

The form in the Gateway pulsed, swelling and writhing, striving to *come through*. An intense crackling hum reverberated throughout the spherical temple. Around Eldon the devotees of the Faith were sagging and pitching to their knees as Sasso *used* their lives, drew upon them in an attempt to enter Varda. Eldon too felt his legs buckling, his mind block weakening, but managed to remain on his feet.

JUST as Eldon reached the point where his wracked nerves were shrieking for surrender she shot a meaningful glance at Wor. The big man's fingers flicked the controls and the pulsating waves of Sassoforce quieted.

High-pitched feminine screams cut the air as the hoist chain unreeled and the victim's feet touched the lavender fluid in the Vat. Her writhing body stirred the pale surface to foam as she was lowered. And then, while Eldon squirmed inwardly in impotent fury, she was gone. Only the cord that had bound her wrists remained. But there was nothing he could have done to save her without abandoning all hopes, all plans.

The restoring tide of the girl's vitality, the very essence of her life, poured through the cables at Wor's touch. In the Gateway the unbelievable, eye-straining shape of Sasso swelled and solidified, thrusting against the thought-barrier that barred it from Varda.

Even through the insulating fabric a tiny portion of the life energy reached Eldon, strengthening him, steadying his reeling mind. It was a *human* force, the antithesis of that emanating from the alien monstrosity, and Eldon resolved that the Rebel girl should not have died entirely in vain. Quickly but unobtrusively he worked his shirt out of his trousers and touched the conducting wristband to the bare skin thus exposed. Instantly the life-current increased, filling him with a new vitality and a terrifying awareness of how crushingly irresistible the Sasso-force would have been in its full impact. The trick of the plotters had unintentionally saved his life and sanity.

All around him color returned to faces drained to death-like pallor by the alien entity. The panting, rasping breathing of the worshippers eased. Two guards stepped forward and the second sacrifice, a man this time, was prepared.

And then his throat constricted in fear. Sin was staring down at him, her eyes narrowed with suspicion. The priestess had been a Superior and was still a telepath! Eldon was afraid that in the throes of resisting the Sasso-force his mind block had slipped. He could only hope no clearly defined thoughts had leaked through.

She gestured to Victor and the renegade Earthman pranced forward, elated at this public attention. She said something to him and he turned toward Eldon, one hand dropping to the jeweled hilt of his ornate dagger. A gleam of joy appeared in his eyes.

Sin spoke further. A petulant, disappointed expression crossed Victor's arrogant face, but obediently he unbuckled his wristband, cutting himself off from Sasso. A buzz of curiosity began among the nearest watchers.

Sin cut it short with a nod to Wor, and Eldon moved his wristband away from his bare skin just in time as the Force of Sasso surged once more through the cables and into the worshippers. Then he was immersed once more in the struggle to retain his own individuality.

This time Eldon knew what to expect and so was better prepared to resist. During the first communion he had been vaguely aware of changes in the Gateway, and now he turned his single bloodshot eye upward, waiting for one particular moment.

The glow changed from green to yellow as once more the terrible entity thrust itself against the unseen barrier created by the thoughts of the surviving Forest People. The barrier weakened, gave, seemed about to snap, and through the cables came impulses of elation. *The Gateway shaded from yellow to pink.*

Ripping noises filled the air, sounds that were oddly familiar. Deliberately, risking his mental defenses to do so, Eldon concentrated upon making mental measurements which were in reality only enlightened guesses at the power and resonant frequency and other characteristics of the multiple bound charges constituting the Gateway.

Eldon felt a hard object thrust against his hand.

"Take it!" Margaret hissed. "Kill Victor! Now!"

With a great effort he forced his fingers to close around the blast rod, and deliberately he fumbled and almost dropped it. He could only stall for time now, for Krasna still stood passive and mindless beside the Vat, still a slave-creature of the Faith.

It was in that moment of perilous indecision that he realized just how deep and all-encompassing his feelings for her had become. He knew that if Sasso *came through* now the fate of Varda and perhaps of his own world too would be sealed. Yet to act immediately would doom the redhaired girl to death or a half-life of mindlessness. He hesitated.

Then he was granted momentary respite. One of the worshippers dropped to the floor. Then another, and still a third. Sasso surged against the invisible barrier, almost *came through*, then recoiled in temporary frustration. The efforts of the entity so drained its worshippers that fully half the group slumped awkwardly to the curving floor. The ruddy tinge of the Gateway faded back to yellow. A wave of malignant hatred poured through for all living creatures who did not acknowledge the overlordship of Sasso.

SIN saw and acted. Unconscious worshippers could not help Sasso *come through.* A nod to Wor stopped the force, and another caused the Rebel captive to be swung over the Vat and lowered. He vanished in the lavender liquid without a sound, without a struggle, unwilling to give the bestial devotees of the Faith the satisfaction they craved.

Margaret's hand closed over Eldon's, thrusting the blast rod into his belt, hiding it beneath his loose fitting coat. A quick glance passed between her and Wor and the big man nodded almost imperceptibly. Almost. Next time.

The hook of the hoist swung back empty and the guards prodded the third victim into position. Quickly they tied her hands, placed a loop of the bindings over the hook, and one of them forced the drug that would counteract the slave potions into her mouth. Eldon held his breath.

For the next to die would be Krasna.

THE GIRL gulped, then twisted her head as the counteragent took effect. She looked up to see Sin leaning from the platform, gloatingly awaiting her screams of hopeless terror. But in the moment of recovery she glared up at the priestess with eyes filled with loathing instead of fear.

Sin's mouth twisted with hate at the girl's defiance. Personal hate, for Krasna had injured her pride and her dignity by escaping from the slave pits. It had been an unforgivable affront, and now the high priestess flung taunting words at her victim.

Krasna's lips moved as though pleading for mercy and Sin bent lower to hear and enjoy. And then the Rebel girl turned her face upward and deliberately spat at her tormentor. Eldon's heart leaped in admiration. It was an unladylike but magnificent gesture of defiance and contempt. Sin jumped back, her face dark with rage, and nodded a signal to Wor. He seized the lever.

Once more Sasso-force pounded through the machine, more fiendishly intense than ever. Once more Eldon felt the ravenings of the alien monster who sensed that this was The Night, and once more battled the overwhelming compulsion to abandon the unequal struggle and with his own thoughts help Sasso to *come through.*

Right then he almost died. He had forgotten Victor.

But Margaret had become sufficiently

adept to hold a part of herself aloof from Sasso's influence, and she saved him.

"Behind you!" she hissed. "It's Victor! Kill!" There was surprise and genuine fear in her voice. She had not expected Victor to come after Eldon.

Eldon abandoned all pretense and whirled.

Under other circumstances he might have enjoyed the disconcerted look that overspread Victor's narrow face. Victor, a few feet away, carried a dagger which he had obviously expected to plunge into Eldon's unprotected back without resistance, as Highness Sin had ordered. Sin's vague suspicions had been enough to order Eldon's death.

"The blast rod! Shoot him!" Margaret whispered urgently, and then she was tumbling aside to avoid the searing backfire of the weapon.

But the moment for which Eldon waited had not yet arrived.

Victor struck out. Eldon sidestepped. And then he fell, tripped by a loop of the cable attached to his wrist. Victor gave a hoarse cry of triumph and moved in. Eldon felt the slashing pain of a flesh wound.

"The blast rod, you fool!" Margaret cried.

But Eldon made no attempt to draw the power weapon. As he regained his feet he snatched a short, heavy sword from the belt of a subordinate officer who was so immersed in the Observance that he was only just becoming aware of the disturbance.

A frightened expression twisted Victor's mouth as he saw his adversary no longer empty-handed, but he knew by the vengeful gleam in Eldon's single eye that this time one of them must surely die. He still held the advantage, for the Force of Sasso confused Eldon's thoughts with alien impressions, interfered with his muscular coordination, drained his strength. And the cable attached to his wrist hindered his movements.

But Victor Schenley's own fear of this man he had crippled but twice failed to kill proved his undoing. One of his panicky lunges caught the cable—and sheared through it.

Eldon almost fainted as the Force of Sasso ceased and for a second his stomach muscles contracted in a tight, cramping knot. But he was freed from Sasso!

The light of the Gateway gleamed red on Victor's weapon. But the renegade had forgotten to close his mind—if he had ever learned how—and with the Force of Sasso no longer confusing him Eldon knew exactly when and where and how the attack would come.

Victor lunged. Eldon swayed clear and caught Victor's dagger hand between his side and the stump of his amputated left arm. Before Victor could jerk free Eldon plunged his blade into Victor's throat.

There was a gurgling moan, the warmth and acrid odor of spurting blood, the clatter of Victor's dagger on the floor. It was over so suddenly that Eldon felt no thrill of revenge, no elation. For an instant he stared at the corpse, stunned. It was the first time he had ever killed a human.

A SCREAM spun him around. Krasna! In the brightening glare of the Gateway her body seemed afire as she swung above the terrible Vat.

With a bellow Eldon plunged toward the elevated chair upon which Wor sat, pushing aside the spellbound devotees of Sasso. He must stop the lowering of the hoist, and at once!

But he had forgotten Margaret.

"Eldon!" she screamed and threw her arms around him, pinioning his single hand at his side. Her pale face was inhuman with fury at the deception he had practiced upon her and fear of the deadly position in which she found herself. There could be no explanation. If Eldon did not kill her, Sin assuredly would.

Krasna shrieked again, this time in pain as her toes touched the liquid of the Vat, and even through the crackling, spitting crescendo Eldon heard her.

The short stub of his arm drew back, swung, and needles of fire raced through it as he struck Margaret's jaw. Her grip slackened and with a heave of his muscles he broke loose. He raised his sword—and knew himself for a sentimental fool. Earth repressions still in his mind would not let him kill a woman. Not even this woman.

The huge grey paw of a Luvan raked the side of his face and he weaved just in time to evade the clutching talons. Three of the monsters towered above him, slow-moving but inexorable. Automatically Eldon threw his sword full into the face of the nearest and ducked beneath its outstretched arms.

Wor looked up from his controls with murder in his eyes and half rose in his seat to rasp his great sword from its sheath.

Eldon swerved aside, avoiding combat with the larger man. The hell-glow of the Gateway was deepening to crimson and the ripping crackles had reached a deafening pitch. Soon, too soon, Krasna would vanish in the Vat and Sasso would *come through*. His last chance would be lost if he allowed Wor to interfere.

With a clumsy leap he vaulted to the transparent platform of the high priestess. He leaned far over the Vat, reaching toward the hook from which Krasna swung. His one hand made pawing motions in the air. But the distance was too great.

Krasna saw him, guessed his intentions, and gave him a look at once appealing and resigned. Then her eyes opened wide at the sight of his maimed body. She turned her eyes upward to where the grossly incredible form of Sasso was *bulging* in the crimson light and shouted. Her words went unheard but Eldon received her thought. She was begging him to ignore her, to leave her to her fate and do whatever he could to halt the alien entity.

But that Eldon could not and would not do. Such a sacrifice would be worse than useless. The crimson tint of the Gateway, the crescendo crackling, the *bulging* of Sasso against the weakening thought barrier, all told him that Sasso needed only the additonal strength of Krasna's life to *come through* in an unstoppable rush.

He crouched at the edge of the platform, measuring the distance as best he could with his single eye, and then the entire power of his legs was unleashed in a leap that carried him far out over the deadly Vat. His one arm stretched outward and upward. For an instant he thought he had misjudged and was plunging to destruction. Then his fingers touched the hook, clutched it, and he crashed against Krasna.

They swung together, pendulum fashion, carried in an arc by the force of Eldon's leap. Out away from the platform, toward the other side of the Vat. Out, and then back again.

Eldon's legs reached, feeling for the narrow rim at the platform's edge. His toes touched it, slipped, held. His body stretched on a slant between hook and platform, every muscle strained. Krasna, shorter than he and unable to touch the ledge, dangled vertically over the Vat, but above the surface.

ABOVE THEM something in the Gateway glared malevolently down. Its silent call reached the high priestess who stood encrimsoned in the lurid glare with outstretched arms reaching in unclean yearning toward the thing to which she had surrendered her humanity. Until then she had been too deep in communion with Sasso to notice the Earthman.

But at Sasso's warning she spun about. A shrill sound of pure rage issued from her throat as she threw herself upon him. She was a harpy, an animal, her teeth and pointed fingernails punishing weapons. In silent fury she clawed and bit, trying to break his hold on Sasso's destined victim. And Eldon was too fully occupied to protect himself in any way.

Wor started up the platform, sword in hand, but Sin paused to wave him back. "No!" she commanded. "At your controls! *Sasso comes!*"

Puzzled, his slow thoughts in confusion at the sudden shift in events, Wor obeyed.

Margaret too joined the fight, scrambling to the platform which would be the focus of Sasso's power. She had picked up Victor's jeweled dagger and with it she now lunged at Sin's back. But not to save Eldon. To save herself from Sin's vengeance and become ruler of Varda. For the Power would descend upon whomever Of the Faith occupied the platform.

The blade sank home to the hilt. Sin opened her mouth, but if she screamed it was lost in the swelling roar of Sasso's coming. The impetus of Margaret's rush carried the Black Priestess' body forward —toward the Vat.

Her body crashed against Eldon and his overstrained body gave way. His toes slipped from the platform's edge, and he and Krasna once more swung out over the Vat—while Sin's white form plummeted on down.

There was a dull splash—and Sin, Beloved of Sasso, was no more. *Nothing* settled through the evil lavender depths.

The temple of Sasso was now in an uproar. Eldon and Krasna hung in slow-swinging arcs, and Margaret stood paralyzed, fingers taloned and shoulders raised.

Through the tumult she and Eldon's eyes met—and held. In what seemed to them both an age, their thoughts took concrete form. Margaret somehow realized that he was her sole obstacle now. Eldon would have to be removed before she could fill Sin's place.

Eldon, too — in this split-second that seemed eternity — had made his decision. From the Gateway came a sound that stopped the blood in his veins. Sin herself had furnished the final needed burst of life energy.

Sasso was *coming through!*

Margaret was evil. But Sasso was the greater evil. With all his Thin World knowledge, Eldon knew that the instant of balance was at hand, the time to strike and disrupt that balance of bound charges.

Margaret leaped forward as his swing carried Eldon and Krasna back toward the platform. She slashed with Victor's knife, slashed at Eldon's fingers.

The thrust was true. The edge bit into bone and severed cleanly. Eldon's mutilated hand slipped from the chains. And he and Krasna fell toward the Vat.

But even as he fell Eldon's hand drove down—what was left of it—and snatched the blast rod Margaret had placed in his belt. Falling, he aimed at the lurid flaming *thing* that was Sasso.

The Sasso-creature sensed his intention, turned its force into Margaret's receptive mind and drove her into a blind attack. With an inhuman scream she launched herself from the platform after Eldon, her dagger thrusting forward and down as she fell.

In midair Eldon pressed the button and with the supreme effort of his life ignored the frothing Vat below and the agony of the rod's backfire to concentrate the resonant power into the Gateway, into the terrible Thing solidifying there, and with Vardan control of mind over matter to warp the discharge of the particular frequency his Thin World knowledge told him was necessary.

A blazing cone from the rod sizzled and spat. The crimson glare of the Gateway flashed through the spectrum, exploded in a scintillating violet flare, and went black. There was the stunning crash of a world being tore asunder and through it an alien cry of rage—and of dawning terror.

In the upper hemisphere of the globe a group of white-glowing pinpoints appeared, arranged in a pattern that had grown familiar. The stars of Varda shining through! With incredible speed the rift in the temple of Sasso spread. Collapse!

As he plunged toward the Vat he knew he had won, knew he had found the proper modulation to disrupt the finely balanced system of resonant bound charges of the Gateway. And he knew the alien thing called Sasso had been caught between worlds, in *no world at all*, doomed to dwindle into the nothingness from which it had arisen by feeding upon stolen lives.

He felt one last wave of malignancy, a wave that faded and left only his own bodily pain. Then that too became indistinct even though his finger still stabbed the button of the ruined blast rod smoking red hot against his palm. And he was falling, not into the Vat but through limitless space.

The shattered remnants of the Globe and the Gateway dissolved in a tearing, melting sensation as though the very atoms of his being were rearranging themselves, a *strain* that made his mind shriek in torment and flee to the verge of madness.

There was a flashing glimpse of a grotto, of crystalline, polychromatic light and tingling warmth—the Chamber. Then that and the pain too was gone and he fell interminably through blackness.

SECONDS . . . hours . . . eons. And he struck with unexpected mildness on a hard, flat surface.

He opened one eye—and the other. He placed the palms of his hands—both hands—against the floor and pushed himself to a sitting posture.

The fluorescent lights of his own laboratory cast shadowless brilliance upon him. The charge collectors still whined, their pitch lowering slowly as he listened, and the air was still pungent with ozone. It couldn't be—or could it?—that only a few moments of Earth time had elapsed?

A woman lay on the floor a few feet away, and he knew that he and she had both been near enough the neutral focus of the forces he had unleashed to escape destruction. And his arm, his eye—even the hand Margaret had so cruelly slashed —these parts of him had somehow in the transit between Varda and Earth his body had been made whole again.

He stared hard at the woman, for it was a different Margaret Matson, hardly recognizable. There were deep lines and wrinkles in her face and her revealing Vardan costume showed only too clearly how her once sleek body had become flabby and misshapen. In that last effort Sasso had fed ruthlessly upon its own worshippers, and his blast rod discharge had prevented their rejuvenation by lives stolen in the Vat.

While his mind was still adjusting itself he noticed the copper bar lying across the contacts of his experimental mechanism, and with Thin World knowledge he knew exactly what effect it had had upon the resonance of the bound charges. After a while he stopped merely looking and went to work.

He picked up a rod of nonconductive plastic and flipped the copper bar aside. Methodically he replaced blown fuses and threw in the circuit breakers controlling the bound charge concentrators. The hum rose rapidly. The machine was not seriously damaged.

A voice startled him.

"Oh! Eldon! You saved me!"

Margaret had regained consciousness. With grim amusement Eldon admitted to himself that she still thought rapidly and bluffed well. But he kept on working, not answering her.

"Eldon!" Her voice was impatient. He turned slowly.

She smiled and held her arms out seductively, and the effect was indescribably grotesque. He felt a malicious urge to bring her face to face with a mirror. But she would discover her condition soon enough. He could look at her now without emotion. There was no longer any hatred in his mind, and no pity either. He turned back to work.

"Eldon! Speak to me!" Her voice trembled between fright and anger. She was not used to being ignored.

But his mind was buzzing.

He knew he could easily be the foremost scientist of Earth, and although the miraculous restoration of his arm and eye would be hard to explain there could be prestige and wealth and power. Easily. Even though the inanimate materials of Earth, more refractory than those of Varda, would not respond directly to thoughts his knowledge could be modified and applied.

And he knew that for El-ve-don of Varda life would not be easy. A savage environment — the task of exterminating any of the mutant Puvas who had escaped —the even more difficult task of weaning the surviving Forest People away from the sullen suspiciousness that generations of hunted terror had made a fixed habit— leading and driving them to become the Superiors once more, the leaders of Varda. It would mean life-long struggle, discomfort and danger, exile from his home world, and work, work, work to start the world of his beloved once more upon the path toward civilization. And there would be those who would always view his efforts with suspicion, even hate and openly oppose him.

HE made intricate calculations with lightning speed and his hands obeyed effortlessly, adjusting the mechanism to limit its field of effect, setting up a deliberate overload that would reduce it to molten metal and shards of shattered glass and plastic. It would never do to leave this minor Gateway open now. Some day, perhaps...

Krasna, too, had been near enough to the neutral focus of escape, and all at once he knew with irrational surety that their child would be—*twins*.

He picked up the copper bar.

"Eldon! What are you doing?" Margaret cried.

He gave her a level stare. It would be a fitting and just punishment to leave her as she was. It would be more humiliating than death.

"I'm going home," he said quietly.

Then he dropped the bar across the contacts.

ME, MYSELF AND I

By KENNETH PUTNAM

So they went back . . . to discuss the matter reasonably . . .

Never before in history had such an amazing, baffling and faintly horrifying thing happened to anyone as happened to Galahad McCarthy . . . but—whaddyamean, history?

DON'T YOU THINK YOU might look up from that comic book long enough to get interested in a last minute briefing on the greatest adventure undertaken by man? After all, it's your noodle neck that's going to be risked." Professor Ruddle throbbed his annoyance clear up to his thin white hair.

McCarthy shifted his quid and pursed his lips. He stared dreamily at an enameled wash-basin fifteen feet from the huge, box-like coil of wire and transparencies on which the professor had been working. Suddenly, a long brown stream leaped from his mouth and struck a brass faucet with a loud *ping*.

The professor jumped. McCarthy smiled.

"Name ain't Noodleneck," he drawled. "Gooseneck. Gooseneck McCarthy, known and respected in every hobo jungle in the country, including here in North Carolina. And looky, bub, all I wanted was a cup of coffee and a pair of sinkers. Time machine's your notion."

"Doesn't it mean anything that you will shortly be one hundred and ten million years in the past, a past in which no recognizable ancestors of man existed? That your opportunities to—"

"Nawp!"

Blathersham University's greatest physicist grimaced disgustedly. He stared through thick lenses at the stringy, wind-hardened derelict whom he was shortly going to trust with his life's work. A granite-like head set on a remarkably long, thin neck; a body whose limbs were equally extended; clothes limited to a faded khaki turtleneck sweater, patched brown corduroy pants and a worn-out pair of heavy brogans. He sighed.

"And the fate of human knowledge and progress depends on you! When you wandered up the mountain to my shack two days ago, you were broke and hungry. You didn't have a dime—"

"Had a dime. Only it was lead."

"All right. All right. So you had a lead dime. I took you in, gave you a good hot meal and offered to pay you one hundred dollars to take my time machine on its maiden voyage. Don't you think—"

Ping! This time it was the hot water faucet.

"—that the very least you could do," the little physicist's voice was rising hysterically, "the very least would be to pay enough attention to the facts I make available to insure that the experiment will be a success? Do you realize what fantastic disruption you might cause in the time stream by one careless slip?"

McCarthy rose suddenly and the brightly-colored comic magazine slid to the floor in a litter of coils, gauges and paper covered with formulae. He advanced toward the professor whom he topped by at least a foot. His employer gripped a wrench nervously.

"Now, Mister Professor Ruddle," he

said with gentle emphasis, "if'n you don't think I know enough, why don't you go yourself, huh?"

The little man smiled at him placatingly. "Now don't get stubborn again, Swanneck—"

"Gooseneck. Gooseneck McCarthy."

"You can be the most irascible person I've ever met. More stubborn than Professor Dudderel for that matter. And he's that short-sighted mathematician back at Blathersham who insisted in spite of irrefutable evidence that a time machine would not work. Even when I showed him quartzine and demonstrated its peculiar time-dissolving properties, he wasn't convinced. The university refused to grant an appropriation for my research and I had to come out here in North Carolina. On my own time and money, too." He brooded angrily on unreasonable mathematicians and parsimonious trustees.

"Still ain't answered my question."

RUDDLE looked up. He blushed a little under the fine wild tendrils of white hair. "Well, it's just that I'm rather valuable to society what with my paper on intrareversible positrons still uncompleted. Whereas everything points to the machine being a huge success, it's conceivable that Dudderel considered some point which I've—er, overlooked."

"Meaning there's a chance I might not come back?"

"Uh—well, something like that. No danger, you understand. I've gone over the formulae again and again and they are foolproof. It's just barely possible that some minor error, some cube root that wasn't brought out to the farthest decimal—"

The tramp put his hands in his pockets. "If'n that's so," he announced, "I want that check before I leave. Not taking any chances on something going wrong and you not paying me."

Professor Ruddle gulped. "Sure, Rubberneck," he said. "Sure."

"Gooseneck. How many times — Only make it out for my real first name. It's—" the tramp's voice dropped to a whisper— "It's *Galahad*."

The physicist added a final scribble to the green paper rectangle, ripped it out and handed it to McCarthy. Pay to the order of Galahad McCarthy one hundred dollars and 00 cents. On the Beet and Tobacco Exchange Bank of North Carolina.

Ruddle watched while the check was carefully placed in the outer breast pocket of the ancient sweater. He picked up an expensive miniature camera and hung its carrying strap around his employee's neck. "Now, this is fully loaded. You sure you can operate the shutter? All you do—"

"I know all right. Fooled around with these doohickeys before. Been playing with this 'un for two days. You want me to step out of the machine, take you a couple of snaps of the scenery—and move a rock."

"And nothing else! Remember, you're going back a hundred and ten million years and any action on your part might have an incalculable effect on the present. You might wipe out the whole human race by stepping on one furry little animal who was its ancestor. I think that moving a rock slightly will be a good first innocuous experiment, but be careful!"

They moved toward the great transparent housing at the end of the laboratory. Through its foot-thick walls, the red, black and silver equipment in one corner shone hazily. An enormous lever protruded from the maze of wiring like a metallic forefinger.

"You should arrive in the Cretaceous Period, the middle period of the age of reptiles. Most of North America was under water, but geological investigation shows an island on this spot."

"You been over this sixteen times. Just show me what dingus to pull and let me go."

Ruddle executed a little dance that a student of modern ballet might have called "Man with High Blood Pressure about to Blow his Top."

"Dingus!" he screeched. "You don't pull any dingus! You gently depress—gently, you hear!—the chronotransit, that large black lever, thus sliding the quartzine door shut and starting the machine. When you arrive you lift it—again gently—and the door will open. The machine is set to go back a given number of years, so that fortunately you have no thinking to do."

McCarthy stared down at him easily. "You make a lot of cracks for a little guy.

I'll bet you're scared stiff of your wife."

"I'm not married," Ruddle told him shortly. "I don't believe in the institution." He remembered. "Who was talking about marriage? At a time like this . . . When I think of allowing a stubborn, stupid character like yourself to run loose with a device having the immense potentialities of a time machine—Of course, I'm far too valuable to be risked in the first jerry-built model."

"Yeah," McCarthy nodded. "Ain't it the truth." He patted the check protruding from his sweater pocket and leaped up into the machine. "I'm not."

He depressed the chronotransit lever—gently.

The door slid shut on Professor Ruddle's frantic last word, "Goodbye, Turtleneck, and be *careful*, please!"

"Gooseneck," McCarthy automatically corrected. The machine seemed to jerk. He had a last, distorted glimpse of Ruddle's shaggy white head through the quartzine walls. The professor, alarm and doubt mixed on his face, seemed to be praying.

INCREDIBLY bright sunlight blazed through thick bluish clouds. The time machine rested on the waterline of a beach to whose edge the lushest jungle ever had rushed—and stopped abruptly. The semitransparent walls enabled him to see enormous green masses of horsetails and convoluted ivy, giant ferns and luxuriant palms, steaming slightly, rich and ominous with life.

"Lift the dingus *gently*," McCarthy murmured to himself.

He stepped through the open doors into an ankle-depth of water. The tide was evidently in and white-flecked water gurgled around the base of the squat edifice that had brought him. Well, Ruddle had said this was going to be an island.

"Reckon I'm lucky he didn't build his laboratory shack fifty or sixty feet further down the mountain!"

He sloshed ashore, avoiding a little school of dun-colored sponges. The professor might like a picture of them, he decided. He adjusted the speed of the lens and focused it on the sponges. Then a couple of pictures of the sea and the jungle.

Huge, leathery wings beat over a spot two miles in from the edge of the luxuriant vegetation. McCarthy recognized the awesome, bat-like creature from drawings the professor had shown him. A Pterodactyl, the reptilian version of bird life.

The tramp snapped a hasty photograph and backed nervously toward the time machine. He didn't like the looks of that long pointed beak, so ferociously armed with jagged teeth.

Some living thing moved in the jungle under the Pterodactyl. It plummeted down like a fallen angel, jaws agape and slavering.

McCarthy made certain that it was being kept busy, then moved rapidly up the beach. Near the edge of the jungle, he had observed a round reddish rock. It would do.

The rock was heavier to budge than he had thought. He strained against it, cursing and perspiring under the hot sun. His feet sank into the clinging loam.

Abruptly the rock tore loose. With a sucking sound it came out of the loam and rolled over on its side. It left a moist, round hole out of which a centipede fully as long as his arm scuttled away into the underbrush. A nauseous stink arose from the spot where the centipede had lain. McCarthy decided he didn't like this place.

Might as well head back.

Before he depressed the lever, the tramp took one last look at the red rock, the underside somewhat darker than the rest. A hundred bucks worth of tilt.

"So this is what work is like," he soliloquized. "Maybe I been missing out on something!"

AFTER the rich sunlight of the Cretaceous, the laboratory seemed smaller than he remembered it. The professor came up to him breathlessly as he stepped from the time machine.

"How did it go?" he demanded eagerly.

McCarthy stared down at the top of the old man's head. "Everthin' O. K.," he replied slowly. "Hey, Professor Ruddle, what for did you go and shave your head? There wasn't much of it, but that white hair looked sorta distinguished."

"Hair? Shave? I've been completely bald for years. Lost my hair long before

it turned white. And my name is Guggles, not Ruddle—*Guggles*: try and remember that for a while. Now let me see the camera."

As he slipped the carrying strap over his head and handed the instrument over, the tramp pursed his lips. "Coulda *sworn* that you had a little patch of white up there. Coulda sworn. Sorry about the name, prof; we never seem to be able to get together on those things."

The professor grunted and started for the darkroom with the camera. Halfway there, he stopped and almost cringed as a huge female form stepped through the far doorway.

"Aloysius!" came a voice that approximated a corkscrew to the ear. "Aloysius! I told you yesterday that if that tramp wasn't out of my house in twenty-four hours, experiment or not, you'd hear from me. Aloysius! You have exactly thirty-seven minutes!"

"Y-yes, dear," Professor Guggles whispered at her broad retreating back. "We-we're almost finished."

"Who's that?" McCarthy demanded the moment she had left.

"My wife, of course. You must remember her—she made your breakfast when you arrived."

"Didn't make my breakfast. Made my own breakfast. And you said you weren't married!"

"Now you're being silly, Mr. Gallagher. I've been married for twenty-five years and I know how futile it is to deny it. I couldn't have said any such thing."

"Name's not Gallagher—it's McCarthy, Gooseneck McCarthy," the tramp told him querulously. "What's happened here? You can't even remember my last name now, let alone my first, you change your own name, you shave your head, you get married in a hurry and—and you try 'n tell me that I let some female woman cook my breakfast when I can rassle up a better-tastin', better-eatin'—"

"Hold it!" The little man had approached and was plucking at his sleeve eagerly. "Hold it, Mr. Gallagher or Gooseneck or whatever your name is. Suppose you tell me exactly what you consider this place to have been like before you left."

Gooseneck told him. "And that thingumajig was layin' *on* that whatchmacallit instead of under it," he finished lamely.

The professor thought. "And all you did—when you went back into the past—was to move a rock?"

"That's all. One hell of a big centipede jumped out, but I didn't touch it. Just moved the rock and headed back like you said."

"Yes, of course. H'mmm. That may have been it. The centipede jumping out of the rock may have altered subsequent events sufficiently to make me a married man instead of a blissful single one, to have changed my name from Ruddle to Guggles. Or the rock itself. Such an intrinsically simple act as moving the rock must have had much larger consequences than I had imagined. Just think, if that rock had not been moved, I might not be married! Gallagher—"

"McCarthy," the tramp corrected resignedly.

"Whatever you call yourself—listen to me. You're going back in the time machine and shift that rock back to its original position. Once that's done—"

"If I go back again, I get another hundred."

"How can you talk of money at a time like this?"

"What's the difference between this and any other time?"

"Why, here I am married, my work interruped and you chatter about— Oh, all right. Here's the money." The professor tore his checkbook out and hastily scribbled on a blank. "Here you are. Satisfied?"

McCarthy puzzled over the check. "This isn't like t'other. This is on a different bank—The Cotton Growers Exchange."

"That makes no important difference," the professor told him hastily, bundling him into the time machine. "It's a check, isn't it? Just as good, believe me, just as good."

As the little man fiddled with dials and adjusted switches, he called over his shoulder. "Remember, get that rock as close to its original position as you can. And touch nothing else, do nothing else."

"I know. I know. Hey, prof, how come I remember all these changes and you don't, with all your science and all?"

"Simple," the professor told him, toddling briskly out of the machine. "By being in the past and the time machine while these temporal adjustments to your act made themselves felt, you were in a sense insulated against them, just as a pilot suffers no direct, personal damage from the bomb his plane releases over a city. Now, I've set the machine to return to approximately the same moment as before. Unfortunately, my chronotransit calibrations can never be sufficiently exact— Do you remember how to operate the apparatus? If you don't—"

McCarthy sighed and depressed the lever, shutting the door on the professor's flowing explanations and perspiring bald head.

H E WAS BACK by the pounding surf off the little island. He paused for a moment, before opening the door as he caught sight of a strange transparent object just a little further up the beach. Another time machine—and exactly like his!

"Oh, well. The professor will explain it!"

He started up the beach toward the rock. Then he stopped again—a dead-stop this time.

The rock lay ahead, as he remembered it before the shifting. But there was a man straining at it, *a tall, thin man in a turtleneck sweater and brown, corduroy pants.*

McCarthy got his flapping jaw back under control. "Hey! Hey, you at the rock! Don't move it. It's not supposed to be moved!" He hurried over.

The stranger turned. He had the ugliest face McCarthy remembered having seen on a human being; his neck was ridiculously long and thin. He examined McCarthy slowly. He reached into his pocket and came out with soiled package. He bit off a chaw of tobacco.

McCarthy reached into his pocket and came up with an identically soiled mass of tobacco. He also took a bite. They chewed and stared at each other. Then they spat, simultaneously.

"What do you mean this rock ain't supposed to be moved? Professor Ruddle told me to move it."

"Well, Professor Ruddle told me *not* to move it. *And* Professor Guggles," McCarthy added as a triumphant clincher.

The other considered him for a moment,

his jaw working like a peculiar cam. His eyes traveled up McCarthy's spare body. Then he spat contemptuously and turned to the rock. He grunted against it.

McCarthy sighed and put a hand on his shoulder. He spun him around. "What for you have to go and act so stubborn, fella? Now I'll have to lick you."

Without changing his vacant expression to one of the slightest hostility, the stranger aimed a prodigious kick at his groin. McCarthy dodged easily. That was an old hobo trick! He chopped out rapidly against the man's face. The stranger ducked, moved away and came back fighting.

This was a perfect spot for the famous McCarthy one-two. McCarthy feinted with his left, seemingly concentrating all his power at the other's middle. He noticed that his opponent was also making some awkward gesture with his left. Then he came up out of nowhere with a terrific right uppercut.

WHAM!

Right on the—

—on the button. McCarthy sat up and shook his head clear of bright little lights and happy hums. He had connected, but—

So had the other guy!

He sat several feet from McCarthy, looking dazed and sad. "You are the stubbornest cuss I ever saw! Where did you learn my punch?"

"*Your* punch!" They rose, glowering at each other. "Listen, bub, that there is my *own* Sunday punch, copyrighted, patented and in-corporated! But this ain't gettin' us nowhere."

"No, it ain't. What do we do now? I don't care if I have to fight you for the next million years, but I was paid to move that rock and I'm goin' to move it."

McCarthy shifted the quid of tobacco. "Looky here. You've been paid to move that rock by Professor Ruddle or Guggles or whatever he is by now. If I go back and get a note from him saying you're not to move that rock and you can keep the check anyways, will you promise to squat still until I get back?"

The stranger chewed and spat, chewed and spat. McCarthy marveled at their perfect synchronization. They both spat the same distance, too. He wasn't such a bad guy, if only he wouldn't be so stubborn! Strange—he was wearing a camera like

the one old Ruddle had taken from him.

"O.K. You go back and get the note. I'll wait here." The stranger dropped to the ground and stretched out.

McCarthy turned and hurried back to the time machine before he could change his mind.

H E WAS PLEASED to notice as he stepped down into the laboratory again, that the professor had rewon his gentle patch of white hair.

"Saaay, this is gettin' real complicated. How'd you make out with the wife?"

"Wife? What wife?"

"The wife. The battle-axe. The ball and chain. The steady skirt," McCarthy clarified.

"I'm not married. I told you I considered it a barbarous custom entirely unworthy of a truly civilized man. Now stop babbling and give me that camera."

"But," McCarthy felt his way very carefully, "but, don't you remember takin' the camera from me, Professor Ruddle?"

"Not Ruddle—Roodles, *Roodles.* Oo as is Gooseface. And how could I have taken the camera from you when you've just returned? You're dithering, McCarney—I don't like ditherers. Stop it!"

McCarthy shook his head, forbearing to correct the mispronunciation of his name. He began to feel a vague, gnawing wish that he had never started this combination merry-go-round and slap-happy fun-house.

"Look, prof, sit down." He spread a great hand against the little man's chest, forcing him into a chair. "We're gonna have another talk. I gotta bring you up to date."

Fifteen minutes later, he was winding up. "So this character says he'll wait until I get back with the note. If you want a wife, don't give me the note and he'll move the rock. I don't care one way or t'other, myself. I just want to get out of here!"

Professor Ruddle (Guggles? Roodles?) closed his eyes. "My," he gasped. Then he shuddered. "Married. To that—battle-axe! That st-steady skirt! *No!* McCarney—or McCarthy—listen! You must go back. I'll give you a note—another check—here!" He tore a page from his notebook, filled it rapidly with desperate words. Then he made out another check.

McCarthy glanced at the slips. " 'Nother bank," he remarked wonderingly. "This time The Southern Peanut Trust Company. I hope all these different checks are gonna be good."

"Certainly," the professor assured him loudly. "They will all be good. You go ahead and take care of this matter, and we'll settle it to everybody's satisfaction when you return. You tell this other Mc-Carney that—"

"McCarthy. *Hey!* What do you mean— 'this other McCarney?' I'm the only Mc-Carthy—only *Gooseneck* McCarthy, anyway. If you send a dozen different guys out to do the same job..."

"I didn't send anyone but you. Don't you understand what happened? You went back into the Cretaceous to move a rock. You returned to the present—and, as you say, found me in somewhat unfortunate circumstances. You returned to the past to undo the damage, to *approximately* the same spot in space and time as before—it could not be exactly the same spot because of a multitude of unknown factors and because of the inescapable errors in the first time machine. Very well. You—we'll call you You I—meet You II at the very moment You II is preparing to move the rock. You stop him. If you hadn't, if he hadn't been interrupted in any way and had shifted that stone, he would have been You I. But because he—or rather you—didn't, he is slightly different from you, being a You who has merely made one trip into the past and not even moved the rock. Whereas you—You I—have made two trips, have both moved the rock yourself and prevented yourself from moving it. It's really very simple, isn't it?"

McCarthy stroked his chin and sucked in a great gasp of air. "Yeah," he mumbled wildly. "Simple ain't the word for it!"

The professor hopped into the machine and began preparing it for another trip. "Now as to what happened to me. Once you—You I again— prevented You II from moving that rock, you immediately precipitated—not so much a change as a—an *unchange* in my personal situation. The rock had not been shifted—therefore, I had not been married, was not married, and, let us hope, will never be married. I was also no longer bald. But, by the very fact of the presence of the two You's

in the past, by virtue of some microscopic form of life you killed with your breath, let us say, or some sand you impressed with your feet,—sufficient alterations were made right through to the present so that my name was (and always had been!) Roodles and your name—"

"Is probably MacTavish by now," Mc-Carthy yelled. "Look prof, are you through with the machine?"

"Yes, it's all ready." The professor grimaced thoughtfully. "The only thing I can't place is what happened to that camera you said I took from you. Now if You I in the personification of You II—"

McCarthy planted his right foot in the small of the little man's back and shoved. "I'm gonna get this thing settled and come back and never, never, *never* go near one of these dinguses again!"

He yanked at the chronotransit. The last he saw of the professor was a confused picture of broken glassware, tangled electrical equipment and indignantly waving white hair.

THIS TIME he materialized at the very edge of the beach. "Gettin' closer all the time," he mumbled as he stepped out of the housing. Now to hand over the note, then—

Then—

"Great sufferin' two-tailed explodin' cat-fish!"

There were two men fighting near a red rock. They wore identical clothes; they had identical features and physical construction, including the same lanky forms and long, stringy necks. They fought in a weird pattern of mirror-imagery—each man swinging the same blows as his opponent, right arm crossing right, left crossing left.

The man with his back to the rock had an expensive miniature camera suspended from his neck; the other one hadn't.

Suddenly, they both feinted with their lefts in perfect preparation for what hundreds of railroad bulls had come to curse as "the Gooseneck McCarthy One-Two." Both men ignored the feint, both came up suddenly with their right hands and—

They knocked each other out.

They came down heavily on their butts, about a yard apart, shaking their heads.

"You are the stubbornest cuss I ever

saw," one of them began. "Where—"

"—did you learn my punch?" McCarthy finished, stepping forward.

They both sprang to their feet, stared at him. "Hey," said the man with the camera. "You two guys are twins."

His former opponent differed with him. "You mean *you* two guys are twins!"

"Wait a minute." McCarthy stepped between them before their angry glances at each other could be translated into action. "We're all twins. I mean triplets. I mean— Sit down. I got somethin' to tell you."

They all squatted slowly, suspiciously.

Four chaws of tobacco later, there was a little circle of dark nicotine juice all around them. McCarthy was breathing hard, all three of him. "So it's like I'm McCarthy I because I've seen this thing through up to where I stop McCarthy II from going back to get the note that McCarthy III wants from Ruddle."

The man with the camera rose and the others followed. "The only thing I don't get," he said finally, "is that I'm McCarthy III. Seems to me it's more like I'm McCarthy I, he's McCarthy II—that part's right—and *you're* McCarthy III."

"Uh-uh," McCarthy II objected. "You got it all wrong. The way I look at it—now see if'n this doesn't sound right—is that *I'm* McCarthy I, you're—"

"Hold it! Hold it!" The two men who had been fighting turned to McCarthy I. "I *know* I'm McCarthy I!"

"How do you know?" they demanded.

"Because that's the way Professor Ruddle explained it to me. He didn't explain it to you, did he? I'm McCarthy I, all right. You two are the stubbornest bindle-stiffs I've seen and I've seen them all. Now let's get back."

"Wait a minute. How do I know I still ain't supposed to move this rock? Just because you say so?"

"Because I say so and because Professor Ruddle says so in that note I showed you. And because there are two of us who don't want to move it and we can knock you silly if'n you try."

At McCarthy II's nod of approval, McCarthy III glanced around reluctantly for a weapon. Seeing none, he started back to the time machines. McCarthys I and II hurried abreast.

"Let's go in mine. It's closest." They all turned and entered the machine of McCarthy I.

"What about the checks? Why should you have three checks and McCarthy II have two while I only got one? Do I get my cut?"

"Wait'l we get back to the professor. He'll settle it. Can't you think of anythin' else but money?" McCarthy I asked wearily.

"Ne, we can't," McCarthy II told him. "I want my share of that third check. I got a right to it. More'n this dopey guy has, see."

"O.K. O.K. Wait'll we get back to the lab." McCarthy I pushed down on the chronotransit. The island and the bright sunlight disappeared. They waited.

DARKNESS! "Hey!" McCarthy II shouted. "Where's the lab? Where's Professor Ruddle?"

McCarthy I tugged at the chronotransit. It wouldn't move. The other two came over and pulled at it too.

The chronotransit remained solidly in place.

"You must've pushed down too hard," McCarthy III yelled. "You busted it!"

"Yeah," from McCarthy II. "Who ever told you that you could run a time machine? You busted it and now we're stranded!"

"Wait a minute. Wait a minute." McCarthy I pushed them back. "I got an idea. You know what happened? The three of us tried to come back to—to the present, like Professor Ruddle says. But only one of us *belongs* in the present—see what I mean? So with the three of us inside, the machine just can't go anywhere."

"Well, that's easy," said McCarthy III. "I'm the only real—"

"Don't be crazy. I know *I'm* the *real* McCarthy; I *feel* it—"

"Wait," McCarthy I told them. "This isn't gettin' us any place. The air's gettin' bad in here. Let's go back and argue it out." He pushed the lever down again.

So they went back a hundred and ten million years to discuss the matter reasonably. And, when they arrived, what do you think they found? Yep—exactly. That's exactly what they found.

FAILURE ON TITAN

By ROBERT ABERNATHY

Terror flared across the Saturnian moons. One of the Woollies, that perfect slave-race, had killed a *man!* But to Big Bill, shambling away from his bloody, suddenly silent master, the ancient pattern of obedience was unchanged.

Illustrated by MARTIN

BIG BILL LUMBERED swiftly forward across the frozen ground, and behind him came the rest of the work gang—a score of bent and mighty manlike shapes, draped like Big Bill from head to foot in long white hair.

They moved in a straggling group, but the rhythmic side sway of the great bodies was more uniform than the tread of marching men. Their red eyes peered ahead through the noonday twilight toward the landing strip two hundred yards away, slashed clean and straight across the ragged low-gravity terrain.

There were human figures — three of them—moving along the edge of the strip that was nearer to the cluster of lighted Company buildings. At the distance they all looked alike, big-headed and thick-waisted in their vacuum suits, but even so, Big Bill identified them with ease. Behind those dull red eyes were perceptions wholly alien to Man's, senses to which the distinctive personalities of the men were things as obvious as are apples or oranges to eyes and fingers.

Brilliant lights flashed on all along the landing strip. Thin nictitating membranes descended over the eyes of the approaching Woollies, and the gang came to a simultaneous halt. They sank slowly to their haunches on the iron-hard, fire-cold surface, and in the act became less like fur-clad men and more like crouching, hairy beasts.

Big Bill hunkered unmoving in his place, but his peculiar senses were probing with an unusual curiosity at the familiar minds of the three men. The one who had just risen from bending over the switchbox that controlled the lights was named Paige, and, when Big Bill's mind touched his, the Woolly felt an odd apathy behind which something tense and secret smoldered like a fire banked under ashes. And the fire was hate.

The second, who stood stiffly near Paige, was called Doc. In his brain too burned hate, a dense and palpable thing to Big Bill, mixed with a fear which turned the hatred inward on the mind that had given it birth.

The third man was Paul Gedner.

He stood a little apart from the others, gazing into the starry sky from which the rocket would come. For the watching Woollies his tall figure was clothed in a tangible aura of power, commanding all their inborn, robot-like obedience. He towered like a sublime and terrible god between the narrow horizons of Phoebe, over the desolate landscape of weird lights and shadows cast by Saturn and the distant Sun. And in his thoughts the Woollies glimpsed dimly something beyond their understanding—a Plan, worthy of godhead in its cosmic vastness, leading toward some unguessable triumph—and it was that Plan which the other men hated and feared.

There was still a fourth human on Phoebe. But that man's mind had gone where not even a Woolly's perceptions could follow it.

Abruptly Gedner gestured, and though the furry watchers could not hear what he said into his helmet radio, they turned as one to stare eastward.

HIGH up in the dusky sky a white star was moving. In seconds it grew through magnitudes; it became a fiery, onrushing comet, then a polished, hurtling cylinder of steel lit up by the glare that went on before it. Swiftly the rocket descended; its underdrive flared briefly out, flattening its trajectory, and it came in over the jagged horizon on a long slant toward the landing strip.

The flame of the drive perished, and an

In a smothered whisper she exclaimed, "Paul—look out!"

instant later the face of the little moon vibrated to the shriek of steel runners on fire-glazed rock. The ship sledded forward in a shower of red sparks for five hundred yards before friction slowed it to a stop.

The men were running toward the ship even as it was still sliding, their little topheavy figures increasingly dwarfed by the great gleaming hull, though they were coming nearer to the slope on which the Woollies squatted.

Big Bill watched intently as a forward port swung slowly open in the smooth side of the rocket. His mind was still attuned to that of the tall Gedner, and beneath his flat skull stirred an excitement, utterly strange to the Woolly, yet in some way pleasant. The feeling was not Big Bill's, yet for the moment it was as much a part of him as it was of the man whose thoughts imprinted themselves upon his. Big Bill was a complete extrovert; his mind, like those of all his race, was a sensitive instrument attuned to the mental

atmosphere around him, and almost incapable of independent ideation. By that token the Woollies were willing slaves of the introverted, insensitive Earthmen.

The metal gangway had descended to grate against the rocky ground. Two vacuum-suited silhouettes appeared in the lighted airlock and began to clamber down, the first with a self-possessed, leisurely poise, the other showing signs of a jerky impatience. Behind them came another, grotesquely burdened with a weight of luggage which would have given trouble to half a dozen men under Earth gravity.

But Big Bill's mounting interest was focused on the first of the new arrivals. He sensed clearly that this was the visitor expected, with various and puzzling reactions, by the three waiting men, and also that the coming of this strange, great rocket, long before the scheduled arrival of the little freighter which stopped at long intervals to load the Phoebean jade, had something to do with the fourth man— the one who now lay out on the frigid rock outside the dwelling of the humans, without a vacuum suit, a tarpaulin pulled up over what had been his face.

All these things, Big Bill knew, had one meaning: the fruition of the great Plan was close at hand.

Abruptly the Woolly rose from his squatting position, disregarding the others who remained motionless, and rolled silently forward on his great splayed feet to within a short distance of the knot of humans. His telepathic sense groped curiously at the mind of the visitor, but told him little, since he was unaccustomed to the interpretation of its vibrations; but his vision served him better. The figure turned to give some order to the porter, who was still on the gangway, and the combined light of Saturn and the Sun fell on the face behind the transparent mask, a feeble illumination that was yet enough for the great red eyes of Big Bill.

He saw that the face was subtly different from any he had known before— more rounded, with less prominent feature, smaller bones better sheathed in flesh, and, more spectacularly and superficially, it was framed in long soft hair which gleamed with almost metallic brightness at the edges of the faceplate.

It was Big Bill's first glimpse of an Earthly woman, and the sight of this alien being set up a queer unease in his little, heteroplasmic brain.

LEILA FREY gazed round her, at the ill-lit Phoebean landscape, with a look of no great rapture. She said flatly, "I think, if I were in charge of Saturn Colonial, I'd give this rock back to the Indians."

The tallest of the Company men said, shrugging, "That's probably what they'll do before another year is out. It won't be that long before the market for genuine Phoebean jade has worked down a couple more income levels, to the point where it can't compete with the just-as-genuine synthetic product."

"That's a pre-eminently dirty trick," said Leila Frey with sudden heat. "Some of my friends bought your jade when you were holding production down and the price was just about out of reach. Now you start flooding the market with the

stuff, and—" She had turned to look directly at the tall Earthman, and the Saturn-light was on his face. Her lips parted in surprise and for a moment she was quite dumb; then she essayed a laugh of pleased surprise, which rang hollow inside her air helmet. "Why, Paul! Fancy meeting you here!"

Gedner's smile showed strong white teeth. "What would life be without coincidences?"

"But this one is rather too good to be true," insisted the girl on a false note of gaiety. "Everybody knew you'd buried yourself somewhere in the wilds. But imagine me stumbling onto your grave!"

Paul Gedner's grin tightened. "Not so surprising, Leila darling. You're royally paid to go around the System digging things up, aren't you?"

Captain Manoly of the *Zodiac* broke in, his voice betraying his irritation. "I believe Miss Frey's luggage has all been landed."

"Fine," said Gedner, glancing toward where Mark Paige was already wrestling with an assortment of trunks and cases far too expensive and extensive to be appropriate on the little mining moon. "You must have thought this was another society assignment, Leila... You're in a hurry to lift, Captain?"

"That's right," snapped the spaceman. "I've got a schedule to keep up." But neither his schedule, nor the unhappy fact that he was seeing none of the impressive sum which Leila Frey's syndicate had paid to persuade the managers of the line to allow a troublesome unscheduled stop, could have warranted his obvious nervousness. He had already cast more than one apprehensive glance into the twilight beyond the little group of humans. Now Leila caught the movement of his helmet and followed the look.

She could not suppress a gasp. Scarcely a dozen yards away crouched a huge white shape, somewhat like a man, more like a gorilla, a strange albino gorilla with a fell of hair like a muskox, covering all its face save the expressionless crimson eyes. Its great three-fingered hands rested on the ground as it cowered and stared.

Leila recovered her composure. "Is this one of your renowned killer Woollies?" she asked coolly of Gedner.

"Not him. Big Bill's my right hand man." Gedner beckoned and the creature rose and padded toward him. "Carry the lady's luggage, Bill.

Paige relinquished his task with alacrity. The great Woolly embraced the entire load with ease, and moved toward the lighted buildings. Leila's eyes followed him, and, accustomed as she was to the sight of Woollies, a faint shudder shook her. The news which had brought her to Phoebe was responsible for that shudder; two days before, the message from the lonely moon had shaken the whole Saturnian system—

"A Woolly has killed a man!"

NOW on all the moons of Saturn, the human colonists paled in terror before their familiar and trusted slaves; families trembled behind locked doors, streets were deserted, industry at a standstill. On the Earth and Mars exchanges, the stocks of Saturn Colonial dropped sickeningly and continued to drop. The whole thriving economy of the Subsystem, based on Woolly slave labor—far cheaper than human workers, cheaper even than robots—rocked on its foundations.

It was impossible, unbelieveable—but frightened millions believed. All experience and all psychological tests pointed to the complete, robot-like reliability of the Woollies. The great race which had ruled Saturn's moons before the Age of Man had, before its unexplained extinction, bred its slave-creatures with superb skill, for vast strength, for adaptability to the diverse environments of the satellites—and for a perfect susceptibility to telepathic control.

But, if a Woolly had killed a man—

The Company had declared at once its intention of sending an investigating commission to Phoebe; it did not request the interference of the Colonial Government, and that, from the Company was equivalent to a stern KEEP OUT in the face of the police and everyone else. But before the corporation heads had recovered sufficiently to issue their statement, the All-Planet News Syndicate had Leila Frey aboard the *Zodiac*, traveling toward Phoebe at sixty miles a second.

Gedner took the girl's arm in one heavily-gloved hand and led her away from the ship at a leisurely pace. Captain Man-oly had already vanished thankfully into the airlock of his vessel.

As if coming out of a trance, Leila made a sudden effort to shake her arm from Gedner's grip. Failing, she walked on beside him in stiff silence. It was the man who spoke, when they had almost reached the largest of the lighted structures.

"So now your employers send you out after scoops," he remarked thoughtfully.

"I just happened to be in the Subsystem, looking for general interest stuff on the colonies," put in Leila quickly, almost defensively. Gedner went on as if she had not spoken, and with like disregard for the fact that every word was ringing also in the helmet phones of the two other men plodding on behind.

"You've been doing well since you got rid of me. But I always knew you had what it takes to get ahead, darling; you've never been anything but a grasping, selfish, irresponsible little monster."

Leila wrenched herself away from him, as they paused at the airlock door of the Company headquarters. "I assure you I haven't changed in the least," she told him icily. "And neither have you. You're still one huge hypertrophied ego. Nothing matters to you except being the boss— Say!" She began to laugh, staccato. "Why, Paul, you've found the one ideal place for yourself here, out of the whole System. A planet little enough to make you feel as big as you want to, where you're almost alone with a crew of subhuman things that don't know anything but obedience..."

Her own words called back the jarring memory of what had brought her here, and she stopped on an indrawn breath. Gedner had stared at her in silence—she knew that of old as a sign that she had come near the quick of his pride—and abruptly she was aware of the ghostly mass of Big Bill, looming erect behind his master.

Out on the landing strip blue lightning ripped through the noonday dusk. The ground vibrated as the *Zodiac* began to glide forward; the rocky landscape stood out in harsh light and shadow, and the glare of atomic flame silhouetted the misshapen figures of the two other men, who had come up and were waiting.

Gedner operated the airlock mechanism, and they passed through; the throbbing vibration underfoot rose to a higher pitch and died suddenly as the space ship left the surface of the moon. In three days, Earth time, it would return to pick Leila up on the return trip to Titan.

After the three men and the girl entered the giant Woolly. The thin translucent lids descended again over his eyes as he rolled into the brightly-lit room.

The room, Leila observed, was large and slovenly, arranged for both business and relaxation, a scarred desk and file-cabinet keeping company with a table, armchairs and a tired-looking couch. Walls and ceilings were naked insulation; the iron floor was unswept of dust and cigarette butts, and patched with rust. But it was a relief for her to feel her great iron-soled shoes, like those of a medieval Russian peasant, assert their magnetic grip. Without further ado, the girl unfastened the bulky ballast belt about her slender waist, wriggled out of the shoulder harness, and let what on Earth would have been a thousand pounds of lead slide to the floor.

Gedner lounged against the table; he had raised the faceplate of his helmet, and his features had the pallor which comes with a long stay on the outer planets. He remarked lightly, "The Company would raise hell if they knew you were here."

"That's not my worry," retorted Leila. "I'm on assignment from A.P."

"Maybe you'd like to interview Sam Chandler. He's right outside."

The girl recoiled from Gedner's easy smile. "No!" she said sharply, and then added, "Later...perhaps."

"The All-Planet people want the details, don't they?"

"For God's sake, Paul!" exploded Mark Paige. But his mouth twitched beneath his hopelessly straggly little mustache as Gedner's gaze met his.

"Shut up," said Gedner evenly. "Miss Frey and I are old friends. We understand each other."

L EILA said nothing, but her red lips were compressed to a thin line as she fumbled with the air-tight zippers of her suit. As she wriggled with difficulty out of the heavy garment, Gedner's hard black eyes dwelt with pleasure on the white silk blouse and shorts she had donned in the stuffy cabin aboard the rocket, on the soft

curves of her breasts and her slender legs ... And in the corner crouched Big Bill, a great white-furred faceless thing with dull red eyes fixed unwinkingly on the girl.

Leila sat down in one of the worn armchairs, but she failed to relax from the tension, the nameless apprehension that had begun to grip her when she first set foot on this little twilight moon. Her gaze flicked from Gedner to Paige, who had picked up her discarded vacuum suit and was arranging it meticulously on the hangers beside the outer door, and from him to the third man, who, without even removing his helmet, had bent over the desk and seemed to be absorbed in the disordered papers atop it. The humming undertone of the air pump, which had started automatically on the opening of the inner airlock door, stopped suddenly as the room pressure reached normal, and left a heavy silence...

She looked back to Gedner, leaning lazily against the battered table, one thumb hooked into the belt that sagged awkwardly over his ballast belt to support a holstered flame pistol. He smiled at her again, and she had a panicky feeling of being alone with him in this bare room millions of miles from civilization.

But what he said was not at all alarming. "Care for something to eat?"

"I had dinner on the rocket," said Leila.

"Cup of tea, then?" said Gedner. Leila nodded, grateful for a distraction. Paige had already moved toward what was evidently the kitchen door, methodically removing his gloves as he went. Presently he came back with a tray and a single steaming cup.

Gedner slid off the edge of the table and turned to Paige. "We'd better flame that strip before it cools off entirely," he said matter-of-factly, and, to Leila, with a gesture at the still-helmeted figure bending over the desk, "Doc Chaikoski here can entertain you while we're busy."

The one indicated looked up quickly, and, though his face was obscured by the reflection of light in his helmet, his very posture, even in the grotesque space suit, spoke of taut hatred as he glanced toward Gedner. The latter took no notice, but turned away to join Paige, who had silently opened a chest in the far end of the room and was dragging out two heavy portable electron torches.

The two men snapped their faceplates shut and went out through the airlock. Leila sat quite still for a little while, glancing nervously from the crouching, silent Woolly against the wall to the equally silent man. At last she exclaimed in exasperation, "Won't you take that thing off your head? Two gargoyles in a room this size are too many!"

The other spoke for the first time. "It won't help much," he said in a toneless voice, but he removed the helmet, set it carelessly on the desk-top, and, turning, began to unzip his vacuum suit. The girl saw a pale, thin, youthful face, shockingly marred by a huge, angry scar which cut diagonally across the cheek, ruined the bridge of the nose, and disappeared under an unkempt shock of dun-colored hair. A terrific blow, perhaps from a hot fragment of metal, must have left that mark.

"My name isn't Doc," There was increasing bitterness in his voice. "It's Leo. It's just that it amuses *him* to call me that, because I happen to be a petrologist."

"Oh," said Leila. She watched him cross the room and toss his space suit onto a hanger, return and sprawl limply in the chair behind the desk. Then she remembered that she was a reporter with the biggest story of her life to get. "Perhaps you can tell me something of what I need to know," she suggested.

Leo Chaikoski stared fixedly at the tangle of papers. "What do you mean?"

"Well..." she hesitated. "Something about the general setup here, to begin with."

"Setup? It's simple enough. Paul Gedner gives the orders to the Woollies and to the rest of us—officially, he's only the Woolly boss, but—well, you seem to know him."

"Yes," said Leila.

"I have a degree from North American Geological, so whenever the Woollies have worked out a jade site, I go out and kick over a couple of rocks to uncover a new one. It's not a job—the surface supply will outlast the market. Paige keeps the accounts and production records and makes out requisitions once in a while and spends the rest of his time with a book and a bottle. Chandler—was—our maintenance man for the mechanical equipment. And the Woollies dig the jade and load it when the rocket comes, and Saturn Colonial pays our salaries."

But Leila seized on the mention of the dead man. She said, "I'm here to get the facts on Chandler's death, you know."

H IS HEAD snapped up; the girl fancied she saw alarm flash into his eyes. Then he looked down again. "You'd better ask the others. They were both there when it happened; I wasn't."

"But you must know how it happened."

"Chandler was out at the diggings, inspecting a drill, when one of the Woollies on the job attacked him. There wasn't any provocation, nor any warning. Paul killed the Woolly with that gun he carries, but Chandler was done for."

There was a guarded look in the scarred face, and Leila was not satisfied. She remembered her training in interviewing—the you-approach.

"What do *you* think made that Woolly run amok?" she demanded pointblank.

Leo rose to his feet with a jerk, as if the abrupt question had carried a physical impact. He said in a savage voice, "I don't think, I—" He bit off the last word and fell silent, the great scar growing more apparent as his face paled. His eyes strayed fearfully toward the outer door; then he looked back at the girl and advancing toward her, lowered his voice. "Listen, I'll tell you. But you mustn't let *him* see that you know... Paul killed Chandler."

Leila sat open-mouthed. But there was no need for her to say anything; the words came now from Leo Chaikoski in a jerky torrent.

"You've seen how it is. *He* controls the Woollies, like he dominates everything else around him. The rest of us know the technique, too—but we can't do anything with them. He's *strong*. He made the Woolly kill Chandler—and he could kill Paige or me the same way—or you. Yes, he could kill you, too, if he wanted to. He has us all in his hands." The young man's voice had sunk lower and lower, and a thread of mortal terror ran through it.

"That's why he can murder us and never

be caught." Leo's scarred face twisted with impotent rage. "I'd kill him...but he always has the gun...and the Woollies. If I had a gun, I could do it..." He grasped pleadingly at the girl's limp hand on the arm of her chair. "Do you happen to have a gun?"

"No," said Leila curtly. Her blue eyes stared into space, past Leo and his fear; her mind raced, envisaging the widening ripples of consequence that were even now spreading throught the whole System from the death of a mechanic. If that death had been murder—had the killer acted without considering those consequences?

Leo's abject terror gave the weight of truth to his accusation—a weird indictment, but no more preposterous than the simple fact that a Woolly had killed a man. But there was still something missing, the fundamental—

"Why?" said Leila suddenly, almost to herself. "I don't doubt that Paul's capable of murder. But it would have to be for profit."

"The motive?" Leo hesitated, then, "Oh, that's simple. *He* sabotaged the radio. Chandler was going to fix it...he wasn't afraid. So Paul made the Woolly kill him."

Now Leila too glanced apprehensively at the door. She exclaimed, "But this makes less and less sense. Why should Paul Gedner want the radio out of commission?"

Leo was silent, avoiding her penetrating gaze; at last he said sullenly, "Chandler wanted to send a message."

Leila's hands tightened on the arms of her chair. "What message?" she persisted fiercly.

"Why shouldn't I tell you what he's doing?" Leo wondered dully. "He's going to kill me, anyway, because I know, and then he'll kill you too—" His words were choked off in a gasp; he sprang back, crashing bruisingly into the desk, and cowered against it. Into a deathly silence came the grating of the inner airlock door. It opened, and Gedner came in, followed by Paige burdened with the two glazing torches. Gedner's eyes traveled from the girl to Leo and back again, and his grin flashed as he lifted off his helmet.

"Having a nice chat?" he inquired softly.

NOBODY answered; in the intolerable silence, Gedner crossed to the desk, picked up a package of cigarettes and inhaled one into life as he began removing his vacuum suit. Leo Chaikoski sidled away from him, slumped into a chair in the corner, and sat staring into space.

"I hope you've found time to admire Big Bill," said Gedner lightly, gesturing at the giant creature, which had not moved or shifted its red gaze from Leila for a moment. "Quite a man, isn't he? You always liked the big, husky type, didn't you, darling?"

"Wouldn't it be better," said Leila in a carefully governed voice, "to leave that beast outside? After—what happened, I mean."

"Big Bill's all right. All the Woollies are all right; you just have to know how to get along with them."

The girl shuddered inwardly; it no longer occurred to her to doubt what Leo had told her. Another silence fell; it was broken by Paige, who, having hung up his outer garments, had stood for a time, glancing about uncertainly, and at last looked elaborately at his watch, moved toward the inner door, and announced, "I'm going to bed."

"Go easy on the nightcap," advised Gedner. He looped his pistol belt carefully over the back of a chair, with the gun hanging on the outside, then sat down on the edge of the desk and drew contentedly on his cigarette. "Our bedtimes are various," he told Leila. "No proper night or day here, and damn little system. The Company doesn't worry as long as we get out the jade."

"The Company's worried now," said Leila, uncomfortably, feeling Gedner's probing gaze upon her. "They're sending a commission to investigate Phoebe."

"A commission!" mocked Gedner. There was silence again for a space, and an infinitesimal change crept into his hard, smiling face; Leila strove in vain to read it. Only at the last moment did she become aware of the pale shadow looming beside her.

She looked up into the scarlet eyes of the monster, and screamed uncontrollably. Shaggy white arms went round her and lifted her into the air; she could feel the muscles bulging like plastic iron against her, pressing her to the furry body that was almost painfully hot. Leila went wild for a few seconds, striking at the white mask of Big Bill's face, struggling uselessly; then she made herself lie still.

"Your idea of a joke..." she choked.

"Quite a man, isn't he?" chuckled Gedner. He made an unconcerned gesture, and Big Bill bent to deposit Leila with care in her place in the armchair again. The Woolly backed away to huddle as before against the naked wall, his mighty three-fingered hands resting on the floor.

Leo Chaikoski had come to his feet, his scarred face distorted, hands clenched at his sides. He made an inarticulate sound; Gedner turned and looked at him for a long moment, then asked softly, "Don't you think it's your bedtime too, Doc?"

Leo jerked out, "You damned...stinking...I'm not afraid..."

"Take it easy," said Gedner. He took Leo's arm in a sure grip, turned him about and walked him firmly to the door. "You're all worked up, Doc. You need a bit of sleep." As if in a dream Leo walked on through the doorway; Gedner watched him go, pressed the stud that closed the door, and turned a key in the lock.

Leila felt herself white and shaking from the reaction, and angrier thereby. It was a minute before she could command her voice; then she told Paul Gedner what he was, in terms that Leo Chaikoski would never have thought of, in English, Spanish, and Martian.

Gedner laughed, thrusting the key into his pocket. "You're all right. But for about two seconds I'll bet you thought Big Bill was going to carry you off, like the gorillas do the beautiful white girls in the story books. Bill could hardly have a gorilla's motives, though—the Woollies reproduce by budding when you feed them phosphorus. He couldn't even eat you alive; you'd probably poison him. That's not a crack; it's metabolism."

Leila was relatively calm again. "I think it's my bedtime too," she said frozenly. "I'm tired from my trip—and this friendly reception—"

"Not yet," insisted Gedner. "We ought to have a lot to talk about. It's been a long time since I saw you." He added, "Or any woman, for that matter." His eyes fell on the teacup, which had toppled

unnoticed from the arm of Leila's chair and rolled away across the floor. "You didn't drink your tea... Maybe you'd like something more stimulating?" He bent to open a drawer of the file-cabinet and take out a half-filled bottle.

"No," the girl said sharply. Gedner shrugged, and put the bottle back. He crossed the room and leaned against the wall beside Big Bill, letting a hand rest on the great Woolly's flattened head and running his fingers idly through the fine white hair. Leila could not face the intent, identical gaze in the eyes of man and monster.

ABRUPTLY Gedner said, "That little crackpot was talking to you, wasn't he?" At the girl's nod, he went on, "He's not particularly sane. They get that way, out in these stations."

She looked at him at last. "He seems to be about as sane as you are, Paul."

"So you think I'm crazy?" said Gedner amusedly.

A surge of anger nerved Leila. "You've always been a little crazy. Now I think you're crazy a lot. Power-crazy."

"That's right," answered the man unexpectedly. Something glowed in his black eyes, smothering the mocking light; he straightened. "And I've got it, now. Here —as you've seen—I'm the boss. And that's not all."

"That's not all!" echoed Leila with a scornful laugh. "Wait till the Company investigators get here. Where will your little kingdom be then?"

"We won't be here to meet them," said Gedner readily. "The *Zodiac* will be back here inside sixty hours. It won't be hard —with the Woollies' help—to commandeer her."

"Now I know you're crazy!" But there was a doubt behind her incredulity. In the confident figure of Gedner she saw the author of the fear and menace that had spread out from this remote moon to grip the whole Saturnian Subsystem. But the *why* was still unanswered.

"I'm glad you showed up here, Leila darling," he was saying. "I'd intended to catch up with you before you got out of the moons, anyway—but you've saved me a lot of trouble. From now on, you're going along with me."

Leila knew a sinking sensation, but she

rallied bravely. "What do you think you're going to do—convert the *Zodiac* into a pirate warship, with a Woolly crew? Those days are gone."

"Nothing so stupid; she'll go on schedule to Titan. I've made some discoveries, and I intend to use them. People have been using Woollies for fifty years, and nobody has realized their full possibilities. I'd already begun to a year ago, when I took this job on this God-forsaken rock; and here I've had the leisure and the opportunity to work the possibilities out."

. "For murder?" asked Leila bluntly.

"I had to get rid of Chandler—he had one of those single-track minds full of ideas about 'loyalty to the company' and so on— But I see you don't understand. Yet you must know better than I do just what's happened in the Subsystem since I sent out the news that one Woolly had killed one man." He paused, and when she did not answer, "Panic, financial collapse, the whole system starts falling to pieces. Before long, there are going to be more such incidents—not on Phoebe this time, but on Titan, right in the heart of Saturnian civilization. You can imagine what will happen then. Now suppose, in the midst of the turmoil, appears a small group of men who have learned to control the Woollies, fully control, so that no untrained human mind can challenge their commands. Like I control Big Bill." He gestured at the immobile monster. "Look at him; he thinks only what I think, he wants only what I want—never before did two hearts beat so completely as one... Suppose, then, that this group—a few friends and I—take over the central offices of the Company, and incidentally the Colonial Government. Then, of course, the secret can come out: that Woollies don't run wild, they don't kill unless they're ordered to, and they won't be ordered to kill anybody who stays in line and does as he's told. There'll be a general sigh of relief, and nobody will worry about the change of administrations."

Leila sat very still, assimilating the picture his words built up. It wasn't impossible; it was the ancient pattern of successful revolution: first bring in chaos, then out of the chaos a new order of brutal force. There was only one flaw... She laughed.

"It ought to work very nicely, Paul. Until the Earth Government hears about it and send a couple of battleships to blast you out of the Universe."

Gedner grinned confidently. "But Earth is in opposition, beyond the Sun. It'll take over two weeks for a ship to get there, if any escapes before we seize the ports. And by the time they can get any Fleet units here, we'll be ready for them, with men recruited—there will be plenty willing to join us—and the defenses of the major moons could stand off half a dozen battleships. They won't dare bomb the cities because of the civilian populations—"

"War with Earth?" cried Leila unbelievingly. *That* was preposterous, unheard-of.

"Why not? In a year, two years, I'll be stronger than Earth!"

LEILA stared at him again. "The population of the moons is about twenty million. Earth has over three billion," she recited as if in a classroom. "'Stronger than Earth'?"

"Your thinking in terms of population figures," said Gedner, "is very crude. Don't you know what the real strength of Earth has been for the past three hundred years? Not a mass of three billion people—but ten or a dozen battleships, the backbone of the fleet. Do you know what a star-class battleship is? A thousand feet of hull, tungsten-alloy armor ten feet thick, twenty-six-gravity mercury engines, fifteen to twenty-one atomic blast guns, a thousand tons or so of atomic explosives. Those are the surface features—but what matters is that they're the biggest carriers and distributors of pure energy that have ever operated in the Solar System. And they remain effective as long as there's atomic energy to power their weapons."

"I know all that," said the girl impatiently.

"All right. What you evidently don't know is that right now, in the year of civilization 745, Earth is almost at the end of its supply of power metals. They've been importing Martian power—solar power—for the last two decades, hoarding their own dwindling stores of the heavy elements, in case of war, and at the same time trying to build up the domestice heliodynamic plants. But it's plain that Earth hasn't the power to fight a major war at present."

"A major war?" said Leila helplessly. "What makes you think it would take a major war to smash your scheme?"

"Evidently," said Gedner, "Doc Chaikoski didn't tell you all he knows."

Leila remembered, with a queer chill, the sentence that had been interrupted by Gedner's return. She opened her mouth and closed it without saying anything. Gedner, who had been pacing up and down paused and gave her a long, intent look.

"I intended you to know, in any case. You'll go with me to Kroniopolis, as soon as the *Zodiac* comes back... Leila, my love, this moon is lousy with uranium."

"That can't be true!" cried Leila, but her voice shook. "The scientists—the whole theory of planetary origins—"

"You've been reading your own Science and Progress supplements. Certainly, the theory says there can't be any heavy metals on the surfaces of the major planets or their moons. But Phoebe isn't a moon of Saturn. Look at its retrograde revolution! It wandered in a long time ago from somewhere nearer the Sun, and wherever it came from there was plenty of uranium. That's the way Chaikoski explained it, at least. He happened onto a deposit the last time he went prospecting for jade, and once he knew what to look for, he found three more. And that's just a sample of what there must be. With that, and the Woollies— Do you see now?"

"Yes...I see," answered Leila slowly. She raised her blond head and met Gedner's look steadfastly. "Paul... did you ever read any history? About six hundred years ago, there was a man called Hitler, who had ideas a lot like yours. He got pretty far with them too, because he had the same advantages you count on: better weapons than anybody else in the world, and a whole nation of people that were almost like the Woollies, trained to obey and not to think. But what happened to him—"

"Isn't going to happen to me," interrupted Gedner, unimpressed. "I've got enough imagination to see where history is heading *now*— not six hundred years ago—and the brains to make a good thing of it. Earth is done for; Saturn and Mars

are going to be the next centers of the Solar System. And inside the next couple of weeks I'm going to be the boss of Saturn." He was .smiling triumphantly down at the girl as she sat in the armchair. For the moment, staggered by Gedner's dream of conquest, Leila had forgotten her own present situation; now, with a tremor, she realized that he was very close.

"How are you going to like being Queen of Saturn, Leila?" he asked softly.

"I...don't know," faltered the girl, rising stiffly, mechanically to her feet as she spoke. Gedner laid a hand on her arm, but she jerked away and retreated from him. "You'd better let me think that over."

Gedner's smile twisted down at one corner; his intense gaze followed her slim figure in the scanty white costume, and his eyes narrowed. "I didn't ask you whether you wanted to be Queen of Saturn. I asked you how you were going to like it."

"It doesn't sound like my kind of a job," said Leila. As she spoke, she was still moving cautiously away, keeping her eyes on him. But at the last moment, Gedner saw where she was going, and swore in fury as he flung himself forward.

"The job's yours," he muttered, "and you start now!" She fought, but his arms were about her with a strength that seemed to equal that of the giant Woolly. When he tried to kiss her panting mouth, she bit his cheek until the blood ran, but he only laughed and swung her clear of the floor. He twisted a hand in her blond hair, pulled her head back and bent to plant a savage kiss on her throat instead.

Suddenly the girl stopped struggling; her eyes dilated, looking past Gedner's shoulder. In a smothered whisper she exclaimed, "Paul—*look out!*"

THE urgency in her voice made him glance up; in an instant he had released her and spun around. To face Big Bill, who had silently risen half-erect and as silently advanced upon the two. The Woolly's flat head was sunk between his shoulders; his huge three-fingered hands dangled below his shaggy knees, and almost all his resemblance to a man was lost. His red eyes glinted coldly in the bright light.

As Gedner wheeled, Big Bill halted his stealthy approach. He reared abruptly to his full seven feet of height, then slowly raised his great mitten-like hands.

Leila, in a dazed huddle on the floor, saw the first look of utter stupefaction on Gedner's face replaced by one of scowling mental effort—and then by a dawning horror. Big Bill sank into a tense crouch. Then Gedner threw himself sidewise, and his hand came up with the gun; and in that instant Big Bill went for him in one terrible rolling rush.

Before the man's finger could jerk the firing lever, one of those huge three-fingered hands closed on his forearm. There was a snapping, and the flame pistol spun away; Gedner screamed out in agony then, and once again as the Woolly lifted him into the air to smash him down against the iron floor.

That was all. Big Bill stood quietly, a stooping white-furred figure with dangling hands, over a red thing on the floor that squirmed painfully and was still. In the silence the sobbing gasps of Leila's own breathing rang in her ears.

Knuckles crashed against the door panels, and Mark Paige's voice came in, edged with anxiety— "Hey, Paul!" Leila stirred from her stunned apathy and picked herself off the floor; and then she did the bravest action of her life.

With heart banging against her front teeth, she walked across the room and knelt beside the shattered body. The great red eyes of the Woolly looked dully down at her. Fortunately, the key was in the first and most accessible pocket.

It took her several tries, with her back to Big Bill, to fit it into the lock. She had picked up the flame pistol and held it in her left hand, pointing away from the door at a wavering angle; that was just as well, for Paige's headlong entry when the door slid open nearly tripped her taut nerves into pulling the trigger.

"Hey!" said Paige again in a low voice. His eyes fell on Leila's shaking hand, and he reached across to take the gun away from her and aim it pointblank at Big Bill. There was a strong odor of liquor on his breath, but his hand holding the pistol was perfectly steady. "Shall I shoot him?" he asked almost casually.

Leila shook her head numbly. "I—I don't think it's necessary."

He was silent a moment, regarding the Woolly. "But we'd better get him out of here." He gestured and frowned at Big Bill, and by sign language and telepathy made the great creature understand. Big Bill retreated to the airlock, fumbled with its controls, and rolled out into the lock. The clang of the outer door brought an involuntary sigh from Leila. One mitten-like hand had left a red smear on the opening lever. . . .

"What happened?" inquired Paige at last.

"I don't know," said Leila confusedly. Her knees had gone boneless; she sank into a chair. "It was just sitting against the wall there—" she pointed "—and then it got up and killed him." She hesitated. "Paul seemed to be trying to control it . . . but I guess he couldn't."

Paige laid the gun carefully on the desk, walked deliberately to the couch, unfolded a blanket, and went to spread it over Paul Gedner and his dream of an Empire of Saturn. The blanket could not quite cover everything.

BIG BILL rolled ponderously through the inky Phoebean night, his huge red eyes picking an aimless path by the starlight. There was a nagging emptiness in his little mind—a vacuum left by the vanishing of Gedner's dominant will. The vanishing Big Bill could not explain. But he knew that he had had no thoughts that were not also those of the godlike master, no desires that were not the reflection of Gedner's . . .

Dimly he remembered the final scene in the humans' dwelling. There had been a strange storm of unprecedented emotions, and Big Bill too had felt a moment of overpowering desire for the slight fair-headed human who had come in the rocket . . . And then came an instant of blind, alien fury to which Big Bill could give no name or meaning, and whose deeds he could not remember.

Nor could he know that, mirroring Gedner's passions, he had only felt and acted as the man would have if he, instead of the Woolly, had been the onlooker.

He had gone mad with jealousy.

The Running of the Zar

By VASELEOS GARSON

Briggs burst out of the cave, running low . . .

Big Joe Stevens asked only two things of Rick Briggs—guts and loyalty. But a man planning to rob the tree-folk of Pluto is in no position to demand anything.

A MAN," BIG JOE STEVENS said, "needs two things to lick this planet. Guts and a friend."

He put his big hands on Rick Briggs' shoulders, staring down at the smaller man, his soft brown eyes searching.

"I know you've got guts. But can you be my friend?"

Rick Briggs' dark eyes narrowed. They swept the big man from his thick zar-leather boots to the tip of his red-thatched head.

Stevens had come to him, drawn by the many stories of the slim dark spaceman's lightning reflexes.

"I need your speed," Stevens said. "It'll pay well if you will come in with me. Half the take on 200 pounds of almost pure resilium—and you know the quoted price. A hundred thousand credits per ounce."

Two hundred pounds of resilium at a hundred thousand credits per ounce!

Rick Briggs' stared at the big man. "For that much I'd share my bed with the devil."

Stevens grinned then, and held out a huge hand, clasping Briggs' small lean one, setting the agreement.

That had happened three months ago.

Now, Stevens lay sprawled in a gully, his body crushed and mashed to a pulp by the atmosphere of the outermost planet, Pluto.

He was dead because Briggs had used his heat-ray pistol to burn a hole in Stevens' armor to let in the pressure while the big man trudged ahead of him, carrying the resilium on his broad back.

Now Briggs lay in his own sweat-drenched armor, the big block of ore beside him. He stared across another gully at Stevens' ship.

Only forty feet straight across to safety and wealth. But the gully was fifty feet deep with almost sheer sides.

STEVENS spared no expense in equipping his ship for the jump from Neptune to Pluto. It was a sleek fifty-foot job, overpowered with an atomic engine built for the swift two-hundred foot four-man space patrols.

"That's a big power plant for such a little ship," Briggs said when Stevens showed him through the little vessel.

Stevens unleashed one of his frequent grins. "I like speed and power to spare when I hit the space lanes. I've dodged meteors with the *Princess* just because she had that reserve of power.

"I picked you, Rick, because I figured you were like the *Princess*. She's little, but she's got more snap and guts than ships four times her size."

Briggs shrugged. You almost had to like a guy like Stevens, even if he was so clumsy he was always barging into things and smashing them up.

Stevens had personality plus, and the mechanics and merchants in Neptune City jumped to help him in servicing the ship. Yes, Briggs decided, you could almost fall in love with a guy like Stevens—if you didn't think that two hundred pounds of resilium was just twice as much as one hundred pounds.

It was Briggs' luck and just too bad for Stevens that the big blond had selected him for his partner in the undertaking. With the pay for one hundred pounds of resilium, you could buy almost anything in the universe. But, with twice that, you could buy anything.

While Stevens worked, Briggs dreamed of the things two hundred pounds of resilium could buy.

Stevens told nothing to Briggs of where the resilium was located, but Briggs bided his time. He'd know sometime and then he could go ahead with his plans.

Finally, the *Princess* was ready.

Trailing her bright tail, the *Princess* leaped upwards from the bright lights of Neptune City's spaceport into space.

After the squeezing shock of the take-off, Briggs unbuckled himself from the hydraulic chair and said, "Here we go, Joe. But where?"

Big Joe Stevens grinned. "Pluto, of course, where else can you find resilium?"

Briggs had known that Pluto was the planet of resilium, but the answer was too obvious.

"Yes," he said, and his dark eyes were thoughtful, "but where are you going to find two hundred pounds of the stuff when the System's Mining Department is sitting on top of all the mines?"

Stevens grinned. "We're not going mining, Rick. We're going hunting, ostensibly for *zar*. That's what our permits call for."

"But the resilium?"

"The resilium," Stevens said quickly, "already has been mined, smelted into almost pure shape. I couldn't get it before. I was alone and I move too slow.

"A man needs two things to lick this planet," he added. "Guts and a friend—a swift-moving friend."

Rick Briggs held back his next question. It wasn't time yet to get too nosy. Give Stevens a chance to see what Briggs is the friend he needs.

Briggs moved over to the spacegraph and checked their position against the stars. He figured with half his mind. With the other, he thought about resilium, the magic metal which gave other metals a resiliency beyond belief.

One pinch of resilium in a hundred-weight of duralloy gave that tough metal tremendously added strength. It would bend against severe pressure, but when the pressure was removed the resilium-treated duralloy gradually would work back to its original shape.

Spaceship companies were desperate for it. It saved innumerable repair bills—saved ship after ship from asteroid damage and loss.

AT FIRST, Pluto was a tiny dot above them, but as they roared closer, it brightened and grew larger until it covered all space above them. Then the *Princess*, automatically adjusting herself to the pull of the planet, spiraled over and the planet lay below them.

"We check in at No. 2 mine," Stevens said. "That's where the Pluto agent is stationed."

"Then," he added, and his grin was bigger than ever, "we go hunting *zar*."

Diggers, the planet agent, was cordial. "Back again, Stevens?" he asked. "You must have run out of *zar* money faster than usual this time."

"Just put in some improvements in the *Princess*, and I didn't realize they cost so much." He handed their permits to Diggers for his stamp.

"Don't forget to stop back," Diggers added. "Pluto has to collect her bounty of one *zar* in ten."

"Have I ever?" Stevens laughed.

Briggs bit his lips. Here was a problem. He'd forgotten the tax on *zar*. But he shrugged. He'd leap that hurdle when the time came. He'd have to stop back, or be the prey of every space patrol ship and lose the two hundred pounds of resilium.

"Zar still running in Cerebus valley?" Stevens asked casually.

"Better than ever," Diggers replied, "So you should have good hunting."

Cerebus Valley was dark and forbidding, slashed by deep gullies. Stevens dropped the *Princess* lightly between two of the gullies.

"We'll hunt first," Stevens decided. "Then we can try for the resilium, and I hope your reflexes are in tiptop shape. I wouldn't want you to lose an arm."

Briggs had heard vaguely of *zar*-hunting, but he never had tried his own prowess at it. All he knew was that the hides of the beasts tanned to a soft shade of green, that the leather was so tough that it resisted the sharpest blade. He'd seen nothing of the real beasts. Three-dimension pictures in plenty of course, but they hardly counted.

Stevens and Briggs stepped out of the *Princess* into the crushing pressure of Pluto, unrelieved by the pressure dome over No. 2 mine. But their sturdy duralloy armor suits didn't even groan at the pressure.

Through the intercom phone, Briggs inquired, "Well, where do we find the *zar?*"

Stevens chuckled. "Follow me."

The blond's bulky figure started slowly down the almost sheer sides of the nearest gully. Briggs waited before he started down.

"You better snap into it," Stevens urged. "We're lucky. I can feel them coming."

Briggs' descent was quick and easy. He was puzzled about Stevens' "feeling" the approach of the *zar*.

He said as much when he hit the bottom of the gully. Stevens chuckled, "Well, how do you feel?"

"I itch," he said matter-of-factly.

"That's the *zar*," Stevens said. "Nobody has explained it satisfactorily, but the *zar* send some sort of emanation ahead of them when they begin to run. The closer they come, the stronger it gets. When your body begins to feel as if it's burning, then the *zar* are just around a bend in the gully."

Briggs' body was already beginning to feel warm, and the itching sensation became more uncomfortable.

Briggs, following Stevens' example, drew his heat ray gun, found himself a slight niche in the rock a few feet above the gully across from Stevens and waited quietly.

The heat sensation grew immeasurably stronger as he waited.

Briggs watched down the trail for the familiar green of Stevens' boots.

So he was somewhat startled when he saw the rush of red, like a river of blood, sweeping down the gully at them.

But when Stevens snapped, "Knock down the leaders!" Briggs methodically began to press the stud of his heat gun, slicing the sharp, pointed heads off the multi-legged little beasts hardly larger than a brown squirrel back on Earth.

What the hell, he thought, red or green, they're still *zar*. The quicker we get the limit, the quicker I can get my hands on that resilium.

HE FIRED slowly and methodically, and his thin lips lifted in a grin as the pile of dead *zar* began to fill up the gully, holding back the animals behind. Some of the little red beasts swept over the barricade formed by their dead comrades, only to lose their heads and tumble, kicking and squirming, to the floor of the gully, as Stevens and Briggs dammed the flood.

"The ones behind will shift to a new gully pretty soon. Then we can count our catch," Stevens grunted through the intercom.

Briggs was sweating profusely, but he was getting sick of the slaughter. The *zar* just didn't have a chance in their blind running.

Then he grinned and chuckled inside his armor.

"What's the matter?" Stevens asked.

"Nothing," said Briggs. But he thought lightly, Stevens'll have about the same chance as the *zars*.

Briggs slid down from his niche to the floor of the gully.

Stevens suddenly started cursing. "Get out of there, you fool. It's sudden death, Briggs!"

Briggs glared nervously at the dead pile of *zar*. He started to kick contemptuously at one of the dead bodies, which gradually was losing its flaming color.

"Don't!" barked Stevens.

Briggs pulled his foot back in time before it touched the animal, disturbed by the urgency in Stevens' voice.

He kept on shooting, knocking off the *zar* as they plunged over the top of the pile. Four of them came over suddenly. He managed to slice the heads off neatly from two but the others came flashing at him.

Briggs snapshot at one, heard Stevens grunting.

Then the second spilled over on its side, its body cut in half.

Briggs grunted as something heavy slammed against him, drove him toward the side of the gully. He whirled to see Stevens' armored suit, and heard the big blond growling.

"You fool, those things are sure death, even when they're dead. Wait till they turn green before going down there."

They clung side by side on the gully wall, shooting until the last trickle of the *zar* stopped.

As they waited Stevens explained, "A running *zar* can cut you to pieces with those clawed feet of his. They dig out iron ore to get at the oxides. How long do you think your armor could stand up? A dead *zar* gives off a corrosive acid gas for hours after it's killed. You can't touch them without danger until they turn green."

Briggs said simply, "I didn't know."

"I should have told you," Stevens added. "It's not common knowledge among other than *zar*-hunters."

They waited, and while they did Briggs polished his plans.

He'd not have to worry about explaining why Stevens wouldn't come back now. Get him in a gully just before the *zar* run, and the *zar* would take care of him, erasing all signs of murder.

Then there would be no division of two hundred pounds of resilium.

HOURS LATER, after hot and bloody work skinning the huge pile of *zar* with their heat ray guns and packing the light skins into the hold, Stevens announced he was ready to try for the resilium.

He slammed the locking door of the hold and said, "There's ten thousand credits worth of *zar*. It's the biggest haul I've ever carried. It'll pay expenses for the trip. The resilium will be all profit."

All profit, echoed Briggs, his mind nervous with excitement. All profit . . . for *me*.

Following Stevens downside and upside crosswise through the gullies, Briggs had his first chance to study the planet he was seeing for the first time.

So far out in the sun's planetary system, it hardly looked as if it belonged there. The surface of the planet was riven by the gullies, as if it had been subjected to a terrible heat that had cracked its crust like a dried up puddle of mud.

Pluto was barren of vegetation, its few species of fauna obtaining their sustenance from the multiplicity of metal ores that made up the planet's outer coat. Its rocky ground cropped up regularly with lava-like formations that had cooled.

But Briggs' study was only casual and temporary. He was too busy with his mind, worrying out a variety of possibilities for use of his take from the two hundred pounds of resilium.

Stevens lumbered on ahead of him, and though the way was tiresome and travel awkward in the cumbersome armor, Briggs was buoyed up by his anticipation.

Stevens turned several times, glanced back. The silver sheen of the *Princess* still was visible against the black rock of the planet.

"It isn't too far now," he said casually through the intercom.

But it was a dozen gullies later before he halted and held up one hand. He waited until Briggs came up.

They stood on the brink of another gully, but this was of a Jupiter scale. It dropped away beneath their feet to lose itself in blackness.

"Some gully, huh?" Stevens asked, laughter in his voice.

"Does it go clean through Pluto?" Briggs asked, almost serious, for he thought he saw a faroff glimmer of light deep in the chasm.

"No," Stevens answered. "That light is a gas flare which guards the entrance to the natives' shrine. That's where the resilium is kept, and that's where your speed will win."

"Natives?" Briggs snorted. "You know as well as I do, there are no intelligent natives on Pluto. Man was the first intelligent creature to set foot here."

"That's what I thought, Rick. That's what I thought, too. But you'll see."

He turned to Briggs, his eyes searching Briggs' face through the duroplast helmet. "Afraid to go down and meet something unknown?"

Briggs' answer was immediate. "If that's where the resilium is, let's go."

They started down, the pointed tips of their armor boots digging toeholds in the sides of the chasm.

Both were almost sobbing with fatigue when they finally reached bottom. It had been tricky and hard work coming down, Briggs admitted. What would it be like going up that sheer wall with the resilium?

It was like twilight on Earth in this chasm, but the light was coming from a towering column of fire which burned steadily and unwinking nearly a mile down the chasm from where they stood.

They leaned against the chasm wall, slowing the gasping sound of their breath and the thud of their hard-worked hearts.

Before they started, Stevens asked,

"Your oxygen supply replenishing all right?" Briggs glanced at the glowing dial of the meter on the armor neck rim just below his chin. The needle was at three-quarters green. "Almost peak efficiency," he said.

"Good. That purifier will take a beating before we get through."

The chasm floor was studded with croppings of lava and loose rock, impeding their progress toward the column of fire.

IT WAS a curious light. At first glance it looked pure white. But the longer Briggs stared at it, the more he saw in it.

It was a column lifted from a pastel rainbow. Wavering through it were shades of pink and blue and orange and yellow so faint. Their hues whispered against the shouting colors he knew so well.

Briggs drew his eyes from the column of soft, almost vanishing colors when Stevens said triumphantly, "May I introduce the natives of Pluto?"

His armored right arm pointed to the darkness behind the column. Briggs stared.

At first he saw only the black maw of a cavelike entrance in the wall of the chasm behind the column of light as it reached up a half mile.

Then he saw blobs of lighter darkness ranked across the cave mouth. It was hard to see what the blobs were with the column of light blinding him.

"Those blobs?" he asked.

Stevens laughed. He unhooked the power lamp from his belt, sent its beam searching into the shadows.

Briggs stared.

The bright beam of Stevens' lamp outlined one of the blobs sharply.

It looked like a stunted, twisted caricature of a tree back on Earth. There were huge misshapen roots snuffling at the ground. A thick twisted bole from which scores of tendrils, some as thin as a finger, others as thick as Stevens' neck, crawled. The tendrils moved as if alive.

"They are alive," Stevens answered in response to Briggs' muttered query. "They are the natives, the metal-sucking natives. They stopped me the last time I was here. This is where your speed will count."

Stevens bent down and picked up a lump of ore. "Watch," he ordered.

Stevens drew back his arm and threw

the ore with a swift snap of his wrist. He threw so fast Briggs had trouble keeping up with it.

But the "natives" didn't. When Briggs' eyes caught up with it, the piece of ore was disappearing into one of the smaller tendrils. The tendril grew up and around it and in a moment, the bit of ore was hidden, leaving only a lump in the tendril.

Then the lump disappeared.

"I just barely got out of the cave," Stevens said.

"Out?" asked Briggs. "How did you get in?"

"They weren't there when I went in. But I heard them snuffling quick enough when I started dragging one of those blocks of resilium out."

Briggs snorted in disbelief. "They're rooted there. They can't move. What did they do? Grow up out of the ground?"

"They can move," Stevens said simply. "Take a look at that little one." He turned his light away from the one that had caught the bit of ore.

The "little one" was about three feet high, but half of its misshapen roots were free of the soil. They groped, like elongated fingers, reaching out farther. One of the roots found a likely spot, and the other free ones joined it.

The "little one" unloosed its other roots, and the newly anchored tendrils began to glide into the soil, pulling the bole and the other roots to a spot twenty feet from its old anchorage.

"That's rather slow," observed Briggs.

"I was in the cave a long time," Stevens retorted.

Rick Briggs picked up a piece of ore himself, tossed it toward the cave entrance. One of the tendrils moved so fast it was just a blur. And the ore was gone.

"I'll have to move fast to get through, but won't they follow?" Briggs said finally.

"Right. You'll have to move very fast, but I'll help you with my heat-ray, and they won't follow you. They know you'll have to come out again."

Briggs shrugged. "Where do I go when I get inside?"

Stevens told him briefly.

BRIGGS turned his purifying unit up to the top notch and unsnapped his heat ray pistol.

"Jets on," he said laconically, and began moving slowly toward the waving tendrils. He saw the tendrils begin moving toward the cave entrance, interlocking to make a lattice-work wall. Stevens was right—this was intelligence.

The heat-ray pistol sizzled in his hand. It carved an opening in the tendrils. Suddenly, he began running at full speed. Though the heavy, bulky armor handicapped him, he still was moving very fast, the heat ray probing ahead of him.

Briggs hit the smoking opening in the tendrils with tremendous force. He was stopped dead.

But only for a moment. The touch of the tendrils which made the metal on his suit blisteringly hot dropped away, and his heavy boots were digging into the metallic ground, shoving him toward the cave entrance. Abruptly, he was free of the tangle of tendrils.

Stevens was chuckling. "That's what I mean about a man needing two things to lick this planet—guts and a friend. It takes two men to lick it."

Briggs just snorted, moving deeper into the cave.

Straight ahead, Stevens had said, *until you bump into a knobbly wall. Then go right. You can't miss the shrine.*

Stumbling through the darkness of the cave, Briggs hit a wall with a metallic clang. His ears rang with the echoes inside his armor. But he turned right then.

The way underfoot was rough, pockmarked with all sizes of holes. Briggs moved gingerly. The pockmarks must be the holes of the "natives'" roots, Briggs decided.

Would the shrine be guarded? he wondered. Then he shrugged and went onward in the darkness. A sudden light to his right lit up a rocky wall ahead of him, keeping him from smashing head on into it.

He turned right again, drawn by the light.

The passage was narrow for about fifty feet, then debouched into a huge cave. Beneath the vaulted roof which reached breathtakingly above Briggs there burned another column of the strange pastel light. But it was only twenty-five feet high, compared with its huger brother outside.

"Are you in the cave?" Stevens' voice asked quietly through the intercom.

Rick Briggs grunted an affirmative. "But I don't see the blocks of resilium."

"Go behind the fire column and you'll find an altar of sorts," Stevens directed. "The resilium blocks make up the first platform."

Looking carefully about him, Briggs moved toward the flame, stared at it for a moment before passing around behind it.

There was an "altar". Built of square and oblong blocks veined with metal streaks, it towered as high as the light column. It was simply built. Rough hewn blocks sat side by side and atop one another. No mortar held them tight.

It looked like an oversize reproduction of an Earth child's pile of building blocks. But Briggs had little patience with the altar itself. The blocks of resilium glowed with their golden light there at the foot of the altar.

His flexible armored fingers ran lightly across one of the blocks. Two hundred pounds of resilium, a fortune in a rectangle two feet long, a half-foot deep and a foot wide.

For a moment, Briggs drifted away from the job at hand. What he couldn't do with two hundred pounds of resilium?

It wouldn't be long now and Stevens would be dead. This block and this secret cave would be Briggs'. He chuckled as he lifted the heavy block, cradling it against his chest.

Briggs sweated and strained the block back along the passage. When a glow indicated he was near the opening, he called to Stevens.

"I'm near the entrance. What happens now? I won't be able to move fast."

"Rest," Stevens suggested. "Then get as close to the entrance as possible. Let me know when you're ready to come out, and I'll burn as many of the roots as I can."

While he rested, Briggs tried to figure an easier way to carry the heavy ore. He didn't like the idea of binding it to him. If the roots caught him, the weight would be too much of a handicap. They'd get him and then he'd never enjoy the fruits of his labor.

He decided finally to carry it as he had from the cave, cradled on his chest.

"Jets on," he said at last.

Stevens' voice cracked back. "Start coming when I say, 'Now.' I won't be able to

help you until you get through. I might burn you by mistake."

Briggs eased himself to the entrance of the cave and watched the tree-like natives. He turned the purifier up to the top notch, took several deep breaths of the rich ozone.

Then Stevens snapped, "Now!"

BRIGGS burst out of the cave, running low, the heavy weight cradled against his chest. Stevens had burned an enormous hole in the intertangled tendrils, but already it was closing.

But Briggs hit the hole while it was still partially open, stumbling and staggering. He was through, when a tendril twined around his leg, spilling him and sending the resilium block skidding before him.

Briggs snatched for his heat gun, only to have the arm caught in another tendril. Then he heard the usually jovial Stevens cursing. Stevens' armored figure loomed over him, wielding the heat-gun at close range. The grips on his leg and arm loosened and Briggs scrambled free.

Stevens was fighting for his life. It was Stevens' trap instead of Briggs. Briggs scrambled to his feet and watched.

Stevens gasped into the intercom, "Drag that resilium away from here as fast as you can. I'll get free."

But Briggs, though thinking that this would be a good time to let Stevens die, decided that an investigation of his death here might reveal the rich cave. He turned back, his heatgun stabbing at the base of the roots until Stevens could stagger free.

Then Briggs and Stevens seized the block of resilium and they went staggering away from the natives. They were following at their slow speed, pulling out their roots and advancing.

But the Earthmen, though encumbered by their heavy armor and the two hundred pounds of ore, easily outdistanced them.

"Thanks," Stevens gasped briefly as they stood at the foot of the cliff where they had entered the gully of the light. "For a while, I thought I'd misjudged you. But you proved to be a friend when you forgot about the resilium and helped me."

Briggs just grunted as he strapped the heavy ore to Stevens' back as the big blond ordered.

The climb back up was rugged enough for Briggs, but the work was lightened by the ironic knowledge that Stevens had burdened himself with a two hundred pound weight which was to be the death of him.

After a brief rest at the summit, the pair started back to the *Princess,* Stevens trudging ahead, the resilium on his back.

Stevens was in high good spirits. "Guts and a friend," he chuckled into the intercom. "When I decided on you to help me, I was the luckiest spacehound alive."

But luck won't help you when you're dead, Briggs amended, biding his time.

The *Princess* was less than a quarter-mile away, its silver sheen like a promise of wealth to come when Briggs executed the first step in his plan.

Stevens stood at the top of a gully, looking down when Briggs loosened the heat gun in his holster.

But he didn't draw it. Stevens said, "We'd better hurry, I feel the *zar* coming."

They slid down the side of the gully, raced across and started up the other side. They were halfway up when the blood-red flood of *zar* coursed through the gully they just had crossed.

Stevens trudged ahead. "They shouldn't be gunning in the next gully yet," he observed.

Briggs drew the heatray pistol and turned it on the armor in the middle of Stevens' back, just below the block of resilium. He had it on low power, so Stevens wouldn't immediately feel the heat of it.

Suddenly Stevens said, "My back stings." He turned around abruptly and saw the heat gun in Briggs' hand. "Blast you, Briggs, I thought you were my friend."

He staggered toward Briggs, but it was too late.

The heat-softened metal ruptured under the pressure. Briggs watched closely as the enrushing pressure forced Stevens body up into the duraplast helmet. Then blood, bursting from ruptured veins and arteries, blotted out the sight with a red curtain over the duraplast.

Calmly, Briggs waited until the flopping armor stilled.

Then he unstrapped the resilium and carried it to the edge of the gully. Then he rolled Stevens' pulped and armored body to the edge and let it tumble down.

The *zar* would take care of it when they ran through the gully again, and it wouldn't be long. He could feel his skin tingling.

Shouldering the resilium, he slipped down the side of the gully, passed Stevens' armored body without a glance and started up the other side. He was near the top when the *zar* swept around the bend. Hurriedly, he clambered up, cradling the resilium in his arms, watching the red flood sweep toward Stevens' body.

BRIGGS turned away when the red flood hit. Then turned back again. Still looking at the flood, he started to walk away from the edge.

His armored foot hit an outcropping of rock. He lost his balance and tried to fling the resilium from him only to be thrown farther off balance.

He fell heavily, one foot catching in a hole, The resilium struck the armored knee of the trapped right leg, and agony danced through Briggs' mind.

When Briggs tried to sit up, he knew the leg was broken. What Pluto pressure had been unable to do, the combination of hole and resilium had accomplished. The armor from knee to ankle had bent . . . The leg hadn't; it had snapped instead.

But Briggs shrugged and dragged his broken leg out of the hole. It wasn't far to the ship. He'd crawl there, pushing the block of resilium along beside him.

Sweating from exertion and pain from the fractured leg, Briggs made it to the next gully.

Then Briggs lay there in his sweat-drenched armor, the big block of ore beside him. He stared across the gully at Stevens' ship. Only forty feet straight across to safety and wealth.

"A man," Big Joe Stevens had said, "needs two things to lick this planet. Guts and a friend."

But Stevens lay dead in his armor, back in that last gully.

Only forty feet straight across to safety and wealth. But the gully was fifty feet deep with almost sheer sides.

Briggs didn't have a friend. But he did have a broken leg.

Briggs glanced at the shining silver ship, and began to laugh though there was no one to hear him . . .

Among The Scented Ones

By BASIL WELLS

His captor grunted . . . and Besan's head was rocked by a club . . .

To Besan Wur this backward planet of stampeding monstrosities and stinking humanoids was Sanctuary. Here he could be free—until they discovered he gave off no odor . . .

Illustrated by MARTIN

A VAST DARK FLOOD SPREAD across the matted green of the broad Saaaran plain. It rolled westward relentlessly, its outer flanks washing around and over the lower hills and lapping deep into the fringes of the jungle. A rolling endless thunder of countless pounding feet went before its tossing crest.

Past the ruins of a score of ancient cities the stampeding herd of green-crested saurians thundered. It seemed a world devoid of intelligent life that they traversed in their unreasoning terror. Only the jungle-grown walls and splintered streets showed that man had once been here...

The great salmon-hued sun was directly overhead as the maddened *denars* poured through a five-mile gap between twin ranges of low hills. Twelve miles further their thundering progress was checked.

And along the line of the northern cluster of hills a giant tube of unrusting metal mesh was laid. Lianas and other vegetation half-swallowed its forty-foot diameter, but inside there was a smooth hard-surfaced roadway where thirty-foot wheels, with cabins for passengers between their twin tires, raced swiftly.

Even as a group of twenty wheels spun eastward through the tube the stampeding *denars* crashed through the stout metal mesh guarding the highway...

BESAN WUR SHOUTED, terror-stricken, as an avalanche of huge green-crested saurians surged toward them through the disintegrating sides of the tubeway. He tasted the salt of bitten lips.

The giant double tires smoked as Nard Rost, the gray-haired Garro at the controls, spun the wheel tightly about and sent it hurtling back along the way they had come.

"That was—close!" Besan's voice was shrill. His fingers were biting into the back of his seat as he peered backward at the hissing horde of *denars*.

"Ras Thib — Walof Jemar — all the others!"

Nard Rost nodded grave assent. At least twelve of the wheels had been swallowed up by that churning death from the open plains.

"There isn't any chance they could have survived," Besan said numbly. "The wheels are flattened and broken already."

Besan gasped and his hand went to his throat. For by now the acrid musty scent of the older Garro pervaded the narrow drum of a cabin. That scent was the natural protection of the men of Saaar; only a mindless stampeding herd of *denars*, or other men, would brave contact with his kind.

Besan Wur's eyes leaked moisture. He nudged the valve that released the countering fumes of the tank under his left armpit. Unlike the older man he was not immune to the product of Garro scent glands.

He was an Earthman, one of a hundred-odd Terrans living secretly among the Garros on forbidden Saaar. His dark hair was artfully dyed blonde along the central stripe, and his oversize ears and the flaring tip of his nose were the result of surgery in his youth. Even his red blood was rendered purple by regular injections of an innocuous fluid.

"I know, Besan Wur," said the older man quietly. "All dead. All our friends and fellow students." He paused. "And soon, perhaps, we shall join them."

His hand indicated the slight bulge of the hill beside which the vehicular tube ran. It was a low hill, less than a hundred feet long and half as wide, covered with the coarse grass of the plains of Saaar. Only a thin belt of trees touching the further extremity of its crest offered any protection.

"Perhaps the trees will shelter us," he said. "If not..."

Behind them the sea of hissing thundering life chewed nearer and nearer. In a matter of seconds it would engulf the hill and sweep beyond it, isolating them among the trees...If they reached them.

"See there, Nard Rost!" cried the Earthman. "Two of the wheels behind us—broke through the mesh—headed for the trees!"

Nard swung into the gap in the wall; the wheel tilted and rocked, the inner drum's gyros groaning in protest, and then they were racing after the other vehicles.

"*Denar!*" shouted Besan Wur, even as an elephantine hammer seemed to crash against the thin metal skin of the cabin.

The great wheel toppled, righted itself, and toppled again as the weight of another *denar's* vast bulk bludgeoned it. The ragged outer fringe of the great herd had reached them even as they came into the shadow of the trees!

With a crash the thirty-foot wheel and its inner cabin went over. The two occupants were unhurt save for a few bruises, and they wasted no time in racing to the shattered port between the two huge tires. Nard Rost led the way, a knobby metal wrench in his fist to clear away the broken shards yet remaining in the frame.

Five feet away the thick bole of a forest giant lifted. They had come that close to its shelter. Without a moment's hesitation the two men raced up the knotty protuberances of the trunk to the lower branches. There, twenty feet above the ground, they paused momentarily.

Well that they had quitted the wheel when they did. The solid secondary flood of the *denar* tide swept over the vehicle, churned, eddied, and pounded onward again unchecked over the flattened scraps of metal and resilient *durnb*.

And now the other wheels suffered a like fate. They too pulped and disappeared. Besan Wur's square face brightened. He shouted something against the all-pervading din of the stampeding lizard horde.

"Relsa Dav!" he shouted into Nard Rost's elongated ear cup.

He had glimpsed the trembling slim form of the girl clinging to a massive horizontal branch a scant three feet above the tossing green crests of the lizards. Now he hurried along a higher branch interlacing with those of the other three where the girl had found refuge.

A moment later he had pulled her to the safety of a higher limb and the girl was sobbing against his tunic's soft brown cloth, her arms about his neck.

He caught a suggestion of moisture in the violet eyes of the older man as he joined them. Nard Rost's mate, Ilva, had perished up ahead there. And with her had died the twenty-four other students and their three instructors bound for a four month's course of practical study in the tin and copper mines of the Durlu Hills.

Only they three had escaped because of the temporary check of the hill and now the sheltering trees. How long the battered lower boles, massive though they were, would remain upright, was doubtful. And the unending flow of squealing whistling *denars* might continue unchecked for more than two or three days!

A S BESAN HELD the soft warmth of the terrified girl in his arms a great gladness fought with the despair in his heart. Relsa Dav, whose least glance in the classrooms of Rhilg University made him more aware of his hopeless love, was alive...And he was an Earthman, a renegade son of an alien race who could never hope to mate with a Garro!

The System that ruled Terra, and a score of other lesser and greater worlds, was responsible for their exile. The System's rigid code of controls over all the activities of its citizens—even to what they ate, and wore, and what they thought—inevitably produced a diminishing handful of rebels with every generation.

The punishment for any infraction of the rules was invariably amnesia; the childlike result of this operation being trained again in the frozen tenets of the System until the least spark of individuality was extinguished. There was no bloodshed in all the System's worlds and prisons were forgotten mounds of crumbling masonry and metal. Instead there were the gentle blanking rays of the System Police and the inevitable hospitalization afterward.

om this threat of complete forgetfulness Besan Wur's father and mother had escaped by spacer to this forbidden jungle planet of Saaar. Her RZX rating and that of Besan's father had not coincided within the narrow limits prescribed. But they had mated and stolen a System police craft in making their getaway.

They found that Saaar was a tropical savage world alive with ferocious and gigantic animals. The System's aversion for shedding blood—even animal blood—had led them to bypass Saaar until the semicivilized natives of that world would have tamed it. So it was a safe refuge for the parents of Besan...as long as they could evade the bloodthirsty denizens of the steaming jungles and broad grasslands!

Strangest of all was the discovery that the cooler uplands of Saaar supported a well-advanced civilization: the Saaaran bipeds who called themselves Garros. Their cities were underground, in the cavern-honeycombed cliffs and deep canyons, and they were linked together by highways that ran through great tubes of a rustless metal mesh. These tubes were designed to prevent the encroachment of vegetation and wandering animals on the roadway—no animal would face the threat of the stripe-headed men's scent but their vehicles were so swift they had little warning of the Garros' approach.

And so they had disguised themselves, as other Terrans before them had done, and mingled with the Garros of the cone city of Rhilg.

"We must leave these trees, Besan," Nard Rost shouted, his voice jolting the Earthman back to reality.

The tree was jolting and swaying as the mighty press of saurian juggernauts lumbered madly beneath. Inevitably it would be torn from its roots if the stampede continued. Nor was there any apparent end to the green-crested flood that rolled out of the northern purplish horizon.

"Think you can climb now, Relsa?"

The blonde-striped head of the girl nodded. Her deep blue eyes smiled into his own purple-tattooed ones.

"Forest widens out that way." Nard Rost's muscular arm pointed out the northwestern loom of hills and the belt of vine-festooned trees linking them with it. "That's our road."

"Hills of Cratur, aren't they?" Besan's voice was tense. He had seen some of the reddish-haired bearlike brutes captured there by Rhilg hunters. They were unlovely elephantine creatures.

"Yes." Nard Rost's answer was short. He had knotted a slender rubbery liana around his waist and now he passed its pliant length to Besan and the girl.

A moment later they were creeping carefully out along a pitching branch's narrowing path, their bodies linked by the slim rope of vine.

Two trees — three trees — they had reached a clump of three interlocking giants when the trees they had first climbed went grinding over and were swallowed up. A moment later another tree toppled drunkenly and the dark avalanche of saurian flesh flowed over it.

Underneath their feet the broken bodies of *denars* heaped higher and higher until a temporary island of mauled bloody flesh fended off the stampeding herd's all-but resistless current.

"Do we stay here?" gasped the girl.

Besan shook his head. "We aren't safe until we reach the hills," he told her. "The pressure is increasing as their broken bodies heap up and these *node* trees are brittle."

Already Nard Rost was leading off. The girl was between them and Besan saw her shudder as she glanced downward into the roaring death. Her shoulders stiffened and she smiled faintly back at him.

"Come along," she said, shouting the words, "or must we drag you?"

Besan grinned back at her. There was a quaver in her voice that her brave words did not dispel. *She has what it takes,* he thought as they inched along precariously high above the *denars*.

THE GREAT SALMON-HUED sun of Saaar was almost touching the distant loom of hills to the west as they slid down a natural ladder of lianas to a rocky ledge. For two hours and more they had been moving through the trees' sketchy byways, expecting at any moment to be hurled into the maelstrom of maddened saurians boiling underfoot.

Now they were safe atop a sheer cliff lifting forty feet above the branch-roofed bed of an unnamed stream...A stream that now flowed with hissing reptilian monsters.

"Tomorrow we cross the Cratur Hills," Besan told the girl sagging wearily now

against his shoulder, "and then reach Rhilg."

Nard Rost shook his head. "I wish we had weapons," he said. "We're safe from animals, yes, but the wild men..."

Besan nodded, lips tightening. For the thousandth time he deplored his lack of the natural defense glands of the Garros. His supply of artificial scent, nestling under his right armpit, was low. Unlike his two companions he must depend on his fleetness of foot and his cunning to escape should he become separated from them.

"We should find a cave nearby," Relsa Dav said hesitantly. "I can't take another step, I'm afraid."

Nard Rost's lips smiled encouragement. "A few moments of rest and you'll be fit again. Besan and I will look around."

Besan squeezed her arm. "Be with you in a minute."

The ridge climbed steeply for a score of feet above the ledge. It leveled off then into a narrow uneven ribbon of rocky brush-spotted earth and fell away again into a jumbled region of twisting ravines, canyons, and wooded ridges. The wind that had been blowing from the south had died and they could see three distant threads of smoke lifting gracefully into the reddening twilight sky.

"Savages." Besan's scalp tightened. The logical path for them to take back toward the dead volcanic cone housing Rhilg lay in that direction.

"Look here, Besan," Nard Rost's voice was muffled.

The instructor was not to be seen. Besan, after a quick look around, made out a crevice in the rocky slope below him. The opening was large enough for a man to squeeze through. He jumped down and entered it.

There was no sign of Nard Rost at first; yet he felt sure that the older man had entered the split rock before him. Then the walls widened, a few feet from the entrance, and he found himself standing inside a large cave. Light filtered weakly from a crevice above.

His friend was examining the dead ashes of a fire. Beside it a disorderly jumble of dead branches was stacked.

"Cold," the instructor said. "And no recent tracks in the dust."

"Should be safe enough for one night."

Nard Rost's voice was doubtful. "If it wasn't almost night I'd say we better move along. But we need shelter—and rest."

"The entrance is too small for *craturs*," argued Besan, "and the night-flying *wadts* should keep away any roving savages."

"Go for the girl," decided the older man, "while I kindle fire."

And now reaction was setting in. Besan Wur felt his knees sagging as he climbed to the upper level. Son of a Terran civilization that for a score of generations had shunned violence and bloodshed, he had forgotten his aversion for the more primitive emotions these last few hours. Again he was feeling the nameless dragging pain of disgust and terror that the savage life of Saaar created in all Terran hearts.

A shadow seemed to move toward him and he yelped, a dry-lipped whisper. He heard a weak, terrified cry from ahead and the shadow was forgotten for the moment. Relsa Dav needed him. He hurried to her side.

"Besan!" She clung to him, sobbing. Her face was a dim oval.

"We have found a cave," he told her. "Come. The *wadts* will be aloft now that darkness has come."

"I hear — things — moving!" The girl's voice quavered.

Besan thought of the shadow and the sense of oppression that had again overcome him. And then he laughed, shakily, as he led.

"Nothing could reach us here save the *wadts*," he said, "and in a moment we will be safe from them."

So it was that they went warily along the shadowy ridge down to the rift in the opposite slope. Twice their soft shoes knocked unseen pebbles clattering downward, but other than that there was no sound.

And from the crevice a flicker of flame revealed that Nard Rost had already kindled a fire. Besan opened his mouth to call out a greeting.

But he never spoke. A great hard-palmed hand clamped across his lips and an arm crushed his ribs together. Dimly he could see a savage face and the naked body of his assailant. There were other shadowy shapes, too. He felt Relsa Dav's fingers torn from his grasp. His knotted fists slammed into the hard flesh of the savage.

His captor grunted. The hairy body shifted and Besan's head was rocked by a club in a bony fist. He sank down into a pain-throbbing gulf that was not completely without sound and sight.

In a detached sort of way he knew that he was being dragged into the cave and bound with stinking rawhide ropes. He lay in a corner of the cave beside the bound shapes of Nard Rost and the girl. And by the fire a dozen half-naked man shapes crouched, harsh voices rumbling.

Relsa Dav was calling to him but he kept slipping further and further away into the blackness of the cavern until he heard her no more.

THE HAFT OF a spear thudded alongside his skull. Besan shook his head and found that he was walking along a sunken game trail in a patch of the yellow-green jungle flooring a narrow valley. His hands were roped behind him and his lips were cracked and dry. Overhead the sun was hand-high in the sky.

From behind him Nard Rost spoke.

"Better now, boy?"

Besan grunted. A sullen growing anger was blotting the fear and acquired timidity of Terra from his mind. If his hands were free...

"I'll do." He turned to see Nard Rost, and behind him the girl, with the balance of the fierce-looking savages strung out behind them.

"They're taking us to their caves," Nard Rost told him.

"To eat, I suppose." Besan turned his face to the front again.

Nard Rost's chuckle reached him. "Nothing so bloody as that. We're to be slaves, cultivating their patches of vegetables and *goorn*."

"Relsa too?"

"Unless Detch—he's the sub-chief who captured us—wants her."

Besan stumbled and the huge warrior ahead of him, the leader apparently, swung his spear again. It caught Besan across the ear and cheek. He staggered and his hatred for this grinning pulpy-nosed brute grew. Once he got his hands on a spear, or a club, or a knife—then let this gargoyle giant watch for his life!

He who had never killed an animal, or struck a blow in anger, was praying to all the unknown powers of space that he might strike the life from Detch's hulking body!

The trail wound between a series of ragged gigantic boulders; black, gray, and red-mottled and layered white. A guard in a thatched shelter high above welcomed them and shouted the word along ahead.

The guard cranked at a rude windlass, the rope disappearing lumpily into the rocks ahead, and when they rounded another black barrier of stone they saw a stout barrier of logs lifting to shoulder-height even as they reached it.

They stooped and passed beneath (apparently the gate lifted no higher) and were in a long, narrow valley.

Cultivated fields and groves of tall slender trees checkered the valley floor. In the low cliffs on either hand black openings gaped, cave entrances, and before these scantily clad children and women moved or sprawled lazily in the sun.

Overhead a rude network of interlaced vines, poles and twisted grasses sheltered the cultivated patches of ground. Besan saw now the purpose of the regular groves of trees—they were to support the guarding nets sagging overhead. It was only thus that the nocturnal raids of the bat-winged *wadts* could be checked.

Detch strutted proudly as he called out to the cave dwellers.

"I have taken slaves," he bragged. "Two strong men fit for the fields. Them I will sell."

A sleek-bodied girl, her central stripe almost pure white, pushed out from among the admiring group before the caves. Her small rounded hands perched atop her generously wide hips and her head tilted.

"The female," she said harshly, "is for sale too?"

Detch laughed. "For too long have you tried my patience," he said. "No, Lifa. The girl is not for sale. She will be my new mate. Go back to your mother."

"No!" Lifa's eyes flamed. From her soiled single garment of cratur hide she snatched a slim knife and flung herself at Detch.

But Detch was familiar with the tigerish qualities of his erstwhile mate. He sidestepped her rush and the ever-present spear lashed out brutally. She went down, a great welt growing along her suddenly white face. Detch kicked her side, and laughed.

"Drag her out for the *wadts* to pick," he ordered the admiring pack of women and children. "Or, if she lives, drive her from the valley."

Besan Wur had made his way to Relsa's side. "We'll get you out of this," he told her.

The girl's face was empty of feeling or emotion. Apparently her mind had temporarily gone numbly blank. Maybe it was better that way, thought Besan. But they'd have to escape soon.

A warrior prodded him with his spear haft. "Get along to the place-of-selling," he ordered.

The place-of-selling was a waist-high slab of brown rock before the caves. Here the savages bartered their weapons, slaves, and the products of their fields. Detch officiated as auctioneer.

Besan brought six spears, two stone axes, a slightly nicked sword-knife—manufactured in Rhilg, Besan noticed — and three small bags of narcotic *goorn* dust. Nard Rost brought Detch but five spears and four bags of *goorn* dust—he was older.

Their buyer, a corpulent narrow-eyed man named Noch, took them to his caves, four of them on valley level, and fed them. Then a collar of heavy wood was laced about their necks and they were driven out into the fields to hoe the newly planted vegetables.

NIGHT CAME ALL TOO SLOWLY in the little canyon valley. Wearily the two men from Rhilg lay in the rear of the servants' cave, their necks chafed and bloody from the heavy collars. The cold scraps of meat lay heavy in their stomachs, and the foul stench of the stew they had forced themselves to gulp down pervaded the cave's thick atmosphere.

By the fire the other slaves chattered. Their collars were smaller and their spirits unhurt. If they worked loyally for their owner they might be taken into the tribe or freed. And they were well fed and warm. Noch was a good master.

"How are we to escape?" whispered Besan. "This yoke is too heavy and clumsy and the entrance is barred at night."

"If we can get a knife and cut the lashings...They're like iron now that they've dried but a knife could slice them. And the slaves must sleep soon."

"And Relsa Dav...that brute taking her!"

"Ssst!"

"Someone coming, Nard?"

"I heard nothing, Besan. I thought it was you."

A hoarsely feminine voice broke in. They shifted to face the rear of the cave where a small section of rock had disappeared.

"I am Lifa," said the voice, and then the woman's face emerged into the fire's half-light. "I wish to revenge myself on Detch. And on Noch who is my brother. They have driven me from the caves."

Besan felt his heart leap. "Good," he agreed. "Cut us free and we will go with you."

"Will you take me to your tribe? If I go as your mate they will welcome me."

Besan swallowed. "I will claim you as my mate," volunteered Nard Rost quickly.

Lifa sniffed. "You are too old. But the other is young and handsome." She slipped into the cave, sheltered by their bodies.

If he could be freed and so rescue Relsa Dav, Besan told himself, it would be worth mating with this stripe-haired wildcat. And she seemed the only way of escape. Probably, if he refused, she would use her knife on the both of them.

"Why, sure," he agreed, his voice strained. "But my friend's daughter must be rescued too."

Lifa was silent for a moment before her muted harsh mirth sounded. He felt Nard Rost's fingers squeeze his arm approvingly.

"Better yet," she agreed. "I cheat them of both slaves and his new mate." She peered at Besan. "Where does your tribe live?"

"In Rhilg," he told her. "In the city of the inner cone."

With an awed gasp the woman drew a well-whetted knife from within her garment and started hacking at the dried bindings of the galling wooden yoke.

"I will be dressed like the aristocrats," she whispered. "Shiny cloth, sparkling rings, polished leather, jewels. Then I can laugh at Detch."

The last strand of Nard Rost's collar

finally being loosed, they slipped into the hidden opening through which the woman had come. The deeper shadows and two heaped-up bundles of dried rushes and grass that they left behind should cover their escape for a time, Besan told himself.

They followed a low, narrow corridor that twisted along a path parallel with the cliff.

"Detch, and the chief alone know of this way," she confided. "Using it they can listen to the conversation of any of the caves and learn who is disloyal. Or they can kill those who sleep within."

"Nice people for in-laws, Besan," Nard Rost jibed.

Besan grunted. "How far to the cave of the—of Detch?" he demanded.

"Here it is," Lifa said, sliding a slab aside. "Won't Detch be surprised!"

Besan pushed through the opening. He was in the rear of a large cave cut into many low-walled chambers by irregular sections of fallen rock. There was a reddish flicker of flames on the walls and roof from the front of the cave. Toward this he made his way.

Beside the fire, huddled in a little pile of *cratur*-hide blankets, was Relsa. She was alone.

Besan hurried to her and explained in a few brief words that he had made a bargain with Lifa. Then he started to lead her back toward the cave's hidden exit.

THE curtains rasped at the entrance and Detch was in the cave. Besan dropped the girl's hand and his eyes darted around the firelit circle of the nearby walls. There were pegs driven into rocky crevices and from them hung short sword knives and hatchets. Other pegs supported a lethal assortment of heavy hunting spears and small bows for birds and rodents.

Besan jerked two of the sword knives from their pegs, his fingers familiar with their ridged leather grips from the required classes in fencing at Rhilg University.

"Is there meat cooked?" roared Detch. He shook his ugly head, his pig's eyes blinking.

"Where are you?" he demanded. "Come out before I beat you again."

"Here," cried Besan, and flung himself at the giant.

In that instant a hot fire seemed to consume the chill in his bones and he felt no more fear. Detch's startled oath and his own sword knife came out together. Their blades clicked.

It was Besan's first encounter with unshielded blades. One of his weapons went spinning in that first swift onslaught and then the practiced skills of his fencing class came to his defense.

He turned the hacking sword and his own blade ripped across Detch's hairy chest. The pain drew a cry from the big savage's throat and his sword knife slashed more furiously. And already the cave was filled with the choking foul haze that was the defense of all Saaaran humanoids.

Detch roared for aid. In a few moments others of the tribe would be coming and they would be trapped. Besan drove his blade through the clumsy guard of the bigger man into the hairy chest.

Detch went down. Besan wiped his streaming eyes and darted toward the cave's rear entrance where Relsa Dav and the others were waiting.

"Good work, boy," said Nard Rost exultantly. "I hoped that you'd prove I was right."

Right about what? Besan wondered, as he helped roll the slab back into its appointed slot.

Nor were they any too soon. From the cave they had so recently quitted there sounded startled cries and shouts of rage. If Detch were not dead they would soon have a party of warriors on their heels.

Lifa hurried before them, leading the way. Once she stopped in a storeroom and tucked several small bags of *goorn* dust into her garment's inner pouch. To her it meant wealth and, although Besan told her Garro law forbade possession of the narcotic, she did not throw it away.

They emerged at last in the valley above the caves and beyond the barrier of logs at its upper end. A dense thicket of thorny brush shielded the entrance and sheltered them from the leathery-winged *wadts* cruising overhead, as they pushed westward toward Rhilg.

MORNING FOUND THEM in a region of rocky gulches and vegetation choked streams but a score of Terran miles from the Rhilg Hills. Far ahead the majestic black cone of Rhilg lifted above the heaped-up jumble of wooded hills and ridges.

But between them and the opposite hills the tide of maddened *denars* flooded onward as they had two days before. They could only hope to find a hiding place until the stampeding herds were gone, a useless plan for they had caught glimpses of a trailing party of warriors several times.

"If we could only find an impregnable position," Nard Rost told them, "until help can reach us."

"You reached them at last?" demanded Besan, tapping Nard Rost's bracelet broadcaster.

The instructor nodded. "About ten minutes ago. Signals are very faint but they're sending a dirigible. By midday probably."

"Besan," said Relsa Dav tensely, "to the right!"

Lifa whirled and her hand stole inside her scanty garment to where the sacks of *goorn* dust and her knife rested.

A smaller rift, a miniature gorge snaking down into the gulch they followed, lay revealed. And sprinting down its rocky floor came four well-armed warriors of the pursuing band! In a matter of seconds they would be blocking the trail ahead.

Besan looked ahead and at the rocky slope to their left. A steep trail, a brushy wet-weather watercourse, led upward to the gulch's bare rim.

"Quick," he ordered. "Up with you!"

They scrambled upward, the girls ahead and Nard Rost after them. The savages realized that they had been seen and their shouts boomed through the air to their fellows behind.

The watercourse climbed yet more steeply so they were forced to pull themselves upward by projecting roots and branches. A moment later they stumbled, one by one, over the lip of the little gulch and paused to catch their breath.

They had reached a table-like flat of some sixty odd feet across. At either end jumbled rocks sloped gradually downward and directly opposite a higher sheer escarpment blocked progress. Their only escape lay to the right, away from their pursuers.

Besan led the way. He chose a course through the broken rocks that tried their wasted strength least. Yet he knew that before long they must halt and attempt to make a stand—

Suddenly he halted and the sword knife was in his hand.

A menacing elephantine shape loomed up in his path, a reddish-haired bearlike *cratur*. And behind the foremost *cratur a* half dozen others jammed the way!

He turned—and saw the snowy-striped heads of the savage warriors already entering the rocks. They were trapped.

Lifa pushed at him. Her purple eyes were blazing.

"Drive them out of the way!" she cried. "One whiff of your scent and they will scatter."

Besan groaned. His tank of scent lay back in the cave village of Detch.

"I can't," he confessed swiftly. "I am— I was born without scent glands."

Lifa's eyes were scornful. She clawed him aside and pushed forward, laying down an acrid barrage that split the lumbering *craturs'* living wall apart. They pushed through into the more open ground beyond the rocks.

Besan's eyes leaked but his brain was busy. If the *craturs* could only be used to stop the savages . . .

"Give me the *goorn* dust," he told Lifa.

"I'll give you nothing," she screeched hoarsely. "I want nothing to do with a freak like you. I'll find a new mate." She turned to run toward the southern hills.

Besan spun her about and ripped the bags of *goorn* dust from their hiding place. Lifa snarled, her nails raked his face, and then her knife slashed at his forearm. The Earthman chopped his hand down on her wrist and the knife jarred free.

"Take her," he told Nard Rost and Relsa.

Back toward the *craturs* he ran until he was within throwing distance of them. As he ran he untied the sacks, and once within range started tossing them accurately at the shaggy red heads of the bearlike monsters.

The *goorn* dust acted swiftly, deadening their senses and, at the same time rousing their notoriously short tempers to a feverish peak. For the moment they would pay no heed to the obnoxious natural weapon of the striped men.

At that moment the pursuing warriors came into sight and darted in among the milling brutes. The *craturs* roared and sprang upon them.

Besan turned and raced back toward the others.

Lifa was gone. She had twisted free from Nard Rost and Relsa and headed southward into the jungle-clad gorges and hills there. And directly ahead a faint trail dipped down into a tree-grown valley on the road to Rhilg.

"We must hurry," he said urgently, and then became aware of Relsa's eyes staring at his bleeding arm.

The blood welling from it was red—the purple coloring had been absorbed and he had not renewed it. He shrugged. Now she would know he was not a Garro—as would Nard Rost. That meant execution as a spy or shipment back to a System planet and amnesia.

Of course he could escape into the jungle before the dirigible came, but that would mean leaving Relsa and Nard Rost unprotected. He shook his head. His decision was made. He faced them proudly.

BUT RELSA WAS not regarding him with the disgust Lifa had shown. Instead her eyes were shining; her lips parting in a glad cry. Unbelieving, he turned to Nard Rost. The weary purple eyes smiled. There was no hatred or disgust here.

Relsa came into his arms, sobbing. "You're Terran too!" she cried.

Nard Rost turned. For the moment they were safe. He found a flat boulder.

"We've known all along, Besan," he said to the dazed Earthman. "Your smell is different. But race or smell mean nothing to us if you have courage." He paused. "And are level-headed under stress."

"That you have proved, even as Relsa's parents proved they were fit citizens of Saaar. With your race's greater knowledge to aid us Saaar can rebuild its cities and resume its rightful place among worlds."

Nard Rost was studying the distant horizon where the great cone of Rhilg loomed. Now he turned to see why Besan Wur had said nothing. He tugged at an earlobe and chuckled. They were not listening.

"Silly custom," he grunted and started wearily off down the trail toward the plain.

The scream of the jets was almost inaudible.

EARTHBOUND

By HENRY GUTH

**Never was there a spaceflight more daring!
Virgil and Lanya sought what everyone else
their age had given up in despair.**

Illustrated by ASTARITA

LANYA GREGGOR, HOLDING
tightly to her brother Virgil's hand,
sauntered with deliberate and exag-
gerated nonchalance through the great
halls of the Martian Museum of Science.
Her eyes were wide with excitement and
pleasure. She was ten years old and Virgil
twelve and this was her first visit to the
museum. Hand in hand, always under the
watchful eyes of strategically-placed uni-
formed attendants they walked ecstatically
through the innumerable fascinating rooms,
stopping to gaze with equally undisguised
admiration at mammoth and complex in-
dustrial machinery and minute, hypersen-
sitive instruments of obscure function.

The attendant smiled warmly as they
walked past him and entered the biggest
room they had yet been in.

"There she is," Virgil said proudly.
"Just like I told you."

Lanya looked. She was dwarfed by the
colossal metal hulk that loomed ponderously before her. She leaned back to scan
its immense bulk from top to bottom.

The bronze inscription plate divulged
the information that it was the "Ghost",
the first ship to land safely on Mars from
a foreign planet. That was the Vón Erick-
son expedition from Earth almost two
centuries ago. According to the history
texts that Lanya had read, that event
brought about the almost overnight trans-
formation of Mars from an agrarian to a
scientific civilization. Trade and exchange
of ideas with Earth, and later with other
planets, had accomplished seeming mir-
acles on Mars.

84

The ship seemed comically primitive to little Lanya. Its huge bulk was almost entirely made up of rocket-drive engine and fuel compartments. She studied the elongated shape that stretched to the vaulted roof like a spear head and rested solidly on the rear jet clusters. High up in the nose she could see the tiny cabin just big enough for three astronauts.

Compared with the sleek, beautifully-designed atomic craft in the rest of the museum, it was grotesque.

"Gosh," breathed Lanya, "it's big, isn't it?"

"Yes," said Virgil, with the full confidence of two years at the Technological Institute. "Very crude design, but necessary because there is so much engine to it. Simple to construct, though, and with a few refinements . . . oh boy!"

Lanya was properly awed. She wouldn't start at the Institute until next year. No matter how hard she studied or how fast she learned, Virgil was always two years of knowledge ahead of her. She had just struggled through higher mathematics and physics, thinking she was getting ahead at last, only to find that Virgil, from the vantage point of his engineering studies, considered the laws of mathematics and physics merely basic.

In the old days, Grandma had said, one didn't matriculate at the Institute until one was as old as fifteen. "How they learn today!" she was always saying when Lanya accidentally exhibited her knowledge. "All so fast you would think they haven't as much time to live as before." She would throw up her hands in mock despair. "This new generation! I don't know what Mars is coming to." But she usually laughed so Lanya knew that Grandma didn't really despair for Mars' future.

Lanya was vague about her father Jonathan Greggor's origin. He seemed to be a physicist and they said he had been sent to Mars from Earth to assist in the development of uranium and plutonium deposits. But her mother, Klee, a beautiful Martian, had induced Jonathan to stay. Lanya knew little more than that.

"Do you think we can do it?" Lanya asked with just the right shade of admiration in her voice. Virgil was much pleasanter company when she took pains to appreciate his masculine superiority.

"Sure," he boasted. "Even better than this one. This old tub is simple . . . we can make ours smaller and faster."

They had a last long, lingering look at the "Ghost", then swaggered out past the grinning attendant.

He wouldn't be grinning if he knew what they knew, Lanya thought.

IN THE Greggor workshop, out away from the house, Virgil and Lanya worked diligently on the ship. A launching rig jutted up out of a pronounced dip in the red Martian sand a quarter of a mile away. Fascinating blueprints, over which Virgil pored learnedly whenever Lanya happened to look at him, littered the shop. Their father's shop equipment was switched on every afternoon to assist in the work. After five months the ship, with rocket engines already installed, was nearing completion.

Lanya's confidence in the venture had been on the wane lately. Before it had been only an exhilarating idea, safely remote in the future. But now, as the ship actually grew before her eyes, it was losing its secure vagueness. It was becoming terrifyingly real.

"Do you think we ought to do it?" she asked sheepishly and hopefully. She trembled at the derision in her brother's voice.

"Girls!" he said. "Always afraid of everything."

"I am not afraid!" Lanya protested indignantly. "I just wondered if we ought. Maybe father *will* buy us an aircraft *this* year."

"Huh! Fat chance! He's so darn busy all the time he doesn't even realize that we're probably the only kids on Mars who haven't a plane. Even Book, the poorest guy at the Institute, got a copter for his birthday last month." He frowned as he always did when talking about how unfairly he had been treated. "We'll show 'em! We'll be the envy of all Mars with this ship." His face lit up in a grin and he gloated, "Muuck thinks that new atom-powered cruiser of his is the best jalopy going, jut because it can range in outer space. He's getting a temporary space-pilot's license this year and all he does is brag. Wait'll he sees this job! We'll make his cruiser look sick, Lanya!" He was apparently carried away by the vision.

Lanya was none too excited about the prospect of excelling Muuck's cruiser. "But, Virgil. *You* haven't a license. How can we make Earth if we can't even leave Mars?"

Virgil scoffed, "They have to catch us first! Besides, they hardly ever stop you, unless you mess up traffic patterns."

"But do you think we should go so soon, Virgil? And do we *have* to go to Earth?"

Virgil turned on his distressed sister impatiently. "Look, Lanya. We agreed to run away from home, didn't we? You haven't forgotten why?"

"Because father neglects us!" Lanya piped emphatically, as though she had been practicing that statement for a long time —which she had.

"Right! And we've never been to Earth, have we? Even though father promises every year to take us."

"No. We haven't."

Virgil's inoffensive domination of his sister was too deply ingrained for her to shake off now. She usually enjoyed complying with his suggestions because his ideas were always much more imaginative and much more fun than her own.

"All right. But I don't know . . ." she sighed, trying to agree and yet not commit herself too completely.

"Well, what's going on in here!" It was Jonathan Greggor, wheeling his speedy copter into the shop. "Give me a hand, will you?"

Lanya rushed to help push the copter beneath the overhead crane.

"Going to try out that new rotor I bought last week," her father explained. "Virgil, send the magnet down, will you, and we'll take this one off."

Virgil leaped to the crane controls. The powerful electromagnet rolled along the high mono-rail and fell into position above the slack copter blades. The rotor was unlocked and the magnet lifted it lightly into the air and deposited it across the room. The magnet dropped hungrily down on the slick new blades.

"What are you kids doing in here?" Jonathan asked automatically as he worked. He glanced at the ship set in its cradle. "Oh, looks like a space ship of some kind. Ancient model though, isn't it? Klee was telling me you were tinkering around out here at something." He reached up to guide the rotor as it came swinging down. "I remember when I was a kid. Always fussing around with things. Built an amphibious car when I was about your age, Virgil." He grinned across the room at Lanya over the copter blades. "I was the envy of our city . . . until Joe Morgan got an expensive custom-built job from his father. What do you two expect to do with that ship when it's finished? Explore the solar system?" He chuckled at his own crude joke.

"We expect to rocket to Earth," said Lanya, who was unaccustomed to lying and thought that an answer to this question was necessary. Virgil scowled at her darkly.

"Earth, eh?" Jonathan said in a way that indicated he was preoccupied and hadn't grasped the significance of the words at all. "Easy there, Virgil . . . all right. Off!" The power left the magnet and it floated up to the ceiling and locked into position.

Virgil looked immensely relieved, but Lanya was puzzled. Their father never seemed to hear a word they said. It was this indifference to the importance of their existence that was the cause of their bold resolve. Maybe running away from home was a good thing to do. Maybe they wouldn't be taken for granted after that.

THE kids seem to be building a space ship out in the shop," their father said that evening as he watched the newcast on the telescreen. "Said they were going to Jupiter or some place." He lapsed into silence to follow the announcement on the telescreen.

"Earth," Lanya corrected from the floor where she was idly fitting together a chain reaction with a three-dimensional atom construction kit. It was an old toy she had long ago outgrown but, because of her father's indifference, she had none of the more advanced educational-therapy playthings.

Klee smiled indulgently. "That's nice," she said. "Have a good time. Jonathan, who was that economist I thought so much of last year?"

"You mean Gulgjar?"

"Oh yes. Well, he's a candidate again in this election. I think I'll vote for him. He's such a good talker."

"Hmmm."

Lanya looked across the room at Virgil and met his eyes with deep understanding. They were the only sane people in this household. Virgil's eyes glittered with the knowledge of their mutual secret. In a few weeks they would be on Earth, and then their parents might not be so dense and disinterested!

"We going to Earth this year, father?" Lanya asked suddenly and experimentally.

"Sure thing! I'll have everything straightened out in a month or so, then we're free to do anything we like. I'd like you kids to see Earth." He turned to the telescreen as the scene switched to the sports arena. "I think Canal City will win again. Beautiful strategy!" He leaned forward expectantly.

"Yes, I've always wanted to see Earth," Klee said without much conviction. "It must be much prettier than Mars. Isn't Desert City ahead, dear? Last week you said their team was the best on Mars."

"Oh, that was last week," Jonathan scoffed. "Just watch this strategy! Unbeatable!" His eyes glowed as he watched the swift, intricate pattern fluctuations of the game.

The same old thing, Lanya thought dejectedly. Always the same insincere answer and then the subject was changed. Virgil crawled across the floor toward her as she connected spheres and rods in a complicated molecular design. He studied the schematic system with lazy curiosity. "This electron is in the wrong orbit," he said at last and removed the offending sphere and inserted it in its proper position in the pattern. "Remember?"

"Thanks," said Lanya without much feeling. "I can't keep my mind on this silly thing anymore." And she added dreamily, "I'll bet they have wonderful scientific toys on Earth. Naddi Cruz has an electronic telescope her parents got on their vacation there. I wish I had one."

"We'll get one of everything when we get to Earth." Virgil promised magnanimously.

KLEE helped pack the food supplies in metal containers, very obviously humoring her children in this game they were playing.

"Why so much, Lanya? You seem to be going on a long journey." Her eyes twinkled amusedly.

Lanya peered at her mother in blank astonishment. Had she forgotten already?

"We're going to Earth, mother. Don't you remember?"

"Oh, yes," Klee said hastily. "And how was it you were going to get there?" She glanced across the dry, desolate span of desert to the distant bulwarks of the canal. "I wonder if it will rain this year."

"The rocket ship we've been building out in the shop," Lanya said with keen disappointment. Her mother didn't remember a thing!

"That's nice. A rocket ship." Klee paused, as though searching for just the right word to express her approval and enthusiasm. "How cute."

Lanya forced back the tears of disappointment that surged involuntarily to her eyes. She grabbed a large container and shuffled out, feeling, not altogether happily, that now the last possible barrier and objection to the running away had been removed. Her mother hadn't taken the slightest interest.

The ship stood now in the launching rig, a gleaming, purposeful projectile, reflecting the red hue of the Martian desert in the blazing sun.

"Mother thinks we're just playing games," she told Virgil who hovered expertly and solicitously about the ship, finding flimsy excuses to polish here and rub there. It didn't seem to shine quite to his satisfaction.

"Games!" he bellowed indignantly. "They'll soon find out it's no game. We'll run away for good. They'll be sorry they didn't pay attention to us!" He rubbed furiously on the metal plates.

"Here are the last of the supplies," Lanya intruded irrelevantly. They had already rehashed, many times, their plan to return to Mars in ten or twenty years as diplomats to negotiate with the highest executives in the Martian government. The splendor of their positions would flabbergast their parents. They would beg to be forgiven. Lanya and Virgil had not decided yet whether they would forgive them or not. Perhaps eventually they would.

Virgil lugged the supplies into the ship and packed them rigidly in the storage compartment. He came out and stood with his sister gazing up at the gleaming hull.

"That does it," he said with apparent satisfaction. "Tomorrow we leave, Lanya."

Now that the venture was so close at hand, Lanya's confidence was less serene. Maybe it was rather risky after all. If nothing else, Virgil might be arrested for charting in space without authorization. Maybe he couldn't fly this ship at all. His piloting had been mostly theory so far. Application was something else again, she feared.

Virgil's face showed doubt too. "You sure you're not afraid to go?" he asked almost hopefully.

"No. It's the only way we'll ever get any recognition around here," Lanya said stoutly.

"Right! I hope Muuck is watching tomorrow. We'll blast out of here like a comet! Make his cruiser look like a freighter."

"I'll bet they have *everything* on Earth," Lanya said with forced enthusiasm as they walked across the dry sand to their flat, rambling house. She looked up to see their father's copter skimming in from the direction of the city. It hovered over them momentarily, then streaked toward the house and settled lightly to the ground. Lanya began to run after Virgil who was galloping across the sand.

"Hello, father," they said breathlessly as they tore into the house behind him.

"Hello, kids. What's new?" Jonathan asked automatically as he always did.

Lanya screwed up her courage. Here was one last opportunity to have someone stop their running away.

"We're all set to take off for Earth tomorrow."

"Oh? That's fine. Wasn't that a rocket launching rig I saw out in the hollow?"

"Yes. That's where we take off at 0900 tomorrow. We'll probably be gone for months and months. Maybe years!"

Jonathan switched on the telescreen. "Is that so? Well, well. Ummm! These blasted commercials!" He snapped the screen off angrily, then turned it back on to the government-sponsored channels.

Lanya looked at her brother and shrugged hopelessly. It was out of their hands now. They had made every reasonable effort to halt the thing—now it would just go ahead on its own momentum.

AT 0830 Lanya trotted beside her brother with determination across the scorching sand to the ship nestled in the launching tower.

"I wonder what we forgot," Lanya said, wishing she could remember something.

"We didn't forget anything! Not a thing! Let's get going now!" Virgil climbed in deliberately without a backward look. He was trying to impress her, Lanya knew.

The girl, feeling suddenly very small and afraid, glanced apprehensively at the metal hull of the ship, then lingeringly at the familiar landscape. Finally, setting her face into a mask of unflinching determination that successfully hid the palpitations of her heart, she climbed into the open port and sealed the lock.

In the tiny pressurized cabin, air-cushioned against acceleration, Virgil was already seated and watching the erratic instruments with absorbed interest. Lanya dropped into the cloud-like softness of her seat and snapped the safety straps securely about her small body.

"I hope Muuck is watching," Virgil muttered under his breath. He turned to his sister. "You ready?"

She smiled sickishly.

They watched the hand sweep slowly across the chronometer and approach 0900. A steady vibration pulsed rhythmically throughout the hull.

"Are you sure you're ready?" Virgil asked, grinning bravely. "Here we go"

The scream of the jets was almost inaudible in the cabin. They floated with eerie slowness from the ground . . . then rose faster and faster. Below, the details of the desert merged into a dull red haze. The horizon began to have a noticeable curvature, which became more and more pronounced. A thick, bunched mass of cloud flicked by in an instant.

A strange pressure knotted Lanya's stomach. Then she blacked out.

* * * * *

"You what?"

"We rayed the thing out of space as a menace to navigation."

"Why'd you stop us?" Virgil's voice was shrill with annoyance and frustration. "We were rocketing to Earth!"

"Earth!" the other voice rasped. "Great

god Bongo! What loony stunt will you kids think up next?"

Lanya forced her eyes open and looked toward the voices. A large, red-thatched man in a space-police uniform was chuckling at Virgil who sat on the edge of a bunk. They were on the inside of a sleek-atom-powered police interceptor.

"Next time you try this stunt, kid," the old space-dog was saying, "paint some identification on the hull. And install a radio, if you do nothing else."

Lanya crawled out of the bunk and approached the two speakers.

"Oho!" the burly space-policeman roared. "The little lady!" He became suddenly serious. "Don't you kids know that at the rate you were accelerating you wouldn't have come out of the fog until your fuel was gone and you were past Earth? If ever. I've been a space-pilot for twenty years but I don't think I could have taken that kind of acceleration for long."

Lanya looked silently at Virgil who seemed kind of sick.

"We thought the air-foam cushions in the cabin were enough. Besides I'm pretty tough."

"Ho ho! Tough, he says!" The red-headed man slapped his knee. "The next time you try it, install some gravity plates and don't expect to defy the laws of nature. You would have been in a fine pickle if the patrol hadn't spotted your flaring jets and put a scanner on you."

"I'm hungry," Lanya said suddenly.

The space-pilot laughed. "She's hungry! Say, you two didn't blast off on an empty stomach on top of everything else?" He groaned as Virgil nodded his head sheepishly.

Lanya accepted the big man's proffered hand and followed him into the galley. The fright and confusion left her as the pleasant savor of food filled her nostrils. She ate hungrily but with proper lady-like delicacy.

"Where are we going?" she asked.

"Home," the big space-dog said.

"Oh. But aren't you going to arrest us, or something?" Lanya made her eyes big and round to show her apprehension.

"Well, ordinarily I would. But I think you two have had enough for the time being. You look fairly intelligent to me. Do you think you've learned anything from this crazy expedition?"

"Identification, communication and gravity plates," Virgil muttered.

"Oh, yes!" Lanya cried quickly. "We'll never do it again. Absolutely never!" She gave an inward sigh of relief as she saw that the man hadn't heard Virgil's careless remark.

Outside the quartz viewport the flat plane of red Martian desert was growing swiftly larger.

"WHY did you do it? Why?" Klee demanded tearfully.

They were seated about the dead and silent telescreen. It was a crucial moment. They could not abandon their principles now.

"We were going to Earth," Virgil said obstinately, "because you always break your promise to take us!" He looked extremely self-righteous as he spoke his feelings at last.

Lanya, inspired by this unexpected outburst, plunged recklessly, "All the other kids have aircraft and we don't have anything! You never listen to anything we say or care about anything we do . . ." Then she was stricken dumb by her own courage.

Klee and Jonathan searched each other's eyes. The father switched on the telescreen, then switched it back off. He cleared his throat five or six times, scratched his elbow, worked the muscles of his jaw, then leaned forward in the chair.

Lanya waited breathlessly. Would he be chastened or angry?

"Supposing I buy you a new copter?" he said. "Will that straighten things out?"

Lanya nodded eagerly. She glanced at Virgil who sat with a stiff face.

"Make it an atom cruiser," he said with finality.

Jonathan's face clouded for a moment. Lanya almost dropped through the floor. She saw her mother nod silently.

"A cruiser it is!" their father cried. Then he burst into a loud peal of laughter, and switched on the telescreen.

Lanya relaxed limply. Then she looked at Virgil. Very firmly and dignifiedly he folded his arms.

But the eye turned away from his parents winked back at her, very solemnly.

EARTH IS MISSING!

87th Century Earth, entombed in a relentless, mile-thick coat of ice—its buried cities groaning in slow-congealing despair—still dreaded far more a bestial horror, known only as The Bear. For that monster with a human brain was threatening to *steal the world!*

Illustrated by SHARP

THE SEARCHLIGHTS PLAYING across the building's dark windows, the police cordon holding back the crowd—the telenews cameras ate it up.

The telenewsmen never seemed to care whether they got in the way of a stray shot or not. They had the video cameras set up right out in the middle of the icy street. The announcer was talking rapidly into his portable mike.

"They've got the building surrounded now, folks! For those who faded in late, this is your teletabloid reporter bringing you an on-the-spot picture. . . ."

The picture was being reproduced on television screens throughout the ice-bound world, in London, Moscow, Singapore, New York—in New York's buried city in particular. It was happening there. New Yorkers crowded around their screens in the bright plastic salons deep in the vita-lamped society levels, in the tidy middle-class apartments several miles nearer the surface, even in a dingy hovel just under the earth's frozen crust, a few blocks from where the scene was being enacted, a sallow-faced tenement family was gathered around an ancient Eightieth Century television set.

"It's one of The Bear's gang, folks! Although the rest of the gang got away after this morning's Radium Bank stick-up, the

By CARL SELWYN

*"I'll get him! I'll get him!"
screamed Lois.*

police wounded one of them. They've trailed him to this vacant building high in the upper levels and—Wait! What's this! A plainclothes man just went in the building! He went in there *alone.* . . ."

* * * * * *

. . . It was dark inside.

Johnny Steel flashed his light on the stairs. There was the same red trail that had brought them here—blood, frozen as it fell. He cut the light off again instantly, pausing till his eyes got used to the darkness again. The heavy pistol was cold in his hand.

Perhaps he *was* crazy, coming in here alone! The Homicide Squad had certainly thought so when he'd ordered them to wait outside.

The stairs were a vague outline slanting up into the deserted building's gloom. At the top, a corridor cut off to the right.

"Floyd . . ." Steel called softly. He'd told no one that he knew the man they were hunting down. "Floyd, this is Johnny Steel. I'm coming up alone. . . ."

His voice echoed through the chill corridor above. There was no answer.

He moved slowly up the stairs. He was a big man, tall and heavy with most of the weight in his arms and shoulders. Near the corner at the top, he paused, listening in the darkness.

"Afraid to come up, Johnny?"

Steel jumped. He flattened against the wall. The hoarse voice wasn't three feet from his ear. His finger took up the slack in his pistol's trigger.

"Your boys got in some pretty good target practice on me this afternoon, didn't they, Johnny?" The voice came from just around the corner. Steel felt the sweat trickling down his neck despite the cold. "You wouldn't tell 'em to take it easy, huh —that I was an old chum of yours?"

Steel finally found his voice. "Floyd, you killed two guards in that Radium Bank. I came up here to try to reason with you— because you used to be my best friend. Tell me who The Bear is—and I'll do my best to help you at the trial."

A husky laugh echoed in the dark corridor. "You know I'm no squealer, Johnny." But now there was a faintly preoccupied tone in the voice. Then Steel heard the faintest scrape of a foot on the corridor floor.

"Floyd!" Steel pled. "Listen to reason!" He paused a moment, listening. But only a moment. Then he backed quickly and silently several steps down stairs. He left the right wall and quickly crouched over against the left. The next instant, he saw a hand flick around the corner at the head of the stairs. A volt pistol roared, blasting the spot where he had been standing.

As the building trembled with the explosion, a figure appeared around the corner, looking down the stairs.

"Floyd! For God's sake—!" Steel cried.

Instantly, the pistol in the figure's hand whipped toward Steel's voice. And Steel couldn't take another chance.

He fired.

The figure hung there a moment like a clubbed ox. Then it crumpled to the floor.

STEEL lowered his pistol slowly. Big shoulders sagging, he walked slowly up the steps. There were tears in his eyes as he stood there looking down at the shadowed form on the floor. Around him he felt the familiar walls of the old deserted building in which as small, boys they'd played cops and robbers together. They had played together in that very street outside, grown up together in that cold miserable place of eternal twilight that was the slums of New York City in 8646 A. D. What chance did a kid have in that environment! Only by sheer luck had he himself been sent to an orphanage in the warm lower levels instead of to a reformatory. It wasn't Floyd's fault that he lay here dead by a policeman's gun. It was the fault of Nintieth Century civilization.

Looking down at the friend he'd been forced to kill, Steel knew that somehow, if it took him the rest of his life, he had to brighten that shadowed world in the street outside—and he declared a private war against the gangsters who led its kids astray. . . .

He walked down the steps and called to his men. "Come on up. It's all over."

But. he knew it wasn't all over. For Johnny Steel, it had just started.

The morgue men bringing the body out, the District Attorney slapping Detective John Steel on the back—the telenews rehashed the story every hour on the hour. "Definitely slated for the Police Medal, the husky young cop who this afternoon brought down with one shot . . .'"

The leather-faced old man sitting across the desk twirled a knob on the office video screen, turning the announcer's voice down. "Johnny"—his hawk face beamed around his pipe—"with all this publicity you're going to be Commissioner when I retire."

Steel shook his head patiently. "Quit trying to change the subject, Chief," he said. He uncrossed his long legs and leaned forward in his chair. "Listen—you say you'll give me a Patrol. But you've sent Patrols up on the ice before. When they get there they can't find a soul. The Bear's got scouts out. They can spot a large group too easy. I tell you it's a one-man job."

Commissioner Brandt sighed. "Johnny," he said and his eyes stopped smiling. "I tell *you* I don't intend to lose another one of my best blood-hounds." He took his pipe out of his mouth to point it at the gold-starred plaque on the office wall. "In the last two years I've sent five good men up on the ice after The Bear. None have come back"

It was true. Steel eyed him a moment. Then he got up and paced the length of the office, hands deep in his pockets. Finally, he walked over to the inter-office video and cut it on. A police sergeant's face faded in on the screen. "Put The Bear file on," Steel told him.

"Yes, sir." The sergeant pressed a button and his face faded with his words. It was replaced by a title card, then the complete sound-picture reel of everything police records had on The Bear.

"Go on," Commissioner Brandt said, watching from his desk. "After you find out more about him, maybe you'll forget this damn fool idea of yours."

Steel ignored him, stared thoughtfully at the screen. What he saw was not pretty.

The Consolidated Tungsten Plant, a $500,000 haul. Central Electric, bankrupt after one robbery. Uranium, Inc. had lost a cool million and its vice president. But the victim topping the list was Vita-Heat. The Bear had pulled five separate jobs there in the last two years. Not only had Vita-Heat lost a fortune in irreplaceable equipment but six faithful employees had disappeared without a trace—no trace except that symbol that struck terror in every insurance executive's heart: An ice-bear's claw, left sticking in the wall like a dagger.

That wasn't all.

Not only had five of Brandt's special investigators vanished when they went after The Bear but sometimes their wives, children, and close friends, too. Often, when The Bear's revenge was through, there was nobody left to receive a police pension. Such was The Bear's long reign of horror—robbery, kidnapping, murder. Worst perhaps was the fact that the body of none of his victims was ever found. But, of course, the endless ice moor up on the earth's desolate crust was a mute and careful sexton. . . .

Steel cut the video off. Commissioner Brandt came around the desk and put a hand on his shoulder. "Johnny," he said, "We've proved there's no sense trying to find The Bear's hideout in umpty billion ice caves on the surface. The only thing we can do is keep on setting traps for him— try to figure out where he's going to strike next. We did it today and we got one of them. Next time maybe we'll get The Bear himself."

"Next time!" Steel turned away disgustedly. "While we're waiting, The Bear's recruiting more kids in the upper levels to do his dirty work. We won't get The Bear. We'll keep on killing these poor kids he gets to work for him." He walked over to the glass case standing in the corner, stared down at the ivory saber-like ice-bear's claw inside, a sample of The Bear's visiting card. Then suddenly he turned back to the Commissioner. "Chief," he said, "will you let me go after him alone or won't you?"

"Johnny, I just can't let you risk—"

"Okay," Steel said. His hand slipped inside his coat, came out with his little silver detective shield. He laid it on the Commissioner's desk. "Vita-Heat, Inc. is offering $100,000 reward for The Bear. It looks like I'm going into the private detective business."

THE DOME of vita-lamps high above the glistening canyons of the lower level bathed the creamy streets in a golden shower as Steel's tunnel car shot out of the midtown exit. He swerved through the traffic on the mirrored boulevard and drew up before a smooth plastic structure that soared above the other buildings on the level. Letters six feet high on the building's face read VITA-HEAT, INC. He got out, strode into the building and took the express chute up.

When the chute door opened, he stepped out into the luminous paneled reception room and went over to the blonde receptionist. "John Steel," he said. "I called Mr. Stahl. He's expecting me."

The blonde charged up a smile for him; then she realized he wasn't staring at her well-filled tunic but at his own thoughts. She repeated his words into her desk microphone, a green light flashed, and she said coldly, "All right. Go on in." Across the room, a panel in the wall slid back.

Steel walked in. The panel closed again quickly behind him.

A fluorescent ceiling's blue-white glow burnished the carved cave-tree wood of an office befitting Vita-Heat's President. Behind a gleaming desk, Hampton Stahl's great bulk rose, pink cheeks smiling. Then Steel saw with some surprise the young woman who reclined in a pillowy chair beside the desk. With more surprise, he recognized her from telenews glimpses of society. It was Miss Lois Harmon, emerald-eyed queen of last season's debutantes, and Steel frowned slightly; he had come here strictly on business. Then Stahl was shaking his hand, introducing him.

Stahl was a big man, tall as well as fat, but his bulk wasn't that with which middle age often covers a big man. His weight was that of a blue ribbon pig, a great white pig swilled on the 90th Century's greatest private fortune. And, Steel thought, the girl was also an expensive looking animal, lean, golden tan, smooth. Her hair was the same golden hue of her cheeks.

"Miss Harmon, you know, is the daughter of my late partner," Stahl said when his visitor was seated. "I'm trying to persuade her to sell me her stock in the company."

"It's because I always argue with him at directors' meetings," the girl laughed. She was as smooth all over as a pedigreed cat. She'd inherited a fortune when her father, one of Vita-Heat's founders, had been killed in a laboratory explosion many years ago. "Now go right ahead with your business," she said, rising. "I've got to go downstairs to the Bank. When you're through," she told Stahl, "you can pick me up there for cocktails." She smiled at Steel, gave him her exquisitely manicured hand and departed. Twenty-four karat, Steel thought. He wondered if she'd have turned out as well however if she'd been brought up in a tenement in the upper levels. . . .

When the panel closed behind her, Stahl turned back to his visitor. "So," he said, "we have another who thinks the risk worth the reward?"

"That," Steel said, "is what I came here to talk about. Mr. Stahl, your corporation has a standing offer of $100,000 for anybody who gets The Bear. I want a million."

The brows shot up over Stahl's piggish eyes. *"What!"*

"Here's my proposition," Steel said, smiling. "Instead of rewarding me—if I get The Bear—I want Vita-Heat to go into partnership with me. A sort of partnership in philanthropy. As my reward, I want Vita-Heat to go to work in the upper levels"

Hampton Stahl adjusted a long cigarette into a silver holder. "I must say, this is—"

"It shouldn't run into much," Steel continued. "You'd be using your own material

and labor at cost prices. It would just be a matter of installing enough vita-lamps up there for people to live by—there's only one to a street corner up there now."

"But—a million dollars!"

"Mr. Stahl," Steel said, "your company's already lost five million and, the way I see it, you're going to lose a lot more if The Bear isn't stopped. I think this partnership business of mine is pretty sound. We both have good reason to want The Bear brought to justice."

Suddenly a cunning look came into Stahl's eyes. "Just what makes you so anxious to get The Bear, Mr. Steel?"

For a moment, Steel hesitated. But he couldn't forget that picture in his mind—Floyd, lying in that deserted building, cornered, hunted down like a mad dog. Sure it was justice—but what had made him a mad dog! His smile faded. "All right," he said quietly, "I'll tell you why I want to get The Bear. It's the same reason I want to get *you*, Mr. Stahl—or your money rather. Those poor souls in the upper levels have two enemies—the gangsters and the big corporations. The gangsters find a young kid up there, give him a gun and make a criminal out of him. And your corporations force him into a career of crime just as much as the gangsters do. You own the tenements. You make those people live in conditions that are so bad you won't even go up there and look at them. You pay $2.00 a day in your mercury mines while you get $4.00 a day rent for your vita-lamps." Steel had to hang on to his temper. "If the upper levels are given a *chance* to live decently, they will live decently!"

Stahl's thick lips curled in amusement. "A pretty speech, Mr. Steel. I admire your philosophy." He sank back in his chair, toying with his silver cigarette holder. "But business, you know, is business. . . ."

Steel stared at him, wondering what was holding him back. He wasn't a member of the Force anymore. Reach across that desk and push his fat face in! Instead, he said, "Okay, I guess that's all then. I'll have to do what I can with just the reward money."

As he stood up an intercom box on Stahl's desk buzzed urgently. Stahl's plump finger touched a button.

"Mr. Stahl!" a voice shrieked from the

box. *"A gang of masked men—they just held up the radium vault in the bank downstairs again!"*

The pink color drained from Stahl's fat cheeks. His thick lips fell open.

Steel's hand darted into his coat pocket and came out with his gun. He started for the door. "Come on!" he said. "If that's The Bear it's the second time he's struck today!"

I T WAS. Sticking in the vaults lead wall was a gleaming white ice bear's claw. That was all—except the chattering crowd, a small army of Stahl's embarrassed guards, and Miss Lois Harmon who had seen the whole thing.

A masked gloved man had suddenly appeared at the teller's cage and at each alarm button—they'd seemed to know the layout perfectly, she told Steel. There were seven of them; four held pistols on the crowd while the other three emptied the contents of the vault into leadex bags. Then they'd marched out, stepped into a waiting tunnel car and streaked into the upper level tunnel. The girl's green eyes were bright with excitement. She seemed to be enjoying this like a telemovie.

"It was wonderful! I only wish they'd kidnapped me and taken me with them."

Steel looked at her with open disgust. Poor bored little rich girl—he felt like turning her across his knee and spanking that $200 girdle. "It was just sheer luck somebody wasn't killed here," he said. "Now you stick around. I hope the police lock you up as a material witness."

The cop on the corner had called the station and the squad was on the way. The gun in Steel's hand was all the authority he needed however. He cleared the crowd away from the vault and walked in. Hampton Stahl followed him, wringing his pudgy hands. "The second time today!" he moaned. "They're trying to ruin me!"

The vault was perfectly safe from radiation now. It was empty, every drawer cleaned out. Steel braced his knee against the wall and pulled out the claw. "We've never found fingerprints on one of these yet." The claw was about eight inches long, white with a faint tinge of pink. He looked at it thoughtfully for a moment. Suddenly he held it up to the light and examined it carefully. He glanced from the

claw to Stahl. Then he reached out, dropped the claw in the fat man's vest pocket. "Well," he said, "have you changed your mind about my proposition now?"

Stahl lifted the thing from his pocket as if it were a spider and threw it on a table. "Anything," he murmured. "They may try to kill me next!"

"Fine!" Steel grinned at him. "But since you were so slow making up your mind, I want an additional clause in my contract now—a little life insurance policy with the upper levels as the beneficiary. You pay off if I get The Bear or if The Bear gets me."

Stahl looked at him in silence. It was hard to tell whom he was cursing, The Bear or Steel. "What makes you think you can even find The Bear's hideout?"

Steel picked up the claw again. "I just noticed there is a tinge of pink in this thing," he said, "and it's only eight inches long. This claw came from an ice-bear cub that was born only a few months ago and the only place they're born this time of the year is near that warm comet crater up on the surface near the Jersey Ruins." He dropped the claw back on the table. "Now, if you won't let anyone know I'm working for you," he said, "I'm going up there on a little hunting trip. . . ."

II

T HE INTERLEVEL LIMITED left the lower warmth and streaked up the great winding tunnel through the neat residential suburbs, through the squalid upper levels, through the ice-locked roots of ancient Manhattan. But Steel barely noticed when the windows in his compartment frosted over. He was studying his glacier maps.

The comet crater was located near the frozen ruins of what was once a surface city named Jersey. He'd been on a snow-deer hunt up there once; an old guide had told him about the ice-bear cubs.

Steel plotted his course from the Surface Terminal to the Ruins, then checked his equipment list—electrosuit, oxygen helmet, volt rifle, rations. He'd charter a little ski plane at the Terminal.

When he finished, he leaned back in his seat and glanced at his watch. Almost there. Had he forgotten anything? Fitted into the oxygen helmet was a little radio unit so he could keep in touch with Stahl. He'd set up a receiver in a vacant room in the Vita-Heat Building and arranged for one of Stahl's guards to be there at all times. He'd also arranged for Stahl to send a copy of their contract—reward or insurance—to Commissioner Brandt. Not that he didn't trust Stahl. . . . Well, it looked as if he was all set. He'd buy a hunting license to put on the ski plane—for all anybody'd know he was out for snow-deer. He'd spend the night at the Terminal Hotel, leave first thing in the morning. . . .

When the Limited's whirring ceased, he put away the maps and picked up his bag. As the outer door slid open, he stepped out into the vast Terminal and headed for the viewway that would take him to the hotel.

The Terminal was a heavily insulated cavern in the ice crust. The landing and departure stalls encircled the huge room where the motley thousands of hurrying travelers bought tickets, waved goodbyes or greetings, or waited sleepily around Dr. Albert Harmon's chrome statue. As Steel passed the statue of the shaggy-haired bespectacled old man, he eyed it thoughtfully. Dr. Harmon's experiments with household and jet propulsion heat had done a lot of good but it looked as if his green-eyed daughter wasn't good for anything but a cocktail party . . . Then he was on the viewway. His spine tingled at the sight outside.

Standing on the crowded belt as it slid past the Terminal's long window, he had a perfect view of the glacier. Glistening in the starlight, the great ice waste stretched to the horizon like a sheet of silver. Tiny varicolored lights swept across the jet backdrop of outer space—freight planes bound for Earth's other buried city-states, for the frozen mines of Neptune, Venus, Mars, or for the nebulous worlds of other suns. Those other suns, pinpoints of light in infinity—when the Solar System had cooled, they had been a beckoning hope. Then their planets had been found even less inhabitable than Earth. Poisoned atmospheres, molten lands, boiling seas—habitation was impossible. It was undoubtedly mankind's greatest tragedy, Steel thought, that it was doomed to call a frozen Earth home forever.

"Look! A liner's coming in!"

A group of tourists ahead of Steel stepped off the belt to the walkway alongside and stared through the plexiglass window at a fish-like space ship that was drifting down to a landing stall nearby. Steel also stepped off to watch.

"It's all automatic," one of the tourists explained to his wife. "A radio beam brings 'em here and lands 'em. The pilots don't have much to do."

Steel watched the great ship settle to the stall's roof, the roof slid open, the ship sank in out of sight, the roof slide closed again.

"Let's go down and watch 'em unload." The tourists moved to a belt nearby that led to the landing stall. And, because he had nothing better to do till morning—Steel followed them.

The moment he got there he knew something was wrong.

"Get back!" A Terminal guard stepped in front of the group of onlookers. "Nobody's allowed near the ship!"

Beyond the quickly formed line of guards, Steel saw an excited group of Terminal executives gathered at the ship's open door. What was up? The ship appeared to be okay. It had come in all right.

"What's the trouble?" somebody asked.

The guard was staring anxiously at the ship himself. "Don't know," he said. "When that ship came in, *there wasn't nobody on it.* . . ."

Steel shouldered his way to the front of the crowd to stare across at the ship's open door. Around him, the crowd buzzed with the news. A woman who had been waiting to meet somebody on the ship started screaming. The ship had come in on the radar beam, on time, but with pilots, stewardesses, twenty passengers, and cargo—missing!

"Pirates!" The word swept through the crowd. The ship had come from Venus. And not five minutes ago the pilot had reported he was arriving on schedule, the trip uneventful. Then the crowd quickly discovered what had happened. A Terminal cop appeared at the ship's door. A hush went over the crowd. In the cop's hand was an ice-bear's claw.

There was a hush, then one whisper in a thousand throats. *"The Bear!"*

Steel turned to a man beside him. "What was the cargo?"

"That—that's what so awful," the fellow said. "It was carrying a load of Venusian tungsoid. And there ain't but two things you can make with tungsoid—electrotubes or *suffo-gas!*"

Suffo-gas! A deadly vapor, its production had been banned on Earth ever since mankind moved underground. One whiff of suffo-gas in New York's ventilation pipes. . . . Steel turned back through the crowd.

He didn't take the belt to the hotel. He walked, big hands deep in his pockets, thinking, thinking things he hardly dared think of.

That ship had been pirated close by. Its route in from Venus was from the southeast. That cargo of tungsoid had been pirated over the Jersey Ruins. He was on the right track and it was a hurry-up job. There was little reason to believe The Bear had gotten interested in electrotubes. . . .

NEXT MORNING when the first yellow rays of the sun's dying ember slanted across the ice, Steel's ski plane circled up from the Terminal and headed south-east.

Crossing the sub-zero ice crevices on foot would have taken months but it was just a short hop by plane. It was a hop, however, that few planes took. Freight and liner traffic from the Terminal immediately headed for the stratosphere. Near the surface, the glacier's fangs probed every cloud and blizzards of liquid air roamed the uncharted chasms. Only an occasional prospector or hunter attempted low-altitude flying here and often these never returned.

This morning, however, Steel was lucky. The weather was clear and ceiling unusually high, the peaks rearing from the shadow-filled valleys like glittering icicles in the pale yellow light. When he checked his instruments by the chart and headed the plane down over the ice field that choked the Jersey Ruins, he grinned silently behind the control lever. Now, if the blizzard would only hold off for an hour or so. . . .

The crumbling ruins of ancient buildings jutted up from the snow, monuments of a long-departed civilization. Although never actually explored, the Ruins were

thought to extend for miles south of the comet crater. More was known about the crater itself since it was only a few centuries old. Its gigantic explosion had knifed a deep valley in the ice mountains that was still relatively warm. Lichen grew on the snow here, bats hung in the caves, and ice-bears had a shorter hibernation. And *The* Bear? Any crevice, any ruined building here might be his lair.

Scanning the drifts below through his windows, Steel looked for tracks, melting snow or rocket stains. As he looked, he kept an eye on his auto-sextant. As it clicked off the changing coordinates of his location, he marked his position on the chart. Vanish he might like those other five cops who'd gone after The Bear, Steel thought, but not without a trace—not as long as the little microphone in his helmet was ready for an instant S.O.S. He'd tested it at the Terminal; Stahl's man was on the job.

On a little plateau below, he saw a herd of bluish white snow-deer. They looked up and then stampeded in all directions as he passed over. Odd he hadn't seen any bears yet.

He was banking low over the half-buried top of a building, squinting down at the white drifts, when he saw the ball.

"Now how the hell did that happen . . ."

He circled lower. It was a ball of solid ice. He could see all the way through it. It was about six feet in diameter, smooth as glass. It was perfectly round, like a huge green bubble. It lay there on the snow, sparkling in the dull light. "Funny ice formation—"

Then the ball *moved*.

Watching, Steel almost rammed a building. He pulled up, staring at the thing. The ball rose slowly, ten feet above the snow. Suspended by nothing. Then it drifted slowly over the wastes, aimlessly, like a bubble in the breeze.

Steel followed it, amazed. A strong air current? But it wasn't affecting the plane. Besides, that chunk of ice probably weighed half a ton!

The thing finally came to rest against an ice crag near one of the wrecked buildings. Steel went in close and hovered, examining it with bewildered eyes. And it was just a ball of ice. That's all it *was*.

Well, lots of queer things happened on

the glacier . . . Shaking his head, he started to zoom away.

Then it happened.

More of the ice balls! Hundreds of them! Curving down upon him from above!

Colorless, unseen until they were upon him, they blocked the plane on every side.

"What in the—!" Steel banked, twisted the plane into every contortion. But at every turn the glistening spheres stood before him, closing in like a net, relentlessly forcing his down.

Fifty feet above the snow, he realized he'd have to ram them. The plane was strong—maybe he could crash through.

Then, as if anticipating this very thought, the spheres moved in suddenly against the plane, pressed upon it from above, forced it down. It was pressed quickly down to the snow.

As it settled into the snow level with the cabin windows, the spheres slowly melted together to form a rough-hewn roof and walls. The plane was enclosed completely.

Steel's heart hammered. His breath fogged his helmet. He stared at the encircling wall, jerked the control lever helplessly. It was only then he remembered his microphone.

"Six-foot balls of ice!" he cried hoarsely. "Some kind of remote control! X-26.9-18.7!" He started giving the coordinates of his location.

"That's hardly worth while now. . . ."

Steel shivered even in the electrosuit's warmth. Slowly, he turned around.

The walls and roof that imprisoned him joined, behind him, the side of one of the ruined buildings, a crumbling structure of weathered concrete. The ruin had a door. In the door, an oxygen helmet topping a snow-white electrosuit, stood a tall thin man. One gloved hand rested lightly upon the butt of a volt pistol holstered at his hip.

"Our little Trojan Horse—those balls of ice," the man continued, "have several interesting properties. They're also a very effective barrier against radio transmission." His voice was coming into the plane on the same radio frequency Steel had been trying to send on.

Behind his helmet, the man's face was lean, thin-lipped, deeply tanned—a tan that wasn't of Earth. That tan had come through a space-ship's viewplate, close in the heat of some foreign sun. He strode over to the plane and took out his pistol to rap impatiently on the cabin window.

"Get out of there! That hunting license on your ship doesn't fool me. A few minutes ago you passed over a herd of snow-deer without firing a shot. The Bear will be mighty interested in why you're up here snooping around. . . ."

THE BEAR—the word hit Steel like an electric shock. He'd thought he was on the right track, he'd hoped, but now that it was proved it was something to think about. He'd found The Bear's hideout and what could he do about it?

He didn't move at first. He sat there looking at the man through the window, his mind running hot trying to figure out what to do. In the middle of the glacier, a six-foot-thick wall in front of him, the man with the gun outside. And his radio useless—his ace card trumped with the game just started. It looked like that insurance policy hadn't been a bad idea. . . .

The fellow banged on the plane with his pistol again. "Come on! Open up!"

Steel opened up. At a wave of the pistol, he stepped out to the frozen snow. At another wave, he raised his hands. The man stepped around him, jabbed the gun in his spine and went over him expertly. He found Steel's pistol and dropped it in the snow. "Now start walking ahead of me. And no foolishness." The pistol shoved Steel ahead through the ruin's door.

Inside it was just like ten million other surface ruins. You walked into what had been about the thirtieth floor above the street and found only drifted snow, shattered walls, a bleached skeleton perhaps. Now, however, Steel had time for only a glance at the familiar scene when the pistol moved him on through another door, then another, and this one, he saw, only faked its weathered appearance. As he went through, a metal panel slid silently shut behind them and he had his first look at the tremendous organization he'd been fool enough to tackle single-handed.

A bright warming glow drifted down from the luminous ceiling. Vent slits in the floor whispered softly, oxygen pouring in. At the other end of the room, a split traveling walk slid noiselessly up and down a shaft past hundreds of offices, workshops, barracks. The place was as big as the Terminal, as lavishly furnished as Stahl's Vita-Heat Building. This place explained why The Bear had stolen as much equipment as money.

He was given little time to marvel here however.

"Take off your helmet," the radioed voice behind him ordered. Steel took it off. When he turned, facing the man and the gun, the man had removed his own helmet. He was smiling, a thin tight-lipped smile with no humor in his eyes. "You seem surprised," he said. "You really didn't expect a bear's den, did you?"

"This is your show," Steel said quietly. "What comes next?" The man held his helmet in one hand, his pistol in the other —both hands full. Steel thought of his own helmet, a mighty handy weapon. If he got a chance—Then suddenly he noticed something else, something that gave him a chance cops dreamed about. The guy's pistol—the safety was *on!*

"Okay," the man said, "if this deer hunting trip of yours turns out to be faked, you'll soon learn what's next." A quick motion of the pistol ordered Steel around on the belt that led down the shaft.

Steel went. As he went, he shot quick glances into the rooms they passed, waiting for the right moment to whirl around and knock that pistol away.

The rooms they passed were filled with workers. There were drafting stalls where scores of men — and women — bent over blueprint tables and charts. There were plastic workshops where people operated compression molds and lathes. Where did The Bear get all these workers! They all couldn't have come from the upper levels! There were glittering laboratories where white-aproned technicians huddled around distillation vats and rows of test tubes. Steel thought of that stolen cargo of tungsoid. Suffo-gas . . . ?

A few yards ahead, on the left, he saw they were approaching an empty room. On the right, a deserted tunnel branched off into whatever labyrinth the place possessed. Okay, this was as good as anywhere else! Wherever he was being taken, they'd be there shortly. Then it might be too late.

Steel crouched slightly, ready to whirl on the fellow behind him.

Then—

"Step off!"

Behind him, the man's hand suddenly grabbed his shoulder and shoved him off the belt into the tunnel.

Steel clenched his teeth. He glanced up the empty, tapestry-walled tunnel ahead. All right then, this was an even better place for it.

But again the man behind him had other plans. "Stop here."

Steel halted, puzzled this time. The tunnel curved on off ahead but here there was only the red tapestry walls. He felt the pistol again on his backbone. Then he saw the man's hand reaching out beside him, lifting the corner of one of the tapestries.

The cloth had covered a window. It looked down into a tremendous auditorium where hundreds of teen-age boys and girls sat in curved rows of seats facing a wide curtained stage.

The scene might have been that of any world-wide juvenile delinquency court. Steel frowned. Dressed in rags, their pinched faces unwashed, the crowd was a cross-section of undernourished kids from the slum levels of every underground city on Earth. They were all sizes and colors and there was excitement in every eye. Steel could hardly believe it. A prep school for crime . . . Steel felt hot rage creeping over him.

Then on the auditorium's stage, the curtain went up and what he saw there hit him like a bucket of ice water.

Ten feet high, its shaggy white hair stark against the stage's black backdrop, Earth's most terrifying creature stood there — an *ice-bear.*

The man behind him dropped the tapestry.

"New recruits." Steel heard him, dazedly. "The Bear's busy now. I hope you don't mind waiting." The fellow laughed. "Okay, get moving."

STEEL turned from the covered window as if waking from a nightmare. He retraced his steps back through the tunnel to the belt as the man behind him directed. He got on the belt again, the man behind him.

But it didn't make sense! It couldn't be! There was some trick to it! But, the proof of his own eyes argued, it must have been an ice-bear. It had been the whole works—

red eyes, saber fangs, razor claws. Rearing up on its hind legs . . .

Steel shook his head. He couldn't figure this out any more than he'd been able to figure out the balls of ice that captured him. Then, suddenly, he remembered something he had been about to do.

He looked ahead down the belt. Nobody there. They had just passed the last of the rooms alongside. Do it now! If he could get back to that auditorium — get within gunshot of that bear—

Suddenly he shifted one foot to the belt beside them that was traveling in the opposite direction. Touching it, his foot stopped him like a brake and whirled him around rapidly.

The fellow didn't even have time to be surprised. Steel's helmet caught him in the face. He went down without a sound.

Quickly, Steel snatched up his pistol. Crouching over the man, he glanced back up the belt. Still nobody in sight. In the other direction, he saw the belt was carrying them down into some dim-lit place, a dungeon, perhaps, where the fellow had been taking him. Nobody in sight there, either. Steel grabbed the man's collar and dragged him—unconscious or corpse, he neither knew nor cared which—down the belt into the shadows.

The floor was level here, undoubtedly the very bottom of The Bear's vast retreat. In the dim light, he saw packing cases stacked along the wall, a heavy freight belt creaking laboriously down the middle of the floor. He dragged his ex-guard behind a packing case and then stepped on the belt that slid back up the shaft. His hand closed fondly upon the pistol in his pocket. He snapped the safety *off*.

Now, if he could get to that auditorium, get to The Bear . . .

He didn't run. He forced himself to stand on the belt and let it carry him up past the crowded workshops and laboratories. He didn't turn his head. He only glanced into the rooms out of the corner of his eye as he passed. It was the worst ordeal he could remember in ten years of detective work. Standing there. Alone. Thousands all around him. His hand grew sweaty on the pistol in his pocket. Then he was at the tunnel and nobody had noticed him.

He stepped in with a gasp of relief. The tunnel was also still deserted. He jumped to the tapestry.

For a moment, he couldn't find the one that hid the window. Then he found it, lifted it with nervous fingers, and stared once more down into the auditorium. The kids were just leaving the auditorium, filing out a door at the rear. The Bear was just leaving the stage.

How was he to get down there? He eyed the wall encircling the auditorium. It curved, just as the tunnel curved. The tunnel seemed to be a closed balcony surrounding the place. Somewhere ahead there must be an exit leading down to the stage. Steel dropped the tapestry and went down the tunnel, running now.

Sure it was quick! Much quicker than he'd ever hoped! Three hours since he'd left the Terminal and he'd found The Bear! His fingers curled around the pistol like a caress.

When he judged he'd half-circled the hall, he slowed down, moving swiftly but cautiously. Then he came to a belt that cut down to the left. It must lead to the stage. He stepped on it.

It did. It carried him swiftly to the wings and peering out across the stage, he saw *it* standing there in the opposite wings. Still reared ten feet high on its hind legs, eyes like red-filmed lights. And with The Bear now was a bull-necked giant whom Steel remembered from police photographs, a boxer of "fixed match" notoriety—Mike Doyle.

The kids were still straggling from the hall. Steel waited behind the curtain till the last one left. Then he stepped out and strode quickly across the stage.

"Don't move, Mike," he ordered the boxer.

The big fellow whirled. The Bear turned.

Steel stopped six feet from them, pistol leveled. "I don't know whether you're real or not," he said, eyeing the huge animal, "but there's a good way to find out. If that's just some kind of trick get-up, whoever's in it better get out fast. I'm going to blast a hole through it."

"It's Johnny Steel!" The fighter's battered face sagged in astonishment. "It's the cops!"

The Bear's neon eyes blazed down at Steel, its huge chest rising and falling slowly, breath hissing in its black nostrils.

It was a sight that few people lived long enough to see close up. An ice-bear could take a man's head off with one claw. If this one was a fake, Steel thought, it was a whopping good one. Its dark lips curled back from a jagged row of yellowed six-inch fangs. From each hairy paw, a rake of white claws slowly unsheathed. Then something happened that almost made Steel drop his gun.

"*Yes, I know Mr. Steel,*" The Bear said.

It was a terrifying sound, guttural, deep in the great animal's throat—but it proved something to Steel after its first shock. He'd heard sound-blending devices before. That was a human voice set in the growl of a bear. The disguise was perfect but it *was a* disguise.

This however did nothing to answer the two big questions. How did The Bear know him? And who was in that disguise? Well, he wasn't going to be long finding out. "Whoever *you* are," Steel said, "I'm giving you five seconds to get out of there." He raised the pistol a fraction of an inch, years of police training, perfect aim from the hip.

Then suddenly—insanely—the powerful Mike Doyle was diving toward him.

Two thoughts flashed in Steel's head as he saw him coming—Mike had picked up a mighty strange loyalty lately to risk his life for his boss—and, Steel knew he couldn't shoot. It would bring the whole gang here instantly.

He jumped aside. He smashed Mike across the head with his pistol. Mike sprawled and slid across the stage, to lay still.

Steel whirled back to The Bear. "Are you getting out of there or not?"

There was no answer for a moment. Then The Bear's voice was a deep whisper. "When I do, Mr. Steel, you're going to be in for a mighty big surprise. . . ."

"Get out of there!" Steel was in no mood for games.

Deep in the matted hair of The Bear's chest, a small door started opening, slowly, mechanically. The whole thing was mechanical, arms, legs, head, everything operated electrically. The door—

The door was the last thing Steel remembered.

A slamming blow. The back of his head. Then blackness . . .

III

WHEN THE BLACKNESS VANished, as suddenly as it had come, Steel didn't open his eyes at first, figuring out what had happened. Mike had obviously came to and crept up behind him. Rabbit punch—Mike was a master at that.

When he got this figured out, he started to work on what to do about it. He lay there motionless, listening. Then he realized he wasn't lying on the stage floor. He was lying on a bed of some kind. Somewhere in the distance, he heard the muffled crackling of a video transmitter. They'd moved him! How long had he been out! His eyes snapped open.

"Well!" a familiar voice said. "Sleeping beauty awakes!" It was the tall thin-lipped fellow, his original captor. He stood beside the bunk on which Steel found himself lying. Across the fellow's thin cheek now was a taped bandage, the result of Steel's helmet-wielding. "I guess its time you knew my name," he said. "It's Dirk." And as he introduced himself, his right fist arced across the bunk, contacted Steel's jaw like a spark-gap and Steel's blackness returned once more . . .

This time however the blackness vanished in a deluge of ice water. Steel sat up on the bunk sputtering, shaking his head dazedly.

Dirk threw the empty bucket in the corner and stood before him, hands on his narrow hips. "If I didn't have orders to take it easy, I'd drown you."

Steel glared up at him. He had to get a few things straight before he stuck his neck out again. He turned from the guy in disgust and glanced about the room.

He was in a small, high-ceilinged place with one door, barred like a cell. The room seemed to be located deep in the cellar region of The Bear's fortress. Across the dim corridor outside, he saw huge boxes and bales stacked against the wall. On the corridor floor, a heavy freight belt creaked sluggishly past the door. Why, this was the same place where he'd been before, at the bottom of the main shaft where he'd left Dirk behind a packing case.

The video transmitter's crackling came from one of the lower rooms on the shaft. It sounded like a long distance set, one used for interplanetary work. It hadn't been operating when he'd passed before. If he'd only known it was there then! A message to Stahl, the coordinates of this place. . . . He looked back to Dirk. "And what happens next?"

"That's for The Bear to decide. When they found me and brought me to, I just came back to even the score." His thin lips grinned.

Steel looked away again. Who was The Bear? Who was The Bear? The question started beating in his head like a drum. His fingers tightened on the metal frame of the bunk. Just when he had him, just when he was about to find out! He swore to himself that if he got another chance, he certainly wouldn't waste time talking.

Then, suddenly, the chance was there.

The Bear stood at the door, horrid face bent down, eyes glowing through the bars. The mechanical voice rumbled, "What does he have to say, Dirk?"

Dirk eyed Steel with evident anticipation. "Want me to go to work on him?" He took out his pistol—the one Steel had taken away from him before, but with the safety *off* now. He walked over and leveled it in Steel's face. "Okay," he said, "we know you're working for Hampton Stahl. Does Stahl suspect this place is near the Jersey Ruins?"

"Certainly," Steel said, ignoring the gun in his face, but meeting Dirk's eyes. "And Stahl's going to have the police around here combing every ruin if I'm not back before sundown." If it were only true . . .

The Bear told Dirk to unlock the door. Dirk unlocked it and the creature ambled in, stooping under the ceiling. Dirk locked the door again.

"And what made you think this was the place to look?" The Bear rumbled.

Okay, get ready. Anytime now. The old business . . . "Well," Steel said, bringing his legs in under him, leaning forward slightly on the bunk, "you ought to know a lot about those little visiting cards of yours." He pointed toward The Bear's own claws. "Take a look at those fake claws of yours there . . ."

The Bear glanced down. Dirk also glanced at The Bear's paws.

Steel sprang at Dirk.

He got his hand on the pistol. At the same time, his knee got in Dirk's belly. His other hand slammed Dirk back against the wall. Good, old-fashioned police work. He snatched the pistol from Dirk's hand and brought it up into Dirk's jaw like a set of brass knuckles.

Then Steel didn't even wait to watch Dirk fall. As he turned from him, he got the pistol right in his hand and fired.

His first shot blasted The Bear's mechanical right arm off. The next one got a leg. The next one got the other leg as the thing toppled over.

As it crashed to the floor, Steel jumped back into a corner of the room, gun on the weird scene on the floor.

Dirk was out cold again. The Bear was a mess. Springs, wires, stuffing, braces, it floundered there a moment till its motors short-circuited. Then inside the great mass of white hair there was a frantic scratching sound.

"Come out of there," Steel said between his teeth.

THE DOOR in the bear chest was pushed open. There was coughing like somebody coming out of a stifling closet.

Then Steel's hand went limp on the pistol.

A cascade of golden hair tumbled out upon the shaggy bear skin. Steel stared into the furious green eyes of *Lois Harmon.*

Steel couldn't have been more astonished if his own grandmother had crawled out of the bear skin.

He couldn't believe it at first. He shook his head savagely. Then the girl got to her feet, shook her bright hair out of her eyes and stood there with her hands on her trim hips, glaring at him. Smooth as a pedigreed cat, even in a pair of dingy coveralls.

"It took us six months to build that electric bear!" Her eyes sparked green fire. "You—you—" Words seemed inadequate. She stepped over and swung at Steel a baby haymaker.

Steel ducked and caught her hand. And the exertion jarred his brain back to work like a stopped watch. "Listen, you lynx-eyed hussy!" He twisted her arm behind her back and drew her to him, twisting till her struggling stopped. "If I hadn't seen you get out of that bear-skin, I wouldn't have believed it. But, if you're The Bear, you're a cold-blooded murderer! I'd **just** as soon shoot you down as not. In fact I'd rather. I—" Then he heard the racket behind him. He whirled around, jerking the girl around between him and the door.

Over her shoulder, he saw a score of men run up and halt at the cell door. They'd heard the shots of course. They took in the situation instantly. Rifles and pistols leveled on him like a firing squad.

Steel, however, had the girl between him and the guns. He put his own pistol against the girl's back. "Careful," he said, eyes on the men outside, "I can get her before you can get me." He'd never used a woman as a shield before, but to him this yellow-haired witch wasn't even a woman. She was a killer. He was a cop. If he could hold this advantage, force his way out of here with her . . .

The girl held perfectly still, facing her gang. "Range about ten feet," she said quietly. And there was something in her almost bored tone, Steel didn't like.

"No tricks," he said, eyes fixed on the trigger fingers outside. He tried to get as much of himself behind her as possible, a difficult thing, however, hiding his shoulders behind not too much woman. "I mean business."

"So do we," the girl said to him over her shoulder.

As she spoke, Steel heard an angry buzzing sound, like a rattlesnake's warning. But there was nothing he could do about such a warning. Instantly, the pistol he was pressing against the girl's back was snatched from his hand.

Steel was too astonished to move. The pistol flew up toward the ceiling, halted, and then moved across the room through the bars of the door. There was nothing holding it up. It moved the way the ice balls had moved outside. Standing there with his empty hand at the girl's back, Steel stared at the gun till it was grabbed from the air by one of the men outside. Then the gang was swarming through the door.

Steel shook his head like a fighter struggling up after the ninth count. The things that happened in this place were beyond reason. How could you fight anything in a place like this! Then the girl had jerked away from him, the mob was upon him, and he was lying on the floor fighting blindly.

In a moment however it was all over. There were too many of them.

"That's enough! Get him on his feet!"

It was the girl's voice. Dazed and beaten, Steel was yanked up, somebody holding both arms and an elbow hooked around his neck.

"We've wasted enough time on you now," Lois Harmon said. She stood in front of him, eyes blazing. "But—it might interest you to know that everything you've tried to do here hasn't amounted to a damn thing! You'll have company here shortly. We're kidnapping your fat boss tonight. We're going to bring Hampton Stahl here and hold him for a cool million ransom—enough to bankrupt Vita-Heat completely . . ."

She turned and stalked from the room, leaving Steel staring after her, the full meaning of her words creeping over him like a chill.

Stahl's ransom—Vita-Heat's bankruptcy! If that happened, the upper levels wouldn't even benefit by that insurance policy . . .

THEY gathered up the wrecked mechanical bear. They carried out Dirk who again had slept through the whole proceedings. They left, locking the cell door behind them. Steel sat on the bunk, watched them step on the belt and disappear up the shaft.

Lois Harmon. Why, she'd been a plant right under his nose when that Radium Bank was held up while he was in the building! For years, she'd been using her innocent-looking beauty and social position to discover the choicest jobs for her gang.

It all boiled down to this—she was The Bear. The Bear had the most terrible record in police annals. And with the unbelievable equipment and advanced science she had amassed here, not only New York but the whole world was threatened. Those inexplicable balls of ice, the mechanical bear, the magic that had snatched that pistol out of his hand—those laboratories and workshops along the shaft seemed capable of anything. Producing suffo-gas was probably a minor task to them.

And—his own motive for coming here, the reward for the upper levels, that would be canceled entirely by Stahl's kidnapping tonight. The pledge he'd made over his dead friend's body couldn't be kept . . .

Up the shaft, Steel heard the video transmitter start crackling again. If he could only get to that thing! Stahl's man was still waiting; if he could only get a message to him!

Steel got up, slamming a heavy fist into his hand. He went over to the door and grasped the bars, testing their strength. They were solid, thick as his wrist. The door wouldn't even rattle. He surveyed the room again. Collapsible bunk, empty bucket, bare walls.

Since The Bear had run riot during the last few years, how many men had she killed? Bank guards, watchmen, company executives, and Jim, Dick, Harlan, Bill—he'd known those cops well. And the reprisals against their families—not one body ever found. It was inconceivable that such horror had stained Lois Harmon's hands. He thought of those hands—strong, artistic, neatly manicured. But it wasn't nail polish that tipped those pretty fingers. It was blood.

Steel sat down heavily on the bunk again. It swayed and threatened to fold up under him and he got up again to kick its slab-metal headboard back into place. Even the State Prison gave its condemned men a decent bunk! He sat down, staring through the barred door at the freight belt that slid slowly, monotonously along the corridor outside. Probably stolen from some warehouse, it was a yard-wide belt of heavy plates none too closely joined together. It creaked mournfully, incessantly. How could he think with that racket going on! He wondered if he could stop it—poke something through the door—wedge it between the plates . . .

Suddenly this idle thought was a spark that touched off a TNT idea.

He sprang to the door and looked out. As far as he could see up the shaft, nobody was in sight. There was no sound but the belt's creaking.

He ran back to the bed. Quickly, he yanked the removable headboard off the frame and then took the footboard off. He lugged the bed frame over to the door.

Still nobody was in sight. He stared at the belt outside, excitement burning in his eyes. If it only worked! He lifted the bed frame, stuck it through the door's bars and held it poised a moment over the moving freight belt. Then, just at the right mo-

ment, as a space between two of the plates passed, he shoved it home.

He jumped back. Something had to give —belt, bed or door. He barely breathed. The belt slowed. What if it stopped? But it didn't stop. It slowed, but still moved inexorably on. What if the frame bent? But it didn't bend. Its tough metal twisted between the bars, wedging itself more tightly. Then inch by screeching inch, the bars in the door bent.

With a sound like a pistol shot, one snapped.

Steel shot toward the door like a loosened spring. He squeezed between the bars and jumped out on the belt. Then he was running up the belt, ignoring its snail's pace, racing up the shaft toward that video room.

In seconds, he was at the door. He halted, paused there, listening.

"Any contact yet?"

"Not yet . . ."

Two different voices—there were at least two men in the room. How many more? But he couldn't risk waiting to find out. Any moment somebody might appear on the shaft. He threw open the door and stepped in quickly, ready to tear his way to that video transmitter.

The room was dark, with only a small light in one corner, the glow of a video screen. In front of it were silhouetted two heads. One had close-cropped hair; the other wore a skull cap. Chairs pulled up close to the video, they were so engrossed in their work they didn't even turn around.

"Shhh!" said the black skull cap.

"We're about to make contact, Mike," said the short haircut.

Steel stood motionless in the darkness. They thought he was Mike, the boxer! And there were only two men in the room. Marvelous! Just walk up behind them and bang their heads together. He stepped silently forward.

He was within arm's reach of the two shadowed figures when the video screen's light suddenly flared. He halted.

"Here she is!" The skull cap bent low over the panel under the screen. Dim-lit hands played the video's controls like a piano.

Slowly fading in on the screen, Steel saw the familiar green sphere that was Venus. The picture was swelling in from a video camera on a space ship somewhere close in the Venusian sector. The picture was closing up, each ice peak gleaming. Behind the planet was a blurred background of white lines—he couldn't figure out what they were. And they certainly didn't matter now. His hands started out for those two necks in front of him.

Then the video screen stopped him again. Stopped him cold this time. He stared at the screen incredulously.

The distant camera had turned from the green planet, turning in from the space ship's window through which it had been shooting, and had focussed upon the cameraman. It was Dirk. Dirk—tall and thin-lipped, with bandages on his face—Dirk, *that* far out in space when not twenty minutes ago he'd been with Steel in that cell below.

How had he gotten out there? How could any space ship have gotten him to Venus that fast?

The other watchers in the room seemed to take it for granted, however. "How'd it go?" the fellow with the skull cap asked.

"No trouble at all,' Dirk said from the screen. "Having trouble with this headache of mine though." He grinned faintly through his bandages. "Second one that guy's given me today. I must be slipping."

"Well, come on in and have a drink," the short-haired one said. "Looks like you did a good job on Venus anyhow."

Steel was so bewildered he completely forget that video worked both ways. If he could see Dirk, Dirk could see him. This didn't occur to him till Dirk's grin faded abruptly and he squinted into the room's darkness from the screen.

"Hey!" Dirk yelled. "Who's that behind you—!" Then, as the two heads before Steel twisted around, "Look out! It's Steel! He's loose again!"

Steel went into action. His fist drove into the face nearest him—the short-haired one's. He knocked him over into the video with a punch that would have knocked out a horse. His left hand caught the other man's collar. His fist started in again.

But this was a blow that never landed.

STEEL'S arm froze in mid-swing. He stared at the face above the collar he was holding as if he'd caught a ghost.

He had.

He was staring into the bespectacled eyes of a man who was supposed to have been dead fifteen long years—Hampton Stahl's dead partner, Lois Harmon's dead father—*Dr. Albert Harmon . . .*

Steel stood there holding Dr. Harmon's collar, fist poised, for a long crazy moment. The skull cap had fallen off, revealing the scientist's shaggy white hair. From his lined face, his gray eyes looked up at Steel, troubled but without fear.

"Well?" he said, as if the next move were entirely up to Steel. His voice was remarkably clear for a man of his age.

"Dr. Harmon . . ." Steel turned him loose and lowered his hand. "Maybe you'd better explain a few things, Doctor," he said shakily.

Instead of explaining, however, the old man shot a hand toward the video table—toward an alarm button.

Steel saw it just in time. He caught the hand and shoved the old man back into his chair. Then he scooped the volt gun from the other man's holster. "Dr. Harmon," he said, "finding you here when you're supposed to have been dead fifteen years explains a lot about this place. The police are going to be mighty interested." Moving around where he could keep his eye on the door as well as on the old man, he reached out and switched the video into the Earth frequency band. Dirk's face had already disappeared. "The police'll be here in about one hour," Steel said.

He twirled a dial to the frequency he'd arranged with Stahl's listener at the Vita-Heat Building. It was hard to believe that a man who had been so well loved as Dr. Harmon could have traded his reputation for a criminal career—but here he was. Obviously, he'd faked his own death and hidden here ever since—another brilliant mind that had followed pure science too far.

A sleepy-eyed guard's face appeared on the video screen. "Get this message to Stahl quick!" Steel told him. "Tell him The Bear is his chum Lois Harmon. Tell him her old man, Dr. Harmon, isn't dead —he's *here!*"

"Wait!" Dr. Harmon jumped up. There was real fear in his eyes now. "You mustn't do that!"

" Hate your ex-partner to be the first to know?" Steel shoved him back in his seat. "And write this down," he told the guard. "Coordinates X-26.9-18.7!" He repeated them as the guard, excited now, raced with his pencil. "Tell Stahl to get the police up here quick!"

On the screen, the guard's eyes were popping. Steel switched the video off. The face faded away. "Now," he told the old man, "I guess that not only gums up your plans to kidnap Hampton Stahl tonight but gums up all of your plans for a long time to come."

"I'm not so sure about that, Mr. Steel."

At the same instant Steel heard these words, he heard an angry buzzing noise. The pistol in his hand was snatched away.

He whirled to see a hidden panel open in the wall opposite. In the door stood Lois Harmon. In her hand was the same queer kind of gun that had taken the pistol away from him in the cell. An ordinary volt rifle with tiny electrotubes lining the barrel. Behind the girl, a small army of men filled the passage.

"You're a very bothersome person, Mr. Steel," she said. "We should quit using a magnoray on you—a volt gun would be better."

Steel stood there holding his numb hand with ice in his heart. The girl stepped into the room, the men moving in behind her. Then to Steel's stark staring confusion, he saw that the thin-faced Dirk led them. Somehow, Dirk had come back from Venus—in *four minutes.*

"Surprised to see me back so soon?" Dirk caught the look on his face. He laughed. "You didn't know I could get back from Venus even faster than I could radio a warning back, did you? That's why nobody ever sees us come and go from here, Flatfoot. We come and go too fast for anybody to see us. Maybe when you learn more about this outfit, you'll quit trying to buck it. Let me take care of him," he told the girl. "Our score's gotten a little uneven again."

"No," she said. "You better take a group up to hold off the police, Dirk. Just in case they get here before we can get underway."

Dirk frowned and then said, "Okay." Glumly, he led some of the men toward the shaft.

The girl motioned for one of the others to take Steel. "Bring him along with us. Come on, Dad." She took her father's arm.

"We've got one hour to make our getaway."

Steel's appointed guardian, built like a bear with the hair shaved off, took his arm, twisted it behind him and dug a thumb into his elbow—torturous stop-and-go button. Another had finally brought the short-haired victim of Steel's punch back on duty. They all followed the Harmon family through the panel and down a long passageway.

IV

STEEL WAS ABOUT READY TO give up. He knew he wouldn't be even faintly surprised at anything else that happened here. He clung to one thought, a praying hope that the police could get here before whatever getaway the gang planned. But, with the crushing ice balls and those weapon-snatchers, Dirk could hold the police off indefinitely, and with this super-speed the gang apparently had at their disposal—the speed that could get Dirk back and forth from Venus in a matter of seconds—they'd be gone long before the police got started.

Steel was so deep in these thoughts, he barely considered what his own fate might be . . .

The passage ended in a place that made New York's central power plant look like a child's play room. Fifty-foot generators towered in the center of the huge room and along the walls were banks of vacuum tubes flashing like fireworks. The group halted before a master switch panel that equalled the Terminal's dispatch board.

"Check the coils, Tom. Get at those insulator switches, Joe." Dr. Harmon quickly assumed command here. "Lois and I'll finish keying in the main control group." Along the rows of tubes and moving in and out of the generator housings, Steel saw other scores of workers, busy as ants at whatever devil's work this was.

The heavy-muscled guard delegated to remain with Steel took it all with a yawn, however, leaning against a battery case and eyeing Steel sleepily. And this was what made Steel want to tear his hair—the utter confidence of everyone here. The fact that the police were on the way seemed to bother them only slightly. They seemed quite convinced they had here the power of a science that need fear nothing the whole world might send against them.

"I suppose you're making your getaway with some sort of electric expulsion system," Steel said finally. From combustion power to jet propulsion—it was just one step further to the ultimate speeds of some expulsion system. There had always been a basic flaw in vehicles having to carry their own means of power. "What bothers me though is where the hell you think you're going." To leave the earth was simple. To have to stay away, forever, in the molten cold or venomous atmosphere of one of the other planets—that should be no happy prospect for any fugitive.

"Where we're going?" Steel's guard laughed quickly. "Buddy, that's something you'll be mighty interested in if Miss Harmon has a mind to tell you about it." And Steel saw the girl walking toward them, wiping a smudge of grease from her cheek. "He wants to know where we're going," the guard grinned as she came up.

She also laughed, a tinkling laugh that Steel hated more because he would have liked it if she hadn't been who and what she was. "Bring him along," she told the guard. "Everything seems to be running smoothly. We'll take a moment off to show him around."

The big fellow gave Steel a shove and followed him and the girl past the generators toward the far end of the room. When they got there, Steel saw there wasn't any wall at the room's end. The room ended abruptly at a two hundred foot drop.

The exit here was only a hole in the wall of a vast cavern, big as a city block. The place had been hollowed out of the earth's ice crust. Its slick green walls glistened brightly under thousands of heat arcs that melted, dried, held back the constantly encroaching cold. On the floor of the cavern, Steel saw what appeared to be a monster space ship, a smooth egg-like thing with a small platform on top. So this was what they planned to escape in! Pile in, melt the ice lid off the cavern, take off! He didn't see *them* at first—they were the same color as the frozen floor. Then he caught sight of the restlessly moving creatures around the ship.

The cavern's floor was alive with icebears, thousands of them, gigantic males, grizzly females, pink-clawed cubs, a living

moat around the precious ship. Not only had *The* Bear chained science to her grim purpose. Here were nature's cruelest watchdogs on guard.

"Okay," Steel said at last. "So I'm impressed. Now will you tell me where you plan to *go* in that ship?"

"Ship?" The girl's smile grew perplexed. "What ship?"

Steel motioned toward the egg-shaped thing below. "That. That's the space ship you plan to get away in, isn't it?"

The girl burst out laughing. Her laughter echoed out across the cavern, tinkling mirth in a place that Hell couldn't have rivaled in Steel's eyes. "Well," she said finally, "you might call it something we plan to escape with. That object is an antigrav projector, Mr. Steel. We'll escape with it all right, but we're going to take the Earth along with us . . ."

During his career as a detective, Steel had heard doomed convicts call the Devil's curse upon mankind; he'd heard dope-crazed crones in the upper levels shriek the curse of witches upon their neighbors; he'd heard cornered gangsters swear dark vengeance—but he'd never before heard words of such raw horror. And the girl said them as a simple statement of fact—with a laugh.

"We're going to take the Earth along with us . . ." This could have been just an insane threat. Cornered, the gang was trying to destroy the world in its own suicide. But Steel had seen the gang's ultra science here, he'd seen their banks of electrotubes —they weren't up to anything as simple as destroying the world by suffo-gas. He couldn't miss the real meaning of Lois Harmon's words. Taking the Earth with *them* meant *moving* it.

Which was still madness! Still suicide! But they didn't think so. They were right now making frantic preparations.

"You see," the girl continued, "we've been experimenting exclusively with gravitational force—the forces of attraction and repulsion that not only hold the atom together but hold the planets of the Solar System in balance." Her smile taunted Steel. "Dad finally devised an ultra-wave screen that could be projected. This screen surrounds the object toward which it's projected, shields off all the gravitational forces acting upon it and allows us to play upon it only those forces we care to use in moving the object from one place to another. You saw how we encircled you with those ice balls when you first came snooping around. You saw how we snatched a pistol out of your hand. In a few minutes, you'll see how we snatch the Earth out of the Solar System."

In a few minutes . . . The girl's face blurred before Steel's eyes. Her words came to him faintly. "But I don't know why I'm telling you all this. You came here, working for Hampton Stahl's filthy money." Then raving fury blinded Steel completely.

He whirled. Ran.

He streaked back into the control room. The first weapon he saw was a wrench. He grabbed it on the run. He sped down the line of electrotubes along the wall, smashing them as fast as he could swing his arm.

Vaguely, he heard the girl's scream behind him. He heard his guard's heavy feet pounding after him. Before him, he saw the horde of workers halt, then swarm toward him. But he kept slashing with his wrench, eyes squinting against the flying glass, smashing his way up the line of tubes toward the main control board. When the wrench was snatched away, he kept tearing at the tubes with his bare hands.

Then he was crushed down by the hundreds of fists and feet that flew at him from every side.

WHEN he was jerked back on his feet, the first thing he saw was Lois Harmon's face. Her face was streaked with tears. Tears of sheer hatred glistened in her green eyes. Her lips parted, trembling, but she couldn't speak. Her tiny fist lashed out, smacking Steel in the face.

She kept pummeling him till somebody pulled her back, fearful apparently that she might hurt her hands on him. Nobody seemed at all concerned whether Steel was hurt or not. Quite on the contrary.

"So you're still after Stahl's reward, huh?" Mike, the ex-boxer, swam toward Steel's blood-filled eyes; he started whipping Steel back and forth across the face with his open hand. A hand as heavy as a sand bag. "When they took me into this crew it was the first decent thing anybody'd ever done for me! They're the first decent folks this damn world's seen in ten thous-

and years! And you try to stop what they're doing!"

"Give him hell, Mike! The voice came to Steel as from a great distance. But there was something about it . . . He recognized it. When Mike's hand paused, he twisted his head around to look at the man who had spoken.

"No!" He tried to blink the blood out of his eyes. The man was Harlan Webb. Harlan Webb, one of those five cops who'd gone after The Bear and never come back! "Harlan!"

"Sure," the man said. "I'm Harlan Webb. We used to be cops together. But we're on different sides now, Steel."

"But I thought The Bear—"

"Sure, that's what we wanted everybody to think about us—Jim, Dick, Bill, the other cops who disappeared, they're up there with Dirk guarding the entrance now. That's what we wanted everybody to think happened to our families when they were brought here too. That's the only way Dr. Harmon could keep what he was doing secret."

"You mean The Bear didn't—"

"Didn't kill them? Is that what you mean!" This was Lois Harmon again. "We didn't kill *you*, did we—when we certainly should have." She pointed about the room. "There's the vice-president of Uranium, Inc. He's been an engineer with us ever since he 'disappeared'. There's the crew and passengers of that space liner that lost its cargo last night." She shook her head furiously. "Our men have killed only as the last possible resort. That rule has been as important as our secret."

"Hush! Hush!" This was Dr. Harmon, holding up his hands, finally making himself heard. His eyes were grim behind his spectacles. "We haven't time for this now! This man has wrecked our remote control up here but we can still operate from the projector itself." He brushed his shaggy white hair from his eyes. "We must hurry before the police get here."

"*But, my long departed friend, the police aren't coming . . .*"

Every eye turned from Steel to the door leading in from the passage. Steel craned to stare over the shoulders of the men who held him.

That great shadow in the doorway was the bulk of Hampton Stahl.

"I thought I had finished with your interference for good, Dr. Harmon, when I arranged that little laboratory explosion fifteen years ago," Stahl said. "I see now, however, that I'll have to destroy you and your work all over again."

Swiftly, when the shock of his appearance died, the men around Steel surged toward Stahl in one mass. And, just as swiftly, when they came at him, Stahl stepped aside, into the room, and twenty of his guards pushed through the door.

They carried volt rifles. Stahl waved his fat hand.

The guards fired straight into the unarmed group coming at them, mowing them down like insects. When the rifles lowered again, a full hundred charred forms writhed on the floor, then quickly lay still. Mike, Harlan Webb, the rest . . .

"After they've shown us around," Stahl said when the volt rifle reverberations died, "you can do away with all the rest of them." Then his thick lips twisted into a smile. "Including Mr. Steel there. It will relieve me of an embarrassing contract."

At Stahl's words now, Steel realized he was standing there alone. Most of the men who had surrounded him had left to go for Stahl. Most of these were now lying in black heaps on the floor. The rest stood among the charred bodies, staring helplessly as Stahl's guards advanced across the room, ready for the slightest excuse to use their rifles again. The terrible silence of their advance was broken only when Lois Harmon sobbed, buried her golden head in her father's arms.

STEEL stood there alone, realizing just how much alone he was. He'd thrown a wrench into the Harmon gang's plans, for which they'd been in the act of doing away with him. Then his rescuers—whom he'd called here himself—had turned out to be an equal menace, bringing the same fate that they'd saved him from. He'd jumped out of The Bear's frying pan into the shortly forthcoming fire of Stahl's volt rifles . . .

"When I received your message and learned who The Bear was," the fat man smiled, halting before Steel, "I preferred not to bother the police with what was really a private matter between Dr. Harmon and myself."

"Private matter!" Dr. Harmon's cold eyes were frightening behind his spectacles. One hand soothed his daughter's head but the other was knotted, white-knuckled at his side. "Yes, you always did look upon my experiments as a private matter. You didn't care whether they benefited mankind or not—if they interfered with your vita-lamp profits, you tried to crush them."

"And crush them I shall," Stahl replied easily, turning to the old man. "When we sighted the coordinate location Mr. Steel so kindly sent us, we blasted the whole area immediately. We blasted the entrance to your hideout before your men had time to use any trick weapons you've developed." Which had been the end of Dirk and the men who'd been up there with him, Steel thought. "At this moment," Stahl continued, waving toward the door through which he'd entered, "others of my guards are searing every room in the place. When we leave here there won't be the slightest sign that this place ever existed. The world will continue to think Dr. Harmon died fifteen years ago."

The guards herded the remaining few of Dr. Harmon's men into a corner.

"Now," the fat man told Dr. Harmon, "if you'll kindly lead us on a little tour of your power plant here, you'll have exactly that much longer to live."

The old man hesitated a moment. Then he lifted his white head, took his daughter's hand and moved slowly ahead past the generator houses. One of the guards shoved Steel after them and the procession started down the long room.

"On the way here," Stahl said chattily to the old man and the girl, "we received a telenews report that a freight liner had just discovered something rather startling in the Venusian space sector. Earth scientists are in a dither." He laughed. "The planet Venus seems to have disappeared . . ."

Steel's eyes widened. He recalled Dr. Harmon's and Dirk's mysterious doings in the video room.

"Perhaps you can explain what happened, Doctor," Stahl said.

"If you wish," the old man answered finally. He walked straight ahead, chin high, voice mechanical and cold. "Venus was in the way of Earth's planned trajectory from the Solar System. We simply moved it—as we've been moving smaller asteroids farther out in space for months. Venus was the last object that had to be cleared from Earth's path to Sun K-16."

"So that's where you planned to take it," Stahl said with some surprise. He laughed. "Who was it that said 'Give me a lever and I'll move the Earth'? So you found it! And I'm quite sure you could have accomplished it without mishap too, Doctor. If you remember, I worked out the preliminary planning with you myself."

"Until you realized what would happen to your vita-lamp monopoly if the Earth had a warm sun again!"

Stahl laughed again, agreeably. Steel however could barely keep his mouth from hanging open. He didn't know what to believe any more. Those blurred white lines behind Venus' picture on the video screen —had they been star trails? A background that Venus was moving past so fast even the video camera's ultra speed couldn't catch it? Was it possible Venus *had* been moved and that the Earth could *have* been moved? These men talked about moving planets as if they'd been moving a house on log rollers. Steel was bewildered.

"Well," Stahl said, "now I'll have your formula for the projector and vita-lamps will become only a sideline. I'll move another planet to Sun K-16—Jupiter, perhaps. When I move it to a livable climate its real estate prices will be something unimaginable. I suppose you applied the principle to space ships long ago."

"They were our first experiments," Dr. Harmon told him. "We have a small fleet in stalls near the surface. We found our only problem was keeping their speed down—to keep them from burning by air friction in taking off and landing." For some reason now as they went down the room, Dr. Harmon went into greater detail in explaining whatever questions Stahl put to him. He was fighting for time, Steel decided, hoping that *something* would happen, anything. Steel also decided it was high time he started hoping that too. He was in for the killing now himself.

When explanations had finished they had reached the end of the room and now stopped at the brink of the vast bear-pit. "And here it is," Dr. Harmon said wearily. "The projector."

THE immensity of the place, the terrible creatures staring up at them, the mysterious machine majestically alone down there—all combined to silence even Stahl a moment. His guards crowded forward, exclaiming to each other and staring into the pit. They did not, however, let their curiosity distract the vigilance of their rifles. The guns remained snug against their prisoners' backs.

"And how did you get the manpower to build all this?" the fat man finally turned back to Dr. Harmon.

"They were easy to find," the old man said simply. He seemed to stare through Stahl—perhaps at the years he had put into this work and its miserable failure. "We found followers everywhere — our workers came from the slums of every city on Earth as well as from the highest society. Most of those we were forced to capture also eventually volunteered to work with us. Those who didn't volunteer we kept in very comfortable quarters, knowing that they—and the world—would be free very soon. We even brought proverty-stricken children here. Helping us gave them their only chance for education." Steel remembered his first sight of The Bear in that auditorium crowded with tenement kids. "The Bear idea was only an advertising trick my daughter thought of," Dr. Harmon said. "It awed the common man and terrified — *you*." His eyes snapped back into focus on Stahl's face.

"And now it's all turned out to my profit," Stahl said. "So suppose we go down and have a look at the projector. You have a way of getting down there, certainly."

Steel found himself also wondering how they *could* get down there. He looked upon it with little surprise however, only one more breath-taking gadget, when Dr. Harmon pressed a button on the nearby wall and a low-railed platform shot up from the top of the machine below. It halted at their feet. Where it had been on the machine below, there was now an open port with a circular stair leading inside, discernable in the distance.

"Very tricky," Stahl said. "But just to make sure this lift doesn't suffer any mishap on the way down, Doctor, I think you better stay up here and operate it while your daughter goes down with me."

Steel's eyes were on the girl's face as she looked at her father. Then she quickly rushed into his arms. The sight made Steel wince. The old man stroked her golden hair and whispered in her ear. Steel started to turn away. Then something flashed, the slightest glint in that icy place where the very walls glinted—he caught a glimpse of what it was, then instantly turned away, afraid somebody else might have seen.

He searched the guards' faces around him and Stahl's face, but they hadn't seen. They hadn't seen Dr. Harmon quickly slip a knife in his daughter's hand.

Steel recognized it for what it was, a thing common in police circles, a tiny knife, small enough to hide in one hand. When a button was pressed on its side a six-inch blade licked out like a watch spring uncoiling.

"The rest of you men stay up here with the good doctor," Stahl said. "Hans, you and Barge come down with me and our lovely guide." The fat man stepped out on the disk-like lift. He caught the girl's arm and jerked her after him.

In the next three seconds, the guards stepped on the lift with them—and Steel remembered the pledge that had brought him here, Floyd lying there dead, the dreary upper levels around that deserted building.

Stahl said, "Okay, let us down, Doctor" —and Steel remembered the confidence that even Dr. Harmon's deadly enemy, Stahl, had had in the Earth-moving venture's safety. Floyd too, working for The Bear, had believed in it enough to die for it. It was the one chance to bring warmth to the Earth again, banish completely such things as the upper levels!

Dr. Harmon pressed the button and the lift started down—and Steel remembered the unwavering courage in Lois Harmon's eyes when her father had slipped her that knife.

In those three seconds, everything that had happened flashed through Steel's mind, and everything that *could* happen. In those three seconds he decided what he *wanted* to happen.

He jumped.

THE LIFT was moving down swiftly. It was going down just a trifle slower than Steel fell. There was little jolt when he landed.

He knocked one of the guards' rifles sailing immediately. The other whirled upon him, rifle raised. But the platform was too small for a rifle. It worked to the guard's disadvantage. Steel grabbed the barrel. A lever. With it, he wrenched the fellow over the side.

He caught of glimpse of Lois Harmon clinging to the hand rail, one hand at her trembling lips, her green eyes huge. Then Stahl's bulk loomed before him and the other guard came in behind him, while from above a volt gun spurted its molten stream past his head.

The guard got his elbow around Steel's neck. Stahl raised both huge hands and brought them down at his face like twin sledge hammers. Steel dropped his weight in the guard's arms, twisted his head, caught Stahl's blow on his shoulder. Then the arm around his neck was blinding him, cutting off his air. A red film swam before his eyes. His ears roared. He felt Stahl's blows numbly against his face. Going down. Going down.

It was more instinct than anything else that made him grip the guard's shirt behind him. It was many a police lesson in roughhouse that doubled Steel forward and arched his back, while he jerked at the guard's shirt with his last strength. He yanked the guard off his feet and flung him up and out over the railing.

When the guard's scream died away, Steel found himself on the floor of the platform, Stahl on top of him, thick fingers grappling for his throat. The platform had stopped falling. It rested at the bottom of the cavern.

"I'll get him! I'll get him!" screamed Lois, leaping toward Stahl, deadly little knife upraised.

Steel fished his legs around and kicked her back against the railing. "No!" he yelled. "Get the projector working!" Dr. Harmon had said: *We can still operate from the projector itself* . . .

The girl turned and fled down the circular stairs, to disappear inside the vast machine.

But Stahl found his opening. He got a grip on Steel's right arm, twisted it behind him and then twisted it back like a bending stick. Steel rolled to keep it from breaking. And found himself staring over the platform's edge into a writhing sea of shaggy hair, upturned blazing eyes, dripping jaws—the bears—ten feet below.

Stahl strained at his arm, shoving with his knees, breath heavy in Steel's ear. Steel's right leg slid over the edge.

Although they couldn't shoot for fear of hitting Stahl now, the sound of gunfire continued from above. It was the requiem for those who remained of the Harmon gang, Steel thought wildly—and for Dr. Harmon.

Steel tried to get a grip on the railing post. The fat man scraped his fingers away. He clawed at the platform floor. But he couldn't stop his sliding. He cursed and prayed and tried to cling to the floor by the sheer friction of his body. Stahl was shoving too hard. Steel's body slid over the side, one last arm hooked in the railing.

The fat man struggled up and kicked at the arm. Then, more than the kick on his arm, Steel felt a sickening shudder pulse through his body—through the platform— through the world . . . .

Stahl felt it, too. His foot hesitated in the next kick. His eyes glaring down at Steel suddenly widened.

The moment was all Steel needed. He jerked himself back up on the platform, rolled and struggled to his knees. Then he saw Stahl wasn't even playing any more. The fat man was staring up at the roof of the cavern as if he was having an apoplectic stroke. It was only then that Steel realized the blinding light in his own eyes.

He squinted up at the strange brightness and saw at the distant top of the cavern, like a huge skylight above them, a great white square, blazing with a light that no artificial fluorescence had ever approached. A light Earth had forgotten.

"The sun . . ."

Stahl's voice was a whisper. Then it sirened into a scream. "Sun K-16! They've done it! They've done it!" His eyes shot back to Steel, like a wild beast's. "But you'll never have it!" he shrieked. His hands shot out at Steel like talons.

This time Steel was prepared. His right fist came up and across Stahl's thick chin. The fat man toppled backward, tottered against the railing, and then went over.

At that moment, Lois Harmon ran up the ladder. Steel caught her and pressed her face against his chest. "Don't look."

But he looked. He saw Stahl ride for an instant on the shaggy white sea below, beat with his hands frenziedly against the mass of animals under him, and then slip down into the mass like a pig slipping into a meat grinder.

His scream was an era dying . . .

THE bright sunlight playing across the shimmering ice waste, the young rivers of melting snow—the telenews cameras ate it up.

The telenews men didn't seem to care whether they had an audience or not. They had the video cameras set up on the sun-drenched Terminal roofs, sending the picture to receiving sets that probably hadn't a single watcher throughout the world. The population of Earth had swarmed to the surface *en masse* and tears of thanksgiving mingled with the melting snow.

"Nobody seems to came that the lower levels have already filled with water," the announcer chattered hysterically into his portable mike. "Nobody seems to care *how* this thing happened. The only thing that matters is that it *did* happen—the greatest thing that *ever* happened!"

"And they'll never know how it happened," Lois Harmon said. "Dad would have wanted it that way." She and Steel sat in their plane on the Terminal roof, listening to the announcer, watching the joyful mob that stretched across the ice as far as they could see.

"Yeah," Steel said quietly, "every clue to the old world will be washed away clean. Everything will begin new." And, he thought, Floyd would also have wanted it that way. This was what he'd died for. Even the memory of that upper level chill would soon be gone." He watched a group of mothers holding their sickly white babies up to the warmth, a horde of small boys and girls whose cheeks already glowed with the strength of a new race.

"Everything new . . ." the girl repeated. She turned, green eyes meeting Steel's, then dropped her golden head against his shoulder.

Steel grinned as he put his arm around her. "Looks like I'd better hunt another job, too," he said. "I guess I'm a pretty bum detective when the world gets stolen right under my nose."

In the brief flash Ron Crag saw the man twist erect.

DUEL IN BLACK

By JOHN FOSTER WEST

In Luna's shroud-like shadows two men lay waiting for each other's move, even their guns obscured. But the dancing space-moths weren't fooled.

YOUNG RON CRAG FUSED THE edge of his claim tag to the metal vein in the quartzite rock with his heat gun, then with heavy-shod fingers he tugged at the small copper disk, but it remained firmly in place.

"That makes you owner according to law, Mr. Crag," he murmured. In the lonely, rugged reaches of Luna's north country a man had to talk to someone. "A real lode looks like. Richest uranium lode I've seen in many a Lunar June. Bring me a nice roll if some of those rotten claim jumpers don't—"

Automatically he grasped the hilt of his gun, loosening it in the holster. He sauntered toward the catatread, parked near

the southern rim of the small crater, near the mouth of the gorge.

He could see several purple, nebulous space moths fluttering around the engine of his vehicle. Crag watched them as he approached the machine; they dipped, fluttered and weaved about the catatread, many of them wrapping themselves about the warm metal of the engine and eagerly absorbing any heat present. They reminded Ron Crag more of translucent amoeba wreathing through the nothingness of space than moths, but some ancient had dubbed them moths and moths they had remained.

They ranged in size from the area of a man's hand to about three square feet. He knew two things about them; they could detect the slightest rise in temperature over a distance of fifty yards, and they did not like the intense, constant heat of the two-weeks lunar days. They apparenly disappeared into craters and fissures during the hotter part of the day, and came out after the setting of the sun.

"Good thing my suit and thermocubes are completely insulated," he muttered, "or there'd probably be about ten thousand of them wrapped around me, drinking up the heat."

He dropped his hands to the two metal blocks built on to the suit high on each hip. Those two mechanisms were almost as important as his oxygen tank. They generated the heat conducted to the material of the suit and protected him from the 153° C of the lunar nights. Of course, he could last awhile with only one of the units functioning. A man got into the habit of checking them during the long nights; his life depended on them—them and the oxygen tank, and sometimes the gun.

THE pale, turquoise disk of Earth rode low in the heavens above the serrated Alps, towering above him, illuminating the rugged fastnesses in a sort of aqua glow. Earth, now at full, lighted Luna many times brighter than a full moon had ever lighted her. But the countless thousands of shadows cast by lava stalagmites, spires, boulders and mountain peaks were pits of nothingness. Crag walked into the Stygian blackness cast by a stalagmite and disappeared as completely as though swallowed up by a dark hole in the moon's surface. He passed on through the shadow and reappeared abruptly on the other side. He himself cast a long, black shadow, more weird because it appeared to be a black pit sliding over the floor of the crater.

Instinctively Ron Crag crouched as the pencil of flame streaked past his head. He could not feel the heat through the insulated suit, but he knew it had missed him by scant inches. He wheeled and darted back into the shadow he had just quitted, his gun leaping into his hand.

He saw a burly form dart into the shadow of a massive boulder across the basin from him. He started to snap a beam at it, but held his fire; the flare would only betray his own position. He could not see the slightest shape, the slightest trace of movement in the inky blackness of the

other shadow. There was some compensation in knowing that the ambusher could not see him either. Without air to diffuse the earthlight, the shadows were sharp and distinct as thought no light existed in all the universe outside their borders.

He glanced in the direction from which his attacker had come. There in the north edge of the crater, in the mouth of the canyon, another catatread was parked. It was an old model, battered and eroded by time and hard usage. Ron Crag thought he recognized the steed; he had seen it once or twice down south, in the parking area back of the Tycho terradome. Realizing the identity of his assailant a sudden terror paralyzed him for a moment, but then it fled, leaving him trembling and angry.

"Howdy, son," a sarcastic voice drawled into the earphones of his radarphone. "You shouldn't talk to yo'self about your rich lodes, else you should be sure your radarphone is cut off, so's pore luckless critters like me couldn't overhear ye."

Crag bit his lip in anger and shame. The killer had heard his remark, got a directional fix on his position and—

"Joe Braun?" Crag grated into the transmitter in his helmet, forcing the quaver out of his voice. "Biggest, dirtiest claim jumper in all North Luna."

"Nobody ever proved a thing on me," Joe Braun guffawed.

"No! Or you'd be at the bottom of some crater," Crag retorted. "This time you've slipped."

"Think so, feller? Think you'll be reportin' this?"

Ron's flesh crept. There were few men on Luna who would match flame with this black-bearded killer. Those luckless ones who had challenged him were now piled at the bottom of various craters.

Crag stared at the black shadow protecting his adversary, gripping his gun. But he knew there would be nothing to shoot at unless Braun shot first, revealing his position. And Joe was no fool even when he faced a greenhorn from Earth. Crag was at bay here in the concealing shadow, helpless, trapped, and calling for help was out of the question. The radarphone would not carry to the nearest terradome.

The catatread! If he could make a dash for the catatread, reach it and throw a light beam into the shadows he could burn the other to a crisp with the large, swivel gun. But then a wave of despondency blacked out his thoughts. It was too far to the vehicle. Even with the lighter gravity of Luna to hold him back, his space suit was heavy and cumbersome, and he could never make it before Joe Braun would throw at least three shots in him. He would be a clay pigeon.

Suddenly he realized the hopelessness of his predicament. He could never match flame with Joe Braun. Ron Crag knew he did not have a chance in an open duel with the ruthless killer.

"What'sa matter, son, afraid?" came the taunt through his headset.

"I guess you know what the penalty is for claim jumping?" Crag snapped. "To say nothing of attempted murder?"

"Shore I do," Joe Braun laughed. "A great big posse'll hunt me down and toss me into a bottomless crater. That's what happens to claim jumpers as gets caught. And you'll get a big, fat reward, huh, sonny?"

Ron bit back his answer.

"But you named one o' the charges wrong, son," childed Joe gently. "You called it *attempted* murder." He chuckled. "That's one thing ol' Joe Braun ain't ever gonna be guilty of. Whyn't ya come outa that shadder an' get it over with?"

CRAG did not answer. He looked toward the catatread. There was not a single rock or spire between it and him to protect him. The cliffs of the Alps rose sheer and precipitous from the level of the crater floor, and for most of the distance to the vehicle the very base of the cliffs was brightly illuminated in the earthlight. But here and there a black shadow did jut out from the base of the precipice, cast by jagged peaks, eight thousand feet above the tiny basin. Those shadows formed an irregular chain of black splotches over the pumice-covered floor between Crag and the catatread.

Crag wasted no time weighing his chances. Blood beat fiercely in his temples as he tensed. He darted out into the earthlight, then retreated back into the same shadow as a livid ribbon of flame streaked by just in front of his visorport. He knew

it was excellent shooting for a hand-gun at that range. It would take Joe Braun ten seconds to recharge and readjust the gun, and in that time—

Ron Crag darted out into the earthlight again, and fled for the nearest shadow a hundred feet away. He ducked into the blackness only split seconds ahead of another bolt of flame. If Braun only nicked his suit, his oxygen tank, or his thermocubes it would finish him, and the gunman was getting his range.

Joe Braun was out in the light now, dashing for the shadow of a spire nearer Crag's catatread. Ron Crag raised his gun and pressed the trip; a bolt of flame cleaved space just behind the hurtling shape.

A disappointed oath ricocheted about the close walls of Crag's helmet. He quickly pressed the charge poles of the gun against the battery posts in his accessory belt and recharged the gun. He then turned the range dial to seventy-five yards, leaving the bolt diameter at one inch. He crouched in the shadow, peering across the intervening area between himself and his assailant.

"Missed, son!" Joe Braun guffawed. "Want to make it to your catatread, eh? Well, two can play the same game."

Crag swallowed an angry retort. Despair was again rising in him like a dense fog.

JOE BRAUN darted for another shadow, drawing ever closer to Crag's vehicle. Crag took careful aim, but his hand wavered ever so slightly. He fired. A streak of flame reached out and nicked—no, it passed just to the rear of the fleeing man, a little above hip level. He could have sworn the bolt grazed the man's accessory belt, but no apparent damage was done. The huge man kept running and ducked into another shadow nearer the catatread. If Joe Braun made it safely to the machine he could turn the young prospector's gun on its owner and burn him down without effort.

The next shadow in the chain was only twenty yards away. Crag covered the distance in three strides. Another bolt blasted space between his head and right shoulder. He snapped a bolt back in retaliation. It cut high and to the left.

Crag glanced frantically at the catatread. It was still too far away to reach in one dash. He knew he could never make it unless he hugged the shadows as he had been doing. Several space moths still clung hungrily to the cooling engine of the machine, but many of them were flopping and writhing frantically in space above the machine. They had detected the violent heat from the flame guns in the instant before their heat was dissipated into space, but that split second was not long enough for the creatures to locate the origin of the heat. They seemed frustrated, flopping desperately about in confused circles. Some of them fluttered into the shadows of the rocks and spires in their search, and their vaguely radiant network of veins squirmed like purple wraiths in the Stygian blackness.

Crag's attention was suddenly yanked back to his predicament, when Joe Braun darted for another shadow. Crag snapped another bolt and missed again. Either the bandit had plenty of guts or he knew Ron Crag was really a poor shot. He did not hesitate in his advance from shadow to shadow toward the catatread. It was a duel to the death, here in the shadows.

Ron Crag dashed to the next shadow without drawing flame. Apparently Joe deliberately held his fire, for the lighted area between this one and the next shadow was much further than Crag could sprint even in ten seconds. And beyond the next one lay the catatread. He crouched against the rock cliffs, glancing first toward the vehicle, then back at the black blot that he knew concealed the killer.

There were only three more spires between Joe Braun and the catatread, three more shadows, three more short sprints. Once the claim-jumper made the machine Ron Crag knew the duel was over anyway. Maybe his best chance was to wait here, aim carefully and take a chance on a lucky hit. But if he missed Braun in the first sprint the man could make it all the way to the spire nearest the machine before Crag could recharge. And if he reached that last spire...

Perhaps he'd better run for it, after all, Crag thought desperately. But he knew with a cold certainty the sure aim of the gunman could not miss him in the long sprint. Perhaps if he shot in Joe's direction just after he broke into the earthlight it might divert the killer's aim enough for a

miss. He decided abruptly that it was his only chance.

WITH trembling fingers he checked the range dials on the gun. His tongue clung to the roof of a dry mouth. Crag crouched, darted forward—then halted so abruptly on the very rim of the shadow that he fell backwards and landed gently on both elbows.

Slowly he got to his feet, his eyes narrowed thoughtfully. Several space moths were weaving through space toward the shadow of the pinnacle concealing the bandit. Crag stared, breathing more evenly now. More and more of the nebulous creatures were rising above the catatread and moving straight as a plumb line in the wake of the leading moths.

He stared at the inky shadows where he knew the killer lurked. The first two or three moths had already reached their destination. He could see their pulsating, irradiant veins curled around some object that had attracted them. More and more of the creatures floated into the shadow,

PS's Feature Flash

CARL SELWYN, author of *Earth Is Missing!*, first appeared in the Fall, 1944, Issue with his *Citadel of Death*, but he may be better known to you-all for his *Space Bat*, in the Winter Issue. That was a job, hey, gang?

This writer has a theory about readers who like to read about writers. They want to be writers themselves. Because this writer tries to give his readers (and editors!) what they want, herewith is offered a complete course in short story writing combined with the biographical sketch our Editor, Dr. Payne, requested.

THERE'S LOTS OF ROOM ON THE MOON
or
HOW TO BECOME A WRITER

Selwyn writhed and gasped, the chill gases of this alien world searing his body, seeping into his tortured lungs. Through the red haze about him, he glimpsed a descending shape, a tentacle thing, snaking down upon him. It encoiled both his ankles. It jerked him high in the air, upside down, head dangling. In the thundering darkness, he felt a solid jolt, an explosive impact that shot through his whole body, searing his raw lungs and ripping from his brain the last memory of that world of eternal peace he had lost forever. Selwyn screamed. It was December 12, 1917. (Lesson 1. Begin with Action.)

Between the Lost Colony's Virginia Dare and Carl Selwyn, quite a few children were born in America but not many on Roanoke Island, North Carolina, and Selwyn's playmates primarily consisted of one small brother and several thousand slightly smaller gray mullet which Pop's fishing fleet monotonously went out for and came in with. Cape Hatteras hurricanes blew the house down with equally monotonous regularity. Mama wondered why she ever left her trained seal act with Ringling Brothers. (Lesson 2. Work in the Background.)

Twenty years later (transitions are easy), Selwyn sat under an oak tree at the University of North Carolina watching his fellow Kappa Alphas stagger off to jobs in filling stations, and cotton gin and tobacco factories.

"Not for me," Selwyn said. (A little dialogue breaks it up.) He went to New York and made two great discoveries—that magazines like the old *Ballyhoo* and *College Humor* bought jokes at five dollars a piece and that the longest cigarett butts could be found in the dark doorways along Fifth Avenue at 3:00 A.M. (Hero's ups and downs.)

Number 16 is not a very lucky number to have in the selective service phase of a world war, particularly when the preceding 15 are halt, lame or husbands. It does, however, get one in on the ground floor and Selwyn was a sergeant long before most of the lieutenants were even drafted. He was also a sergeant long after most of the lieutenants were lieutenant colonels. Selwyn was five years in the chairborne infantry. He wrote public relations for Captain Bligh and training films for Major Martinet. He married a Vassar girl who didn't approve of enlisted men and who divorced him when he finished O.C.S. (Love interest, complications.)

Haggard, worn, but with chin held high above the frayed collar of his faded army shirt, Selwyn waited in line for his readjustment allowance check. He took stock of himself. His meager talents. His futile past. His aimless future. (Torture of the soul.) As he signed his name for his twenty-dollar relief-check, he considered his present shameful state. He slammed his fist upon the desk. The interviewer jumped. Selwyn picked up his check and hurried away. (Decision.) He went across 42nd Street to a flower shop. He wired a dozen camellias to a girl in Greenwich Village. He went in a phone booth, called his uncle collect in California and said he'd take that job writing for Metro-Goldwyn-Mayer. (Happy ending.)

Readers who like to read about writers will note a flaw in this combined biography and short course in short story writing—there is no unity of purpose. You don't need one. Not if you have an uncle at M.G.M.

——CARL SELWYN.

disappeared for a moment, and then reappeared for a moment, and then reappeared as a vague glow, fluttering toward the mass their companions had already formed.

Ron Crag watched. The killer was apparently oblivious to their presence. Ron wet dry lips with his tongue, while his fingers slowly reset the dials on the gun. Range: sixty yards! Diameter of beam: four inches! Slowly he raised the gun and took careful aim, eight inches to the right, eighteen inches above the radiant cluster of space moths. If he was wrong, if he... It was a gamble and if he was shooting at the wrong space Joe Braun would get him with the flare of Ron's gun. Even if he only wounded him, the other would get him.

"Worried, feller—" the harsh voice began.

A coruscating tube of flame leaped at the shadow across the canyon; for a moment it illuminated the area around the bandit in a brilliant glare. His taunting voice broke off with an agonized gasp. In the brief flash Ron Crag saw the man twist erect, his empty hands grasping heavenward. He took three halting steps and tumbled into full view in the earthlight. A great, charred hole was burned completely through his chest, and already the space moths were shifting to the wound, eagerly absorbing the escaping heat from the suit, and from Joe Braun's body.

Ron Crag slowly approached the crumpled form, gun ready. One glance at the sightless eyes, the bearded face and open mouth behind the visorport was all he needed to confirm what he already knew. Joe Braun had jumped his last uranium claim; Joe Braun had pulled his last gun.

He leaned over the body, examining it closely. His gamble had panned out. One corner of the thermocube on Braun's right hip was fused and a pinpoint hole was evident. The heat bolt Crag thought struck the killer's accessory belt had not missed after all.

"I'll be a fork-tailed comet!" Ron Crag breathed. He glanced affectionately at the squirming, purple creatures. "Thanks, friends," he murmured.

Then he set out on shaking legs for the catatread.

THE VIZIGRAPH

Gorgeous little Mink breathlessly, daintily approached her first date—with a haunting, voiceless shadow in the exotic gardens of Terra . . . But why the pots and pans?

THAT'S the blurb we should have written for the Ray Bradbury story. Now we realize our error. With the above effusion, everybody would have howled, "Phooey, what an ed! What a lousy way to handle the best story old PS has ever published! T'row him out!" Because, instead, we led off with the claim we did, some folks started to be critical—

But we're not sore, really. In fact, we love you all. For all, or nearly all the regulars sent in their stuff promptly—typed double-spaced on one side, and everything. As a reward we're gonna shut up quick.

Bradley, pick one. Anger, pick two. Zimmer, pick three. Thanks to Telis Streiff, we sign our selves off this time as your
—PERAMBULATING LOLLY POP

"PEEK-A-BOO!" SAID CHAD

1311—25th Street,
Galveston, Texas

DEAR EDITOR:

The small, green thing thrust its four-dimensional head through the iron door of the editorial office.

"Payne, hey?"

"Umm."

"He's back, hey."

"*Him?*"

"You want I should burn it, hey?"

"What—and lose a million readers? How many times must I tell you, Boris—*don't think*. Your job is to select the covers. Back to the art department with you!"

The awful thing flipped a letter to the handsome, markedly intelligent editor. (*Who knows, I might send you a story some time?—Author.*) (*We're holding our breath—Ed.*)

"Covers, oboy, hey!" it screeched, and slithered away, its multiple tentacles writhing in anticipation.

THAT LETTER IS THE ONE NOW BEFORE YOUR VERY EYES! WHAT WILL IT SAY? AH, TAKE HEED, MY CHILDREN . . .

Ray Bradbury is my boy. *Zero Hour* is a gem—slightly superior to the same writer's *Million Year Picnic*, and, therefore, the best yarn yet to appear in PLANET STORIES. I have to restrain myself from writing reams of deathless prose in praise of it; I'll content myself with a few adjectives and phrases. To wit: unique, clever, original, unusual handling, mature, intelligent, literate, appealing—

James, my Roget, if you will. Peek-a-boo!
I shall mercifully refrain from commenting upon the other stories in the Fall PS. Egad! Must there be a woman in *every* story? ("Her thin coveralls were plastered against her, revealing every swelling curve and indentation . . ."), regardless of type, locale, motivation, and author? Finding a lush female in every spaceship is about like encountering a pearl in every oyster. And, judging from the heroines hereabouts, I vote for oysters. An oyster in every spaceship, say I, and a couple of space pirates in every garage.

La Vizi was fine, as usual, but, if I may, I should like to take issue with Mr. Sigler and his pseudo-science. This learned gentleman seems to be about one hundred years behind the times. This is, I realize, no place for a discussion of races. However, the science of anthropology has shown, beyond any doubt, that there is no difference in the ability of any race in the known world. Whether or not there are races at all is a moot question—perhaps they represent simply an extreme form of adaptive evolution. Be that, as it may, his statement that the peoples of India "prefer squalor and dirt," in the face of such leaders as Nehru, is rank nonsense. Mr. Sigler seems to be a devotee of Nietzsche. I seem to recall another admirer—his name was Hitler.

Give the pix to McKinley, Clements, and Anger. They really deserve something better.

Hang on to Bradbury, by all means. He is a *most* valuable asset. Requests: Kuttner, Rocklynne, Neil R. Jones, Paul, Bok, and the abolition of stereotyped heroines and ridiculous boy-girl relationships on scientific expeditions.

Best of luck, Mr. Payne, and let's keep PLANET where it belongs—up with the best.

Regards,

CHAD OLIVER

TWO MILDEWED PEANUTS, AND A GREEN APPLE

84 Baker Ave.,
Dover, N. J.

DEAR EDITOR:

Whoops! Bradbury does it again! *Zero Hour* not only rates as one of the best yarns of this or any year, but it proves once more that a neat little human-interest story can score a knock-out over tales stuffed to the gills with supertechnical jargon. My family—reasonably normal people with scant sympathy for the wonders of STF—were just as favorably impressed as yours truly when I plunked 'em down and read *Zero Hour* out loud to 'em. The tale lends itself well reading aloud, no kidding. Try it, folks . . .

Brother Bradbury is going like a house afire these days, with yarns in *Harper's, Collier's* (or was it *SatEvePost?*) and such slicks, and a hardcover anthology of his weirdies just published. More Bradbury, please—lots more! (*See below—Ed.*)

The raygun, the green-skinned grulzaks, the flame-spouting rocket, the pretty blue background—PLANET's cover this issue bears a strong resemblance to the March, 1943, number. (*That was by Rozen—Ed.*) If this is Anderson's work, he's definitely on the up grade.

Bill Oberfield's *Escape From Pluto* was excellently written, thought this 'umble one, tho it could've ended about 300 words sooner without spoiling the effect. Congrats, Bill! Let's see more from you.

The Vizigraph ain't got the blood and corn and dynamite it had way back in the good ole days,

said he with a tug at his yard-long beard. No feuds. No screwy take-offs on PS's stories. Bah. Ye ed's fable about the bem who wrote the letter on sheet platinum was as readable as any letter this trip. But here goes my vote: (1) Lin Carter. Anybody who's willing to put his comments into verse deserves a pic. (2) R. R. Anger, partly 'cause he likes me. However, avid collectors might be inclined to tilt an eyebrow skyward at RRA's statement, "Under the editorship of Wilbur S. Peacock PLANET attained a standard so high that few STF mags have equaled it. . . ." Not that Peacock wasn't blamed good, but really outstanding yarns of the Bradbury caliber were fewer and farther between during the mid-war years, or so I'm told. (We-e-ell . . .—Ed.) And, while it may be true that "any real stafan will buy any STF mag as long as it publishes one good story per ish," how many really fanatical science fiction fans are there? The point may be in dispute, but PLANET's hero-babe-BEM cover formula probably accounts for half the circulation! (3) Marion Zimmer.

Two mildewed peanuts and a green apple to Sigler. If he considers the Japanese the only Asiatic race having "the ambition to build and colonize," why is he opposed to them?!!?? I wonder, Ed, (Sigler, not Payne—Ed.) whether YOU wouldn't seem "shiftless" if YOU had been born in India, in squalor and poverty, and knowing nothing better, under a caste system which stifled individual ambition And, if the planets are to be colonized by missionaries and adventurous explorers, who'd "exploit the material resources," as you so confidently predict—well, all I can say is Gawd pity the Martians!

Hot dog. I won a pic. Thanks, people. Thanks, PLP. Ummmm. Eeny-meeny-miney-mo. Kennedy chooses page 68; second choice, page 87. Ummm. Originals are lovely. Brighten up dingy den. Scare bill collectors away, also.

Undaunted by rejects (zounds! come up sometime and see my stupendous collection of little pink and blue and yellow slips!) Kennedy vows to submit some more bright-eyed, reeking, hopeful little yarns for PLANET's consideration—as soon as he recovers from grave inferiority complex brought on from reading too much Bradbury. En garde, Brother Payne!

The best to yez one and all,

JOE KENNEDY

(JoKe, you're not the only one to develop the Bradbury fever. Here's his comet's-tail across the literary firmament:

The Big Black and White Game, first published in AMERICAN MERCURY and then selected for BEST AMERICAN SHORT STORIES OF 1946.

Homecoming, first published in MADEMOISELLE and then selected for the O. HENRY MEMORIAL PRIZE STORIES OF 1947.

Dark Carnival, a Ray Bradbury anthology published by Arkham House. Stories in two anthologies, The Night Side by August Derleth and The Sleeping and the Dead by Stephen Grendon, both published by Rinehart.

The Man Upstairs, in HARPER'S MONTHLY, March, 1947.

The Meadow, a radio script for the World Security Workshop, produced over WCBS, January, 1947.

So don't blame us if we get excited about the guy. We have two more jobs by him coming up, just as soon as we can run them. It is our sober judgment that they are decidedly better than Zero Hour!—Ed.)

TAKE IT FROM OBERFIELD . . .

400 Ontario Street,
Wheeling, W. Va.

DEAR EDITOR:

What's'e mean, Telis Streiff? "One more fan—gone!"??? Does this mean that one pink spot on a green BEM makes it a pink BEM? I don't get it.

The main reason for this letter is Bradley's letter in the Fall Ish. A very interesting letter. It looks like a hunk of nice, red meat and I feel like a wolf, so here goes.

Why is the most economical direction for taking off from Earth straight up? Why not eastward? Better still, eastward at midnight above the equator. Since the surface of the earth is moving in the same direction as Earth's progress around the sun, the surface speed (about 1,000 m.p.h.) would be added to the orbital speed (about 66,000 m.p.h.), giving the ship a velocity of something like 67,000 m.p.h., not counting the power-induced motion of the ship. This speed, of course, would be in relation to a point that does not revolve about the sun and probably applicable only to travel within the system.

So a ship having a power-induced speed of about 1,600 m.p.h., plus the motion induced by the axial rotation of Earth, would, in the orbit of the moon, exactly neutralize gravity with its centrifugal force. A power-induced speed of 2,000 m.p.h. or more would, if applied at the point opposite the sun, send the ship on ahead of Earth with the orbital speed of the earth to neutralize the sun's gravity and the axial speed plus the ship's power induced speed to tear it away from the sun's grip and send it outward through centrifugal force. The ship would travel a considerable distance around the sun before reaching the desired planet.

Unless you wanted to "fight back" against the orbital motion of Earth, which would be a waste of energy, the straight upward path would also take you some distance around the sun before reaching your destination. You would be traveling sideways at about 67,000 m.p.h. and ahead at the power-induced speed of the ship, not that this sidewinding matters in airless space. What does matter is that you would have to travel four times as far as you would in the eastward takeoz before the 1,000 m.p.h. induced by the axial rotation of Earth, acting without the aid of power-induced motion in the same direction, could neutralize the pull of Earth's gravity.

The eastward takeoff, by the way, would serve to travel to inner planets by turning the axial rotation of Earth against its orbital motion because you would take off from the sunward side. Here, the surface of Earth is moving contrary to the orbital motion and would reduce the ship's orbital speed, in relation to the sun. Additional power-induced speed would reduce this orbital motion even further until the ship loses all orbital speed. With no orbital motion you would have no centrifugal force to neutralize the pull of the sun and you could just fall, brother, fall! Of course, any energy saved in this way would be used up in the return trip. As I learned in a previous life, when I was with the Space Patrol of a great civilization that lived before Adam, you can't "get something for nothing," even in space.

Bradley, in bouncing his ship off the moon, forgets that the gravitational pull of Earth would hamper his fall toward the moon and that, in going beyond the moon, he would have not only the gravity of the earth, which extends much further than the moon, but that of the moon as well to overcome.

Pre-Adam, we didn't go to the bother of toting all that junk way out to the moon, just to build big ships with little motors. We built big ships with little motors on Earth, where we had plenty of air and water and supplies and power near at hand. Then we fastened little ships to the big ones, like spare jets, hauled the big ones out and set them in their orbits, and returned to Earth with the small ones. These methods seem easier.

Here you have one man's opinions and they might be wrong. Bradley has other ideas, and they could be wrong. I am sure the authors would put logic into their yarns if someone would tell them whose logic is correct. Einstein's, you say?

One question. If, as theory has it, the stars burn by nuclear fission and are constantly transforming matter into energy, what becomes of the Mass constant, Energy constant theory of the universe?

Grrrrrrr!

WILLIAM (BILL) OBERFIELD

COVER UP THE COVER GALS?

865 20th Ave. So.
St. Peterburg, Fla.

DEAR EDITOR:

Ah, me! What is so rare as a day in June? Offhand, you can probably think of a couple of thousand things but I've gotta start this letter somehow, so shuddup. I feel in a jolly mood today, so I guess I'll favor you with a letter. *Lucky* people.

Struggling past the cover (and it *was* a struggle. Great Ghu . . . a bronzed hero in a red shirt, with green britches and yellow boots, holding a babe in a pale green .. .. er ... *dress* against a bright purple sky. Gawd. Getcha back into it, Payne! Clean them covers up.) Hmmm. I seem to have left myself, at the beginning of this paragraph, without a sentence to stand on. I'll make a new paragraph.

There. Now, as I was saying . . . er . . . what *was* I saying? Oh yeah—Good issue. Very good. Even without a Fox yarn, too. Incredible. The latest episode in McDowell's Interplanetary Color Scheme was the best yet—even better than *Red Witch*. The ending was a little too pat, tho, doncha think? Here Brother McDowell had built us up to a powerful suspense . . . all earth was uninhabitable because of the protozoa .. . . the last citadel of the earth people was being besieged by the amazon hordes . . . inside the citadel, Nesbit was planning a revolution or something and then *blooie!* Everything falls into place perfectly. And they lived happily ever after. Despite the corny and improbable ending, the story was McDowell's best yet.

Now, this Fennel thing. Can't rightly say that I've ever heard of him before, but *Crust* was good. Darn good. Let's have more by him— eh, Payne?

Crash Beam. Okay. So-so. A rather unobtrusive little thing. *Zero Hour.* Despite all the hulla-balloo it was only fair. A nice, quiet horrible little thing. Brrr. *Test for the Pearl.* Good. I jus' *love* them O. Henry endings. *Asteroid Justice . . .* corny. *Assignment in the Dawn.* Fairly good. Kinda sad ending. *Against Tetrarch.* Quite good. Dunno why, but I liked

it. *Escape from Pluto.* Another good 'un. Good for Oberfield! *Girl of the S. S.* Very good. Let's have more by Haggard. He's O.K.!

Now let's tune in on the Vizigraph. Not so good this time. There, there Paul . . . don't cry. You tried. Anger, Streiff, Sneary, Clements, and a few other people had good letters. Bradley had an interesting (albeit technical) li'l missive . . . Sneary seems a bit gay . . . Streiff must use at least a thousand dots in his letter . . . What, no letters by Guerry Brown, Pace Jewett or Oberfield. Tsk.

Well, this thing has dragged on long enough. Guess this'll hold you for the time being, Payne. I'll drop in again on my next trip around the galaxy.

Lincerelv,

LIN CARTER

DIE, I THOUGHT I'D LAUGH

2962 Santa Ana St.,
DEAR EDITOR: South Gate, Calif.

Tell Anger to go sit on a atom. Peacock and Whitehorn were good editors, but they never gave us what you have. Nothing like *Million Year Picnic,* (*A Whitehorn selection—Ed.*) Anderson on the cover, or The Fall Issue. It has the highest average of stories that I can remember. Except maybe for the one that had *Star Mouse.*

Now for a little literary criticism. You called *Zero Hour* the best STF story you had seen. Maybe some will agree with you. I don't. Don't get me wrong, I liked it, I'm beginning to belive Bradbury is a nother Nelson Bond, but it wasn't a clasic. It is easy to understand why you said what you did. The last two stories by Bradbury have been raved over, and rightly so. So I suppose you thought you had a nother one. But there were three killers in it for me.

No. 1. You saying it was good ruined it for me. I expected to much.

No. 2. There was no suspence to it. You know what was going to happen, partly becouse of the story which gave it away in the first page and partly the picture, which gave the whole story away. Any fan with brains could have writen a rough out line of it from that pic.

No. 3. And last of all, I don't belive in the characterization. First little kids love there folks unless they are really mean to them. They wouldn't be talked into doing away with them in just one day. And second, the kids are of the future, and so our stf stories will be there average thing. Like our comic books. Well can you see kids of today letting Japs in to kill their folks??? Well kids of the future will fear planetary invaders just as much, or I'll miss my guess. And beside all that, kids of the future will doubtless be a lot smarter.

Bradbury did bring in the future "time savers" and house-hold gadgets very nicely. He still is tops for my money. You just over rated him.

I nearly rolled off the couch tho at the ending of *Black Silence.* I'm harden to the the hero getting the girl in 99.9% of the stories, but this fool winds up with seven. Ha! Die, I thought I'd laugh. McDowell should rate a bonus for that story. The best advanture tale you have run in a long time, but then McDowell's name gets respect anywaere. And ofcourse you will have to have a sequel to it, called *Crystal City.* (*Oh?—Ed.*) But lest not have it to far in to future. I suppose you have used Matt up as a hero, but how about one of his sons. (Wonder if he will know them all.) Say about 30 years after this

story. Have the silican attacking. (*Go on, go on—Ed.*)

Say, one would almost think you did what I said. In my last letter I remarked that there were few stories were the Martains won, and here you bring out a story inwhich they do. *Beneath the Red Worlds Crust* by Fennel was very good. Like his stile. He used the old chase plot to good advatage. Turned out alot better than the tital made me belive. Why so long. *Martian Waters* would have been better. If you are going to get away from the flub-blub stories of the past three or four years clean up your titles too. Tho you did pretty well this time, only two.

Say by anychance is A.A.O.Gilmour who wrote *Against Tetrarch* the old time STF writer Anthony Gilmour? (*Dunno—Ed.*) I was wondering, the stile seems good, but sort of like the old days.

All the shorts were good, tho some might have appeared in fanzines and none would have notest. (By that I mean they sound like ones written by fans. About the same size to.)

As for the *Viz.* Very good, but reather short. Don't you belive thos people (they aren't fans) that tell you to shorten it. It still is better than some of the stories. My votes are, #1. Bradley, #2, Zimmer, and uuuuu lets see. Not Streiff, he wouldn't vote for me, annnn, Carter was good but . . . you wont let me vote for—no I didn't think so . . . well. Clements would get it except for saying Fox was getting better but his stories were degenerating. Well as you all ready have some no doubt, give it to McKinley, hope it make Telis jealous. He (Telis), as far as I know a male. A male *what* is a nother thing.

Your art work this ish was from fair to bad. Your new men (?) Napol and M. Elkan are pretty good, Vastal (p. 37) neet and well done, Martin(?) on p. 55 was fair. He seems to like nudes. I do to, but not so much in PLANET, unless they match the story at least. (Wonder what would hapen if there was a strong wend! P. 67 (Robot story) was very bad. Kiemle for "The Test" pretty good. P. 84. (Pluto) ask . . . Vestal, fair (pp. 90-1). As I said about the best you have which is none to good.

Of say, I wrote that young Britisher. Cost me all of 25¢ to air mail it to him. I'm not happy the way the letter looked. Oh well, it might chear him up, and I might get a answer. And a stamped letter from there will go nice in my collection too.

Well before you become board to directors I'll leave.

Yours,

RICK SNEARY

TELIS TELLS ALL!

548 North Dellrose
Wichita 6, Kansas

DEAR PERAMBULATING LOLLY POP:

"Ho hum," I said. "Boy, am I tired!" So I went in on the bed and laid down. ". . . now where is that copy of the latest PLANET?" I asked myself brittely. I looked down on the floor under the record cabinet. "Oh, there it is." But before I could pick it up the red-shirted hero on the front threw down his gun, and stood up three-dimensionally on the mag. He glared at me and said, "What for do you read this trash, hey?" I gasped, "Why . . . er . . ." "Yasee," he said, "ya don't know." "Well, really, you know, it isn't any of your business," I told him, regaining my wits. The blonde female picked herself up off of the ground where Nick had dropped her. "What manners you've got!" She glared. By now the Martians were off the cover, walking around the room and exploring it. "Take this issue, for instance," said Nick, ignoring the girl. "Turn to page 4." I did. Up pops the five girls and Matt. I recoils suddenly. . . . "Well, I'm glad I'm out of *that* story," sez Margot. "Boy, did *I* have a crummy part, or did I have a crummy part. . . ." "You did," sez pistol-packin mama. Matt looks up at me and sez, "The story started out O.K., but got awful toward the end, don't ya think?" "Yes," I agreed, not wanting to offend him. "It could have been much better," I goes on. Nick pulls on my big toe, so I looks down. "Turn to page 37, now," he tells me. I do. Kearns staggers off out of the picture and yells, "I did it, I did it!" "Did what?" I sez. "Reflected it right back at him!" he yells. Nick motions to one of the Martians, who carries Kearns over to the fish tank and drops him in. My Barb gets hungry and starts chasing him around the tank. "Page 40," sez Nick, pulling at my hair. I turn. Mink looks up at me and sez, "Who are you?" and then goes on, "Are you Drill?" "Er—yeh," I sez. "That's a nice story you were in," I compliments her. She sits down on an album of Beethoven's 9th Symphony and sez casually, "It was O.K." "O.K.," I screams. "PLP sez it is magnificent! Have you no respect for PLP?" "Is he over nine?" she sez eagerly. "Er—let's turn to page 47," I sez changing the subject. I do. Sam slugs Ned one and he staggers off the bed on to the floor. I pick him up and set him down beside Matt. "Oh, you nasty villain you," sez Sam nasally, lisping all over the place. "Take that!" He hits Mink, I drop him in the fish tank, and the Flame Tetras start chasing him around the rock in the center. I drops Nancy in, too, so he won't get lonely. "Page 55," Nick reminds me. I turn. Mona jumps up and runs out of the picture and hides behind me. "Save me!" she cries, so I seal her up in an envelope where she's safe. Can't find the envelope around anywhere, tho, or I'd send her to ya. Mink yells "Hey! This is fun, turn to page 67." I do. This stuff goes on until my five-gallon tank is full, my tropicals are all over the floor, the Martians are massacring the Chameleon men, Ned has killed off Waltk, The Master Miners are tracking down the girl in the Silver Sphere, and Kemble is trying to repair his spaceship, mumbling to the master mind (me) "I wonder how I got off Pluto in the first place. Seems to me that the heat from my rocket jets would have melted this blank-blank mercury." "Ah," sez I sagely, "that is not for us to answer. I'm sure Oberfield the Great knows, but will not tell us for fear of snapping our puerile minds." I feel something in my shirt, reach my hand in and pull it out. It's a robot with a gun in one hand and a club in the other. He screams, "I thot I had nerves of steel, but they turned out to be lead!" There isn't room in the fish tank for him, so I stick him in the Files of The Parks Streiff Construction Co.

Now I settle back into my bed and hide under the covers to read LaViz alone . . . whoops, almost alone . . . as I throw out a Brachadanio Reerio. Give McKinley first place in choice of originals, as per usual, and I don't see why everybody is confused over my sex. It worries everybody except me, and I'm happy, so what's the fuss? Give Sigler second and Sneary third. That

PoGoStIc of Mac's (McKinley) is truly an interesting weapon, for actually it serves as this more often than in any other capacity. Why, I remember once on Gorhas Six when I was fighting it out with a bunch of fierce, terrifying, horrible Gorhasian Paper Sacks, with only a flame gun for defence, that the great Mac came to my rescue with the whole Norvalian Navy behind him! The great Norvalian Navy! Ahh, it was an inspiring sight to see him pulling those two battered life boats behind him. Oh, well, he saved me. I think. I'm reasonably sure. Some times. You're silly. I'm not silly, you're dumb. I'm not dumb, your idiotic. I'm not idiotic, you're stupid. Yeh. Only on Tuesday. But SOME SNARKS ARE BOOJUMS! he hawhehahahabhabrrgg . . .
　　　'bye

　　　　　　Telisincerely
　　TELIS STREIFF (male) (*At last!—Ed.*)

SAYS LETTERS THROW US

　　　　　　　　　670 George St.,
　　　　　　　　　Clyde, Ohio
DEAR EDITOR:

　. . . So he says to me, A futuristic Gregory Peck ain't so bad, but when he's six fingers on his gun-hand, that's too much. And I says, Maybe he's the BEM in disguise. He says, Naw, his hair ain't messed up atall. He's the hero!
　We were, of course, squinting at the Fall PLANET cover which, despite the above, is the best PLANET cover I've ever seen. The girl was especially— Yes.
　After gulping over the cover, I leaf through and glance critically at the illustrations. Napoli is getting worse and Vestal is as usual good. Elkan is fair, but Kiemle' should drop dead. Martin bad, Whozis on page 67 fair (*Hardison—Ed.*), Whitman good, Whozis on page 115 good (*Hardison—Ed.*). Vestal, though, is your best bet.
　Now, the Vizigraph. I always save the stories for last. The dessert, so to speak. Bradley's letter interesting, but he is practically quoting from Willy Ley's *Rockets*. And I rather think the nebulous gravities of other planets would interfere with the "coasting." Sneary writes a lot, but don't say much, though I agree that Vestal is tops in your unoutstanding art dept. We should shut Streiff and his claustrophobia in a shoe box until he learns to delete those millions of periods he loves so well. The boy is interesting if only he'd make his letters look nice. R. R. Anger should be told the facts of life, namely, that every STF reader is not a fan. Many people read STF just for the fun of it, while fans think that their sole mission in life is to breathe over editors' shoulders and criticize writings they can't even hope to match. I know. I'm a fan.
　The same goes for Sigler. Carter's poem neat. Any connection between it and the cartoon that followed? (*No—Ed.*) McKinley illustrates the axiom that friends always vote originals to each other, a deplorable practice, to be sure. Only sometimes you can't get away from it. Said he, wondering if friend Sneary has any vacant wall space remaining. Wood is dippy. Friend Clements is the usual Vizi type who has a nice letter, to be sure, but says practically nothing. But then, we can't ALL be brain-trusts. Miss Zimmer is lucid in places so give her first chance at the originals, with Anger second and Carter third. You can choose stories okay, Mister P., but letters throw you. (*Want us to be more choosy?—Ed.*)

Stories: *Black Silence*, Mr. McDowell's latest in his Spectrum Series, tied with Fennel's "novel" in first place. I simply LOVE stories like the former that kill off most of the world population, leaving a few people to build up the civilization again. Personally, I think it could happen here. Fennel's story very good and finely written and plotted. *Zero Hour* wasn't quite as good as advertised, but Bradbury's style is wonderful! Tied for third were *Escape From Pluto* and *Test for the Pearl*. Oberfield shows a depth of touch not quite reached in his first Planetale. I expect more and better stories from him. Garson good, though I was looking for a trifle more after such a build-up. *Against Tetrarch* was fourth. Well written, but the others mentioned seemed just a little bit better. After his big build-up, Walton let me down with *Assignment in the Dawn*. It was just too slow and heavily written. Barrett, Thiessen, and Haggard might just as well have been left out.
　Feature Flash swell. Always nice to learn how writers live, hoping I can somehow duplicate the experiences and "arrive" as a writer. Me and how many others?
　Random thoughts: Wonderful how with so few, well-chosen words the contents-page story "blurbs" are written. Inside-front cover detective advertisement drawing good. When is PLANET to be published six times yearly? Three months IS an awful long time between issues. Prologue to Vizi, Mr. P., was fine. Only "fen" is plural, not singular. (*Thanks—Ed.*) Although I'll grant you that fans are mighty singular. (*Ouch—Ed.*) Cartoon welcome but unfunny. Too many advts. Why did Fennel want the pic for his story? (*His first sale to us—Ed.*) Pic was terrible. (*Oh—Ed.*)
　　　　　Regards,
　　　　　　　　　TOM JEWETT

OH, SHAW!

　　　　　　　　　1301 State Street,
　　　　　　　　　Schenectady 4, New York
DEAR EDITOR:

　Apparently it is not yet unfashionable, in the Vizi, for the reader to relate the usually difficult and always incredible process by which he acquired the latest issue of PLANET. Well, I did it before—in my own personal good old days—and I can do it again. Here's exactly how I bought the Fall ish:
　I entered the magazine store, picked PS off the shelves (along with the latest issues of "Encore" and "The New Yorker"), gave the clerk a dollar bill, received thirty-five cents change, and made my exit.
　Fascinating, isn't it?
　However, since I have long since passed the stage where I indiscriminately buy every issue of every stf magazine, you might conceivably have some interest in the factors that influenced me to buy this particular one as soon as it came out. These were as follows: (A) The cover, on which the old scene was relatively well-painted (incidentally, since the gal was wearing her nightgown, I thought that perhaps this time it might all be a bad dream). (B) The contents page display of a large and various variety of short stories. (C) The sudden realization that you were still giving us those nice deep pages, still charging only twenty cents, and in general, more than any competitor and plenty of mags in other fields, are still giving the customer his honest money's worth. All of which is highly commendable. However . . .

Just one suggestion, before I get on to weightier matters. Why not put colors in the titles of *all* your stories? It wouldn't require many changes: Purple Crash Beam, Zero Hour for the Blue Invaders, Justice on the Yellow Asteroid, Test for the Grey Pearl, etc., for instance. I know they don't all fit the stories; what of it? Then you could change the mag's title to RAINBOW STORIES. Much prettier. If anybody complained that it wasn't stfictional, you could tell 'em it was short for "Somewhere-Over-the-Rainbow Stories."

Besides, PLANET STORIES isn't stfictional, either. Non-readers could take it to mean Stories About Earth.

The stories this time fall naturally into five classes. I'll take the worst first—though I'm not sure which of these first three groups is really worst.

Sheer Amateurishness in Idea and Execution: *Crash Beam, Escape from Pluto* (obvious as all hell, especially with that illustration), and *Girl of the Silver Sphere*. Yes, the last one, too, even if Haggard is a name. No plot, no point—no!

Could Have Been Good But Was Bungled in the Writing: *Assignment in the Dawn*. The naivete of a man who can write something like "Did she like his body? That was the important thing," is appalling. Also this: "Roland . . . stared. 'Martians! You mean—from Mars! The planet?'" Bro-ther!

The Usual Blood and Blunder (worst of the four famous characteristics) and Not Very Good at That: *Asteroid Justice, Against Tetrarch, Test for the Pearl*. Not for me, thanks. The last one named, especially, pulled out the oldest gag in the book. As for "Justice," Mr. Thiessen should learn something about that subject. His ending is cribbed direct from Lewis Padgett's fine mystery novel, "The Brass Ring."

Thud and Thunder (lesser of the four evils) But Quite Readable: *Beneath the Red World's Crust*. Well written of its type. But that business with Susan's blouse was *really* unnecessary, Erik!

Good Stories: *Zero Hour*. Very good, in fact. Marred only by that straight-from-little-Rollo first paragraph. Far from anybody's best, though, and you're looking for trouble labeling it that. Those who disagree will cuss you; those who agree will be disappointed in all future stories. *Black Silence*. An easy best in the issue, this would be terrific in any issue. A magnificent job of story-telling. It was—dare I say it?—down to earth. Well-plotted, unusual, intelligent, even realistic. I even liked the hero's name. The episode with the bull was outstanding in an outstanding yarn. See, fellows, you don't *need* mad monsters and swoony love scenes! One blot: "She was dressed in boots and breeches, but they couldn't conceal her sex." Yes, Emmett, *we* know! But do it again, chum, do it again!

Two very good stories and one fair out of ten. Enough to keep me buying, but not exactly a bright and shining record.

The illos were almost universally stupid in conception, and poor to fair in execution. The lonely exception was Elkan's for *Zero Hour*. Pretty good.

Marion Szipper—er—Szimmer, that is, wrote the best letter. This is, after all, the type of thing that made the Vizi famous and still forms its backbone, and Marion did a better than average job. Clever, in fact. I hereby nominate Marion the fanne I'd most like to be marooned on an asteroid with. (Even if she weighs 200 pounds; she sounds like a right gal.) Give Bradley second for an unusual and intelligent piece. Seems to me the planets would rarely be in positions that would enable us to use his system, and that it would be just as easy to coast to the final destination, once started, as to a midway point. But he obviously knows more about it than I do. Einstein has *me* beat. And give Pears third because he's a good egg and I like him.

This wise guy Sigler, now, is stupid—though he may be educated. From this sort of thing it is but a step to the most vicious race hatred. Can you quote *facts*, Sigler, to prove that Asiatics are any different from anyone else—that their IQ's are lower, or something? I don't believe you can. I don't think *anyone* "prefers" to live in squalor and dirt. Have the Indians ever been given a chance to solve their own problems? This sort of letter doesn't even have the merit of being controversial; it's just disgusting. Somebody shoot Sigler.

The rest of the letters were about on a level, enjoyable but unexceptional.

Had enough?

LARRY SHAW

(The *original* PS Hermit)

SIGLER SPIELT AUF

1028 N. Broadway,
Wichita 5, Kansas

DEAR EDITOR:

In regard to the lead novel would say that even dear(?) old Adolph would regard seven or more wives as cruel and inhuman punishment. I believe though that silicon-based life spores would live on silicides instead of carbon compounds. Under the conditions mentioned in the story, for as little as one pound of those spores to have dropped on the earth would have required an original amount of approximately 177,619,907,336,190,098,158 tons. Yes, it gave me a headache figuring it out, but what I want to know is, where could such a quantity originate? That has always seemed the weak point in such theories to me.

Ray Bradbury's story wasn't so hot but it was so much better than his harem-style stories, that he is to be congratulated.

I notice that Mr. McKinley doesn't like my math. Does that cancel the fact that it showed the author was all wet?

I would suggest that Erik Fennel do a little research before he writes any more stories as I can't get interested in a story that blithely ignores all fact. According to Mr. Fennel, Mars has absolutely no surface water at all. That will certainly be a surprise to astronomers who have been photographing the polar icecaps for nearly a century.

I would like to know why your artists never read a story that they illustrate. One story has a girl dressed in some kind of suit with an oxygen helmet. However, to the artist it's just the same old naked dame? (*Old?—Ed.*) If a picture is to illustrate a story then it should follow the description of the author.

I am getting tired of the state of mind that pretends that a bra and a G-string equips a woman completely for any weather and locality from the surface of Pluto to the sunward side of Mercury. If the artist had to wear that costume down a city street in winter, he would start howling for a suit of coonskin pajamas.

PLANET is supposed to deal with science, yet ever since you have taken it over it has printed pure tripe. I get a feeling of nausea in my stomach when an author ignores facts that a child should know about science and makes his own assumptions, contrary to all common sense.

How about insisting that all authors do a little research on the subject before they write any more stories and how about getting more stories out of the ordinary?

Of course, some will say the story is the thing but how can a story be science-fiction if the writer refuses to use fact in his story? I expect any day now to read a tale in which the old Roman empire is really situated on Mars instead of Earth. With the writers you have, anything is possible.

EDWIN SIGLER

WIGODSKY WEAKENS!

306 Evans Avenue,
San Antonio, Texas

DEAR PAYNE-DEMONIUM:

Here's a very silly, silly rhyme:
McDowell's getting better all the time.
Seriously, though, *Black Silence* is wonderful. *Beneath the Red World's Crust* is a great improvement over Fennel's stinking *Atavism*. *Crash Beam* was a surprise, anyway. *Zero Hour*, while not one of the best science-fiction stories I have ever seen, was very good. However, it was strictly fantasy. (*Huh?—Ed.*) *Asteroid Justice* was mediocre. *Against Tetrarch* was ditto. *Assignment in the Dawn* was fine. *Test for the Pearl* is the best Garson has ever written. *Escape From Pluto* was superb, for a first try. *Girl of the Silver Sphere* is O'Henry-ese—by a Haggard. No relation to Rider?

The best illustration is the Kiemle on p. 76. Vestal's improving. Napoli should have his ears cut off.

Give Sneary all three originals.

Thanks to this issue, your magazine has climbed to second on my list.

Yours truly,
MICHAEL WIGODSKY

GRULZAK'S SUPPER—ONE SHMOE

1116 Fulton St.,
Woodmere, N. Y.

DUH!!—PLANET'S PAYNE:

Last ish some shmoe named Streiff said *Vassals of the Lode Star* was a direct steal from Kuttner's *Dark World*. *Vassals* is swell, but it can't even compare to *Dark World* and only remotely resembles it. Anybody that says what Telis said should be a grulzak's supper. *Black Silence* is O.K., but I wouldn't having a mind as to 13 wives. *Beneath the Red World's Crust* stoonk even though Fennel is a good writer. *Crash Beam* was fair. *Zero Hour* wuz superduper. Thiessen didn't do *Asteroid Justice* justice. *Against Tetrarch* was O.K. Gilmore should write more. *Assignment in the Dawn* wuz good. *Test for the Pearl*, *Escape From Pluto*, and *Girl of the Silver Sphere* were very fine. The Vizigraph and the Feature Flash were super. Dos vos a good ish.

STFantasincerely yoors,
JIM GOLDFRANK

Made in the USA